by Jim Michael Hansen

Night Laws
Shadow Laws
Fatal Laws
***Deadly Laws** (2007)*
***Bangkok Laws** (2008)*

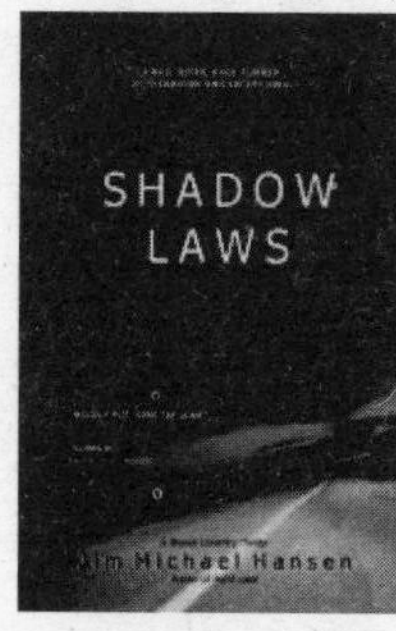

What they're saying about Jim Michael Hansen's
Fatal Laws

"Jim Michael Hansen will keep you glued to the pages. A very well-told tale that is guaranteed to satisfy any thriller or suspense fan. You'll be looking for his other books, *Nights Laws* and *Shadow Laws*."

—Anne K. Edwards, NEW MYSTERY READER MAGAZINE
www.newmysteryreader.com

"Third in the *Laws* series (*Night Laws* and *Shadow Laws*) and hopefully there will be a lot more to come. . . . Another well-written . . . book that keeps ratcheting up the ante. Definitely recommended."

—Jack Quick, BOOK BITCH REVIEWS
www.bookbitch.com

"Mr. Hansen's thrillers keep improving with every book he

writes. I have found his plots and action to be edgy and twisted. . . . His stories are rich with plausible actions and motives . . . This particular novel's ending will slap you upside your head with a two-by-four, it's so unusual. We rated it a solid five hearts."

—Bob Speer, HEARTLAND REVIEWS
www.heartlandreviews.com

"Jim Michael Hansen has amazingly kept each book fresh and invigorating. Like the other two [*Night Laws* and *Shadow Laws*], I was taken on a roller-coaster ride . . . The familiar characters that I was re-introduced to were just as intriguing, funny and smart as they were the first time I met them. This book gets the reader to run from page to page the way the detective runs from clue to clue. But be prepared . . . the last twist at the end even had me shaking my head!"

—Kathy Martin, IN THE LIBRARY REVIEWS
www.inthelibrearyreviews.net

"*Fatal Laws* is most assuredly a page-turner."

—Naomi de Bruyn, LINEAR REFLECTIONS
www.linearreflections.com

"I wondered with great anticipation what I would find between the covers of Jim Hansen's new work, *Fatal Laws.* I have come to love detective Bryson Coventry . . . True to form, our author has once again penned a mystery that will keep your heart racing and your mind struggling to figure out the evil behind the hideous deaths. As usual, and what I have come to expect from his work, he has paid careful consideration insuring every element that makes up a mystery of depth is covered, played up, exciting your senses and making you hunger for more . . . A page-turner, shivering read that will chill you to the bone . . ."

—Shirley Johnson, Senior Reviewer, MIDWEST BOOK REVIEW
www.midwestbookreview.com

"Expect the unexpected. That is the best advice I can give before sending you to a bookstore to purchase Jim Hansen's superb suspense novels. *Fatal Laws* is the third novel in the author's Bryson Coventry series; perhaps it is the best of the bunch so far and that's not an easy feat to manage. It is not unusual for an author to reach a 'sophomore slump' after one or two stunning novels, Jim Michael Hansen proves that he is in a whole other class! *Fatal Laws* is amazing!"

—Tracy Farnsworth, ROUNDTABLE REVIEWS
www.roundtablereviews.com

"Jim Michael Hansen has come up with yet another heart-pounding thriller . . . His unique style of writing keeps the reader captivatingly interested. All the while, each chapter is like a roller-coaster ride . . . Great job Mr. Hansen!"

—Wanda Maynard, SIMEGEN
www.simegen.com

NIGHT LAWS

ISBN 13: 9780976924302
ISBN 10: 0976924307

Denver homicide detective Bryson Coventry is on the hunt for a vicious killer who has warned attorney Kelly Parks, Esq., that she is on his murder list. Something from the beautiful young lawyer's past has come back to haunt her, something involving the dark secrets of Denver's largest law firm. With the elusive killer ever one step away, Kelly Parks frantically searches for answers, not only to save her life but also to find out whether she unwittingly participated in a murder herself.

"*Night Laws* is a terrifying, gripping cross between James Patterson and John Grisham. . . . Hansen has created a truly killer debut. The characters are compelling, the research dead-on, and there's just a touch of humor to take the edge off one of the grisliest serial killers in recent memory."

—J.A. KONRATH, bestselling author of *Whiskey Sour*, *Bloody Mary* and *Rusty Nail*, www.jakonrath.com

"A chilling story well told. The pace never slows in this noir thriller, taking readers on a stark trail of fear."

—CAROLYN G. HART, *N.Y. Times* and *USA Today* bestselling author of the *Death on Demand* series and the *Henrie O* series, www.carolynhart.com

"[A] well-plotted thriller that knows its audience and gives them what they want in spades. It's an airport read, a high-concept thrill-ride, the kind of popular thriller you can pick up, read, enjoy and put back down again."

—Russel D. McLean, CRIME SCENE SCOTLAND www.crimescenescotland.com

"Jim Hansen has crafted a tough and hardbitten legal thriller, compelling and intricately plotted by an author who clearly knows his terrain ."

—BARON R. BIRTCHER, *L.A. Times* and IMBA bestselling author of *Roadhouse Blues, Ruby Tuesday* and *Angels Fall* www.baronbirtcher.com

"Fast-moving, sharp storytelling, likeable characters who talk like real people, a page-turner all the way to the end."

—SELLEY SINGER, author of the Jake Samson detective series and the Barrett Lake mystery series, www.shelleysinger.com

"*Night Laws* is a creepy, scary, nail-biting read. Jim Hansen and homicide detective Bryson Coventry deliver a one-two punch."

—SARAH LOVETT, author of *Dangerous Attractions*, *Dark Alchemy* and *Acquired Motives*, www.sarahlovett.com

"A brand new thrill ride through the Mile High City."

—EVAN MCNAMARA, author of *Superior Position* and *Fair Game* www.evanmcnamara.com

"*Night Laws* is a truly impressive novel."

—NANCY TESLER, author of the *Other Deadly Things* series www.nancytesler.com

SHADOW LAWS

ISBN 13: 9780976924340 (Trade Paperback)
ISBN 13: 9780976924395 (Audio Book)

Denver homicide detective Bryson Coventry, and beautiful young attorney Taylor Sutton, are separately hunting vicious killers but for very different reasons. As the two dangerous chases inadvertently intersect, both of the hunters get pulled deeper and deeper into an edgy world of shifting truths where there is more at stake than either could have imagined, nothing is as it seems and time is running out.

"As engaging as the debut *Night Laws*, this exciting blend of police procedural and legal thriller recalls the early works of Scott Turow and Lisa Scottoline."

—LIBRARY JOURNAL

"*Shadow Laws* is a thriller that will keep you turning the pages while you remind yourself to breath."

—Andrea Sisco, ARMCHAIR INTERVIEWS
www.armchairinterviews.com

"This is what excellent storytelling's all about."

—Byron Merritt, FWOMP BOOK REVIEW, www.fwomp.com

"Without a *shadow* of a doubt, Hansen knows murder."

—Paul Anik, I LOVE A MYSTERY
www.iloveamysterynewsletter.com

"From the opening scene to the wrap up, *Shadow Laws* is one edgy thriller. Edgy characters, edgy plot, skillful storytelling—a page-turner for sure."

—L.B. COBB, author of *Splendor Bay* and *Promises Town*
www.lbcobb.com

"Hansen's story surges with action like a screaming Ferrari with no brakes. His plot captivates and terrifies, while the characters vault from the page—alive and kicking—dueling with sizzling dialogue. Throughout the tale, Hansen's razor wit snicks and slices with wry cunning, giving the reader a complex, intriguing and satisfying ride."

—MARK BOUTON, author of *Max Conquers the Cosmos* and *Cracks in the Rainbow*, www.markbouton.com

"In Jim Hansen's latest legal thriller, *Shadow Laws*, he does it all: vividly evokes a setting, Denver, from its sleazy Colfax Avenue bars to its slick Cherry Creek mansions; brings to life a quirky bunch of characters; and twists a plot so capably that the reader hasn't a chance to put the book down until it's finished."

—ANN RIPLEY, author of the *Louise Eldridge* gardening mysteries

"Jim Hansen's books just get stronger and stronger. *Shadow Laws* is part police procedural, part legal thriller, and completely satisfying."

—MARK TERRY, author of *Devil's Pitchfork*
www.markterrybooks.com

COMING NEXT

DEADLY LAWS

ISBN 9780976924333
(2007)

Third-year law student Kayla Beck receives a disturbing telephone call. A stranger gives her an ultimatum—follow his directions and possibly save a woman's life, or ignore the call and condemn the woman to certain death. What happens next catapults both her and Denver homicide detective Bryson Coventry into a deadly world where secrets are more important than truth, shadows are more important than light, and survival is more important than everything.

"The imaginative departure from the time-tried plotlines will satisfy and have readers looking for other books by this author."

—Anne K. Edwards, NEW MYSTERY READER MAGAZINE

"This is the best *Laws* yet." —Jack Quick, BOOK BITCH REVIEWS

"Just as with the previous three books, this one grabbed me from the first page."

—Kathy Martin, IN THE LIBRARY REVIEWS

"[T]his is one top-notch read. Again, Mr. Hansen adds just the right amount of mystery, suspense, romance, horror and nail-biting adventure to keep you turning the pages."

—Shirley P. Johnson, MIDWEST BOOK REVIEW

AFTER *DEADLY LAWS* WATCH FOR

BANGKOK LAWS

ISBN 9780976924319
(2008)

As Denver homicide detective Bryson Coventry finds himself entangled in the collateral damage of a killer who uses the entire world as his playground, newly licensed attorney Paige Alexander lands her very first case—a case that could possibly destroy the most powerful law firm in the world; a case involving a deadly, high-stakes international conspiracy of terrible proportions; a case that started in Bangkok but will not end there.

FATAL LAWS

Jim Michael Hansen

DARK SKY PUBLISHING, INC.

Dark Sky Publishing, Inc.
Golden, CO 80401
www.darkskypublishing.com

www.jimhansenbooks.com
www.jimhansenlawfirm.com

ISBN 13: 978-0-9769243-6-4
ISBN 10: 0-9769243-6-6

Library Of Congress Control Number: 2006908787

Cover photography / Getty Images

10 9 8 7 6 5 4 3 2 1

Made in the USA

Dedicated to
**EILEEN, RUSS, YVONNE,
TARA AND RACHEL**

The author gratefully thanks and acknowledges the generosity, encouragement and contributions of the following fantastic people, without whom the *Laws* novels would be nothing more than dusty paper stuffed in a old desk drawer:

Paul Anik, Baron R. Birtcher, Rebecca Blackmer, Kathy Boswell, Mark Bouton, Naomi de Bruyn, Aldo T. Calcagno, Tony M. Cheatham, Angie Cimarolli, L.B. Cobb, James A. Cox, Lisa D'Angelo, Linnea Dodson, Anne K. Edwards, Geraldine Evans, Tracy Farnsworth, Sgt. Mike Fetrow, Carol Fieger, Denise Fleischer, Barbara Franchi, Norman P. Goldman, Eric L. Harry, Carolyn G. Hart, Joan Hall Hovey, Shirley Priscella Johnson, Harriet Klausner, J.A. Konrath, Katherine Shand Larkin, Andrei V. Lefebvre, Sarah Lovett, Karen L. MacLeod, Kathy Martin, Wanda Maynard, Cheryl McCann, Russel D. McLean, Evan McNamara, Byron Merritt, K. Preston Oade, Jr., Stephanie Padilla, John David Phillips, Sally Powers, Lt. Jon Priest, Jack Quick, Nayaran Radhakrishnan, Patricia A. Rasey, Ann Ripley, Kenneth Sheridan, Shelley Singer, Andrea Sisco, Bob Spear, Mark Terry, Nancy Tesler, Safiya Tremayne and Laurraine Tutihasi; and

My many friends at Barnes & Noble, Borders, Books-A-Million and countless other fine bookstores throughout the country; and

The many people I have had the pleasure to meet at my author events; and, most importantly,

My readers.

Chapter One

Day One – September 5
Monday Morning

TWO HEARTBEATS AFTER BRYSON COVENTRY rang the bell of the expensive contemporary mansion, a naked woman walked across a marble vestibule towards the door, in the process of throwing a long-sleeve shirt over a perfectly tanned body. She had one button done when she opened the door, and looked a lot more like a movie star than a murderer.

Coventry introduced himself as he shifted his 34-year-old frame from one foot to the other, explained that he was with Denver homicide and asked, "Are you Tianca Holland?"

She said nothing.

And instead studied his eyes.

"One's blue and one's green," she said. "I couldn't figure it out at first."

Coventry shrugged.

"One of my many flaws." He couldn't look away. She wasn't just attractive, but dangerously so, with hypnotic green eyes.

She turned. "Come in."

He followed her through a vaulted space with marble columns, exotic plants and modern art. She appeared to be about twenty-seven or twenty-eight. A black tattoo wrapped around her right ankle, something in the nature of a tribal band. Her hair was damp and hung perfectly straight, about six inches below her shoulders. Right now it seemed light brown, but no doubt softened to blond when it dried.

The white shirt was flimsy silk.

An incredibly muscled ass pushed it back and forth as she walked.

"You work out," he said, raking his thick brown hair back with his fingers.

She looked over her shoulder.

"Nice of you to notice."

"It would be pretty hard not to," he said. "Did I say that out loud?"

She laughed.

"Yes, you did."

"Sorry."

She stopped and turned, so abruptly that he actually walked into her. "You're here about Angela Pfeifer, right?" she asked.

"Right."

"Does that mean her body's shown up?"

He nodded. "We found it yesterday."

"Where?"

"In a shallow grave, near a railroad spur north of downtown."

"How'd she die?"

"Stabbed."

"More than once?"

"A lot more than once."

She retreated in thought and then asked, "Was she wearing any clothes?"

"No."

She exhaled. "So, it's official then. She's actually dead."

"I'm afraid so."

She turned, continued walking, and said over her shoulder, "I didn't do it and don't know who did. You're wasting your time with me."

THEY ENDED UP IN THE KITCHEN, which had to be a thousand square feet or more, replete with granite countertops, stainless steel appliances, and distressed wood cabinets. A wall of floor-to-ceiling windows showcased incredibly landscaped grounds, including no less than three waterfalls cascading into an aqua blue pool.

Off in the distance, more than a hundred yards away, a couple of gardeners were hard at work.

The woman handed him a cup of coffee.

He said, "Thanks," took a noisy sip and added, "Nice place."

She studied him.

"It keeps the rain off my head."

She reached into an upper cabinet and pulled out something that looked like a small cigarette. Then she stuck it in her mouth, turned on a burner, and lit it. The unmistakable odor of marijuana immediately permeated the air. After a couple of hits, she offered it to him.

"I better not," he said. "You go right ahead though."

"Our secret, right?"

"I don't see why not."

She took another hit, paced back and forth and then looked him dead in the eyes. "I didn't do it."

Coventry nodded.

"The word is that you two were lovers," he said. "You had a falling out and she disappeared shortly after that. Now her body shows up and we see that she's been dead for some time—months."

She looked at him.

"Since our falling out."

He nodded. "Right. Since about then."

She took another hit from the joint, sucked it in, held her breath, and then blew it out. "I'm glad she's dead. I'll tell you that much."

Coventry paused midway through a sip of coffee.

"She was a major bitch," the woman added.

He raised an eyebrow.

"How much of a bitch, exactly?"

The woman retreated in thought. "Enough that I hated her at the end."

"Hated her enough to kill her?"

The woman didn't hesitate. "Oh, yeah, easily." She headed out of the room. "Follow me. I'm going to show you something."

SHE LED COVENTRY INTO THE MASTER BEDROOM. Thick drapes covered the windows and kept the space so dark that he could hardly make out anything, except for the oversized canopy bed. Then, as his eyes adjusted, the vague shapes of dressers and lamps emerged.

She left the room dark and told him to lie down on the bed.

He hesitated.

She only wore the shirt, with nothing underneath.

And she was high.

"I'm not sure that's a good . . ."

She pushed him and he fell into the bed. "Relax," she said. "I don't limit myself to women, but that's not what this is about."

He stayed where he was, wondering what she was up to. One thing he did know, though, he liked the sound of her voice. She somehow turned each word into an incredibly sexy and intoxicating melody. Each time she talked he didn't want her to stop.

"So you're bi?" he asked.

"Bi, tri, wherever the mood and the liquor take me."

She must have pressed a remote control because the large box at the end of the bed hummed and a screen rose up. She hopped onto the mattress next to him and propped her head and shoulders up on a pillow.

Coventry did the same.

Then the screen lit up—a large flat-panel unit with exceptional clarity. On that screen, two women kissed with open mouths, deep and long, with lots of tongue. It took Coventry a moment to realize that one of the women was Tianca.

"That's me and Angela," Tianca said.

Coventry swallowed.

"Oh."

He watched. Slowly, the women undressed each other and then licked each other's nipples. Coventry knew he should look away but couldn't. Instead he wondered just how far things would go. It didn't take long to find out. Angela was on her back now, with her legs spread wide, as Tianca worked her over with her tongue. After what seemed like a long time, they switched positions.

He lay there, next to Tianca, as she withered in orgasm on

the screen.

But there was more than just sex between the two women.

There was passion.

When it was over, a half hour or more later, she said, "You see how much I loved her? Well, that's the same amount I hated her, at the end. So if you're looking for motive, congratulations. You just found it in spades."

She removed the DVD and set it on top of the player.

"I'll leave this here, so you'll be able to find it if you ever feel the need to get a search warrant and take it," she said. "People's Exhibit A."

BACK IN THE KITCHEN, THEY DRANK MORE COFFEE and talked, but not about the case. Then she showed him around the grounds.

As far as he could tell, Tianca hadn't yet replaced Angela with anyone else in her life, female or male.

He looked at his watch and was shocked to see it was almost noon. Shit, time to go. She walked him out to the Tundra and, just as he was about to pull away, she tapped on the window.

He powered it down.

She leaned in.

"I threatened to kill her. Did I mention that?"

"No, you must have forgot."

"Talk to Natalie, down at Femme, in Glendale," she said. "She'll tell you all about it. It's always exciting, isn't it?"

"What?"

"The first time you meet the next person you're going to sleep with."

Chapter Two

Day One – September 5
Monday Morning

CARRYING A LEATHER BRIEFCASE without a single thing inside except a ballpoint pen and a freshly sharpened No. 2 pencil, Haley Wilde squeezed her 25-year-old body into the elevator, saw that the button for Floor 45 was already lit, and took a deep breath as she ascended to the lofty offices of her new employer—Hart, Sanders & Day, LLC.

She didn't feel like a lawyer.

Even though, technically, she had been one since 2:00 p.m. on Friday when she got sworn in.

She wore a gray pinstriped skirt, a matching jacket, a crisp white blouse and black leather shoes with a one-inch heel, all purchased with plastic on Saturday. She had minimal makeup and styled her shoulder-length brown hair close to her head, to give it a trim professional look, even though she didn't particularly like it that way.

The clothes felt foreign, as if they belonged to someone else.

They were a far cry from the usual jeans and T.

She pushed through the glass doors into the reception area, got informed by a way-too-cute receptionist that the office manager hadn't arrived yet, and was invited to wait in the lobby.

Instead, she walked down to the 44th Floor to see if Renee Rand was in.

HAVING SERVED AS A SUMMER LAW CLERK for the firm a year ago, between her second and third years of law school, she wasn't exactly a stranger to the office—although, she had to admit, most of that two-month tenure was spent stuffed inside a windowless cubical surfing Westlaw and cranking out memos.

Summer law clerks came and went.

Most of the firm's attorneys didn't have the time or inclination to find out much about them, other than whether they could do the work and do it quickly.

Renee had been different.

She'd taken an actual interest in Haley.

Haley stopped in the kitchen to get coffee, hoping to see someone she knew, but found no one. She filled a cup, took a sip, found it to her liking and then trekked down the hall to Renee's office. As she got closer she saw that the light was on.

Excellent.

She walked in, beaming, anxious to see the look on her face. Except it wasn't Renee sitting behind the desk. Instead, it was someone else, a young Asian woman with captivating almond eyes and shiny black hair, dressed to impress. She appeared to be more curious than startled when Haley walked in.

"Oops," Haley said. "Wrong office, sorry."

Embarrassed, she ducked out before the woman could say anything, then got her bearings and realized it wasn't the wrong office after all.

She edged back over to the door and stuck her head in.

"Sorry to bother you," she said. "I'm looking for Renee Rand."

"Renee Rand?"

"Yes."

"She hasn't been here for months," the woman said. Haley must have had a puzzled look on her face, because the woman added, "Haven't you heard?"

No she hadn't.

Heard what?

THE ASIAN WOMAN TURNED OUT TO BE a third-year associate named Christina Huynh, an exotic woman of moderate build and an incredibly small waist, who wore expensive designer glasses. Ivy league diplomas and awards filled the wall behind her.

"No one's seen or heard from Renee since April," Christina said.

"Why? What happened?"

Christina looked stressed. "No one knows for sure, other than she just suddenly vanished."

Haley wrinkled her forehead. "Vanished where?"

"She had an eight o'clock dinner meeting scheduled with two of the firm's partners at The Fort one night. You know where The Fort is, right?"

Haley shook her head.

No, she didn't.

"It's sort of out in the foothills off Highway 8, south of Red Rocks," she said. "It's one of those fancy-schmancy places where people go on special occasions. They serve buffalo, that's their big thing."

Haley shrugged.

She still didn't recognize the place.

"Anyway," Christina said, "they found Renee's car in the parking lot. But she never showed up inside the restaurant."

"What are you saying? That someone took her?"

Christina nodded.

"That's the theory."

"Who?"

Christina held her hands up in surrender. "She didn't have a boyfriend, or money problems, or health problems, or anything that might explain it. Reportedly, she had been in a good mood all day, suspecting what was going to happen."

"What was that?"

"The partners were going to tell her that they were putting her name up for partnership at the annual meeting that was coming up in a couple of weeks," Christina said.

Haley pondered it.

Renee would have been ecstatic.

That's all she ever wanted.

And had worked her ass off for eight years to get it.

No one deserved it more.

"Who were the partners she was going to meet?"

Christina wrinkled her forehead, reaching deep, then said, "Jason Foster and Derek Bennett, if my memory's correct. Why?"

"Nothing, really," Haley said. "I'm just going to ask them about it, if I ever get a chance."

Christina shook her head in doubt.

"The cops assigned to the case were way out of their league," Christina said, "so the law firm actually hired a couple of private investigators and threw some serious money at it. In the end, no one knew much, other than what I just told you. Renee disappeared somewhere between her car and the front door of the restaurant. How and why no one knows. Maybe we'll learn more when her body shows up."

Haley looked out the window.

Then back at the attorney.

Haley must have had a look on her face, because the attorney added, "She's been gone for more than five months."

Chapter Three

Day One – September 5
Monday Morning

JACK DEGAN DIDN'T KNOW IF HE WAS AN INDIAN, a Mexican, or just a really dark white-man. Nor did he give a shit. Most people took him for an Indian on account of the high cheekbones, the thick black ponytail and the scar that ran down the right side of his face, all the way from his hairline to his chin. It had been there ever since he could remember. He had no idea how he got it, but did know that he wouldn't erase it even if he could.

It was part of him.

Somehow he'd earned it.

Now it was his.

Driving south on I-25, the traffic thinned after he passed Colorado Springs and the speed limit increased to 75. He set the cruise control at 88, looked around for cops, found none, brought a flask up to his mouth and took a long swallow of Jack Daniels.

It burned his mouth and then dropped into his stomach.

Damn good stuff.

A knife with an eight-inch serrated blade sat on the seat next to him. He picked it up and twisted it around in his hand as the arid Colorado topography shot by. To the left a river snaked through the land. Hundreds of ugly Cottonwoods—nothing more than 50-foot weeds, in his opinion—sucked up to it.

A hint of yellow had already snuck into the leaves. Fall was coming. Lucky for him, he'd be in California before the first snow fell.

THIS MOST RECENT HUNT was going to be a little tricky. He was searching for an Hispanic woman, nice looking, under thirty, heavily tattooed. Tons of tattoos, that was the most important thing. The more goddamn tattoos the better.

That would be a tall task in Denver.

But in Pueblo, not so much.

There was more Hispanic pussy down there than the law allowed. Not to mention a biker bar on every street corner—tattoo magnets.

He rolled his six-three, 225-pound frame into the blue-collar town mid-afternoon and checked into a sleazy rat-in-the-closet hotel, paying cash—the kind of place where no one noticed anything and remembered even less. He tried to take a short nap but some hooker in the next room kept screaming fake orgasms. So he drove around to check out the tattoo shops, just in case the perfect woman happened to be hanging around one of them. He'd hit the biker bars tonight.

He drove by three tattoo shops, saw nothing but guys, and kept going. Then he found a shop with two women inside, one of them working on the other. He stopped across the street, wrote down the license plate numbers of the two cars in front of the shop, and then pulled in and killed the engine.

Rap music filled the air.

When he walked in, the woman giving the tattoo looked up.

"Hi, I'm Mia," she said. "Go ahead and look around. If you got any questions just holler."

She fit the bill, perfectly—Hispanic, mid-twenties, with long brown hair pulled into a ponytail. She wore a tank top with no bra, showing off strong arms covered in ink. The woman getting the tattoo would work too, although she would be second choice. She was getting the new artwork on her left breast, a small rose or flower of some sort.

"Just looking," he said.

"Besides the stuff on the walls," she said, "there's books on the desk, too. We can make anything any size you want. We can change the colors, customize them however you want."

"Great," he said.

Pattern pictures covered the walls, hundreds of them.

He walked around.

Keeping one eye on the women.

Trying to not be obvious.

Then something weird happened.

He spotted a pattern he actually liked.

"What's this?" he asked, pointing.

Mia stopped working and turned her cute little face towards him. "That's an Indian war symbol," she said.

He didn't even hesitate.

"I want it."

She nodded. "That'll look good on you. I'll be about another half hour here, then you're up."

Perfect.

"Say, would you mind if I watched, and see how you do it? I've never had one of these things before."

The two women looked at each other.

Neither cared.

So he pulled up a chair and watched.

As they chatted he found out all kinds of useful little facts. The woman giving the tattoo—Mia Avila—owned and operated the shop. She opened it two years ago at age twenty-two after coming out of the wrong end of a marriage. The woman in the chair—Isella Ramirez—was married with two kids. The ink on her tit was a birthday present from hubby-face.

Mia Avila would be the one he'd take.

Assuming the opportunity presented itself.

Chapter Four

Day One – September 5
Monday Afternoon

BACK AT HEADQUARTERS, BRYSON COVENTRY sat through a series of afternoon meetings drinking decaf while his thoughts wandered to Tianca Holland. He liked her eyes, her voice and the way she tossed her hair.

He needed to see her again, soon.

If not again today, then tomorrow for sure.

There was something between them, unspoken but yet tangible. He couldn't remember the last time a woman's pull had so strong of a grip on him, especially right from the start.

After the last meeting, he swung by Shalifa Netherwood's desk. At age twenty-seven she was the newest detective in the Unit, personally stolen by Coventry from vice a year ago. But she had already cut her teeth on two of the scariest guys to ever hit Denver—David Hallenbeck and Nathan Wickersham.

"Want to take a ride?" he asked.

She looked relieved at the opportunity.

They were headed to the stairwell, almost past the elevators, when Shalifa jumped in front of him waving a bill.

"Ten dollars if you take the elevator," she said.

He stopped.

"Why?"

"Just to see if you're capable."

"I am," he said, trying to walk around her.

She blocked him again.

"Ten bucks says you're not," she said.

He studied her.

"Remember, I'm the cheapest guy on the face of the earth," he said.

"I already know that."

He grabbed the bill and pressed the down button. When the elevator doors opened, he hesitated, then stepped inside and pressed the button for the parking garage. Shalifa—visibly startled—stepped inside with him.

Before the doors shut he jumped out.

Then returned the bill down in the parking garage.

"Try me again tomorrow with a twenty," he said.

THEY HEADED NORTH ON BROADWAY in his Tundra, with the windows cracked just enough to let in air but not noise. The weather couldn't have been more perfect, eighty and sunny. He flicked the radio stations, finally stopping at "Two Out of Three Ain't Bad."

"Does this car even get black music?" Shalifa asked.

He raised an eyebrow and realized that sometimes he actually forgot that she was African American, born and raised in Five-Points.

"What? You don't like Meat Loaf?"

"No, I like steak," she said.

He chuckled and then added, "He was in Rocky Horror Picture Show."

"Who?"

"Meat Loaf. He was in the Rocky Horror Picture Show."

"What's that?"

"What do you mean—*what's that?* You never saw the Rocky Horror Picture Show?"

"No, what is it?"

"Have you ever danced the Time Warp?"

She looked at him weird. "No more coffee for you," she said. "Tell me about your meeting with Tianca Holland this morning."

He did.

Leaving out the bedroom scene.

"She did everything she could to incriminate herself," he said. "Either because she's innocent and doesn't care what we find, or because she's guilty and wants to appear so innocent that she doesn't care what we find."

"So which is it?"

"I don't know. I need more time with her."

FIFTEEN MINUTES LATER they ended up driving through weeds and dirt down an old abandoned BNSF railroad spur north of downtown. Coventry parked the vehicle and they hoofed it down the tracks for about fifty steps. Then they walked north for thirty yards until they came to the shallow grave where Angela Pfeiffer's body had been found.

"What are we looking for, exactly?" Shalifa asked.

Coventry shrugged and raked his hair back with his fingers. It immediately flopped back down over his forehead.

"Whatever we missed the first time," he said.

Three geese flew overhead.

The grave had been shallow; in fact not more than six inches deep. Either the digger tired easily—say, a woman—or didn't really care how deep the grave was, just so long as the body was hidden from sight.

Ten yards farther past the gravesite was a concrete retaining wall, about four feet high. Coventry got on top and scouted around. The ground on the other side came up to about two feet from the top of the wall.

Coventry jumped back down on the track side of the wall and called Shalifa over.

"How much to you weigh?" he asked.

"Why?"

"Just indulge me," he said. "How much?"

"I don't know," she said. "One twenty-five, maybe."

Good.

That was about the same weight as the dead woman.

"Do me a favor and lay down on the ground," he said. "I'm going to see how hard it is to lift you up and get you over this wall."

She looked at him as if he was crazy.

"I don't think so," she said.

"Come on," he said. "It's for the case. If I was going to dump a body here, I would have put it on the other side of this wall if I could." Still, she hesitated. "Come on, lay down and be dead."

She did.

"Okay, here we go," he said. "Stay limp." Then he reached down, picked her up and muscled her to the top of the retaining wall, finding it more difficult than he at first thought, but not an all-out effort.

She hopped down and brushed herself off.

"Satisfied?"

He was.

"Most women wouldn't be able to do that," he said. "Most men would."

Shalifa continued to brush the dust off her ass and said, "That doesn't mean it was necessarily a woman. It could still be a guy. Maybe he just didn't see the wall because it was night, or saw it but could care less."

That was true.

But he found himself saying, "The best place to bury the body is on the other side of the wall. A man would have gone to the bother. A woman might not have."

"So the position of the grave points to Tianca Holland as the killer?" she asked.

"It's a strike against her."

From the railroad spur they headed to Femme, which turned out to be an upscale lesbian bar in Glendale, not far from Shotgun Willies.

The bar was closed but they rapped on the door until someone answered.

The woman they were looking for, in fact.

Natalie.

Coventry explained the situation, including the fact that Tianca Holland herself had suggested that they talk to her.

"I don't know why she'd do that," Natalie said. "I'm not going to lie about what happened."

They ended up sitting in a booth, drinking diet Cokes.

Coventry asked if the place had a men's room, was told, "Of

course, that's city code," and then used it. When he came back Shalifa and Natalie were chatting like old friends. Natalie was soft and curvy and reminded Coventry of Sophia Loren, back in her early days, say the *Man of La Mancha* era.

"Okay," Natalie said, "Angela Pfeiffer was your basic hard-core slut, except in a classy, upscale package. She'd come in here alone about twice a month, pick out whoever she wanted, take her home and screw her brains out. Then dump her and start all over again. She openly bragged about having some rich lover wrapped around her little finger, someone she milked for money."

"So she had lots of enemies," Coventry said. "Meaning the women she dumped."

"I don't know if I'd go that far," Natalie said. "Getting dumped was sort of understood when it came to Angela. Most of the women accepted it going in."

Coventry nodded.

Okay.

"So what happened with Tianca?"

"Well," Natalie said, "one night Angela's in here, drunk out of her mind, and has about three or four women hovering around, trying to get in her pants. In walks another woman, a striking, exotic woman."

"Tianca," Coventry said.

Natalie nodded.

"Yes," she said, "although I didn't know her name at the time. They immediately got into an argument. It escalated and they ended up in a catfight, and I'm not talking about some dainty little slap and cry, I'm talking about a serious confrontation. They wound up wrestling on the ground with everyone in the place crowded around, hooting and hollering and egging them on."

"Does that happen often here?" Shalifa asked.

Natalie looked shocked.

"No, never—this is a class place. Anyway," she said, "Angela got the upper hand. She got the other woman—Tianca—on her back and then straddled her and pined her arms up above her head. Now the crowd was going nuts and shouting for her to sit on her face. So she scooted up and ground her crotch on the woman's face. That's when the woman, Tianca, started shouting that she was going to kill her. That went on for a long time, five minutes or maybe even longer. Finally the bouncers pulled them apart."

"So Tianca definitely said she was going to kill her?" Coventry asked.

Natalie nodded.

"Yes, absolutely."

"You heard it yourself?"

"Yes I did. And I saw her face. She meant it. There's no question about it, not in my mind at least."

Chapter Five

Day One – September 5
Monday Morning

THE LAW FIRM DIDN'T WASTE ANY TIME turning Haley Wilde, Esq. into a billable-hour machine. The head of the Employment Department—Baxter Brown, Esq.—showed her to her office, drank coffee with her, smiled and made her feel at home. Then he left her with a wrongful termination file to review, in preparation of answering interrogatories, admissions and document requests which needed to be in the mail by this time next week.

"If you run into any problems, shoot me an email," he said. "I'll be in depositions until Thursday morning but I'll be checking my emails twice a day."

Then he left.

She felt wonderfully full.

By eleven o'clock just about everyone on her hall had popped in at least once to say welcome. A couple of the guys stopped in twice. The associates gave her the thirty-second scoop. Sure, the firm's stated goal for newbies is 1,750 billables a year. But plan on 2,000 minimum. And, if you're actually crazy enough to want to make partner some day, plan on 2,200 to

2,500. "When you get up in the middle of the night to take a piss, think of a case and bill the client for your time."

Shortly before noon, a new face showed up in her door—an attractive man in his early forties with blondish hair and energetic blue eyes. He wore a gray suit with an expensive hang, and looked exactly like what a lawyer at the top of his game should look like.

The kind of person who could walk into any room and dominate it.

The epitome of success.

She recognized him from somewhere but couldn't quite place it. Then it struck her. He was none other than Austin Gray himself—the president of the firm and reputed rainmaker extraordinaire.

"Got time for lunch?" he asked.

THEY ENDED UP WALKING PAST A CROWD of waiting people at Marlowe's and got escorted to a nice booth near the back with a white tablecloth. Within minutes their food arrived, a steak and nonalcoholic beer for him, and a shrimp salad for her.

"With your arrival today," he said, "we now have 123 lawyers. One of my primary responsibilities, as the head of the firm, is to be sure that we all remember we're a family, and not just a bunch of individual cogs in some kind of overgrown machine. It's our attitude towards one another, and towards our clients, that spells either survival or extinction. So I make it a point to personally know everyone in the firm, hence our lunch today. But more importantly, I make it a point to be sure that everyone in the firm, from the copy clerk to the department head, knows that my office door is always open."

Haley nodded.

"That's good to know."

He smiled.

"You know," he said, "I'm a little jealous. I wish I could be back in time, reporting for my first day of work. You have the whole world ahead of you."

She wasn't sure if it was smart to say what she wanted to say. But decided to anyway.

"I'm a little scared," she said. "I'm not sure I'm ready."

He understood.

"It's an intimidating place at first," he said. "But we were all green once, just like you. Then we grow. You will too, trust me. Just take it one day at a time."

She took a drink of water.

Then decided to see if his door really was open.

"I heard this morning about what happened to Renee Rand," she said. "She was one of the nicer people towards me, when I clerked here last summer."

He wrinkled his forehead.

"She had a big heart," he said, "on top of being a brilliant attorney."

Haley agreed.

"I can't help but think about one of the projects she had me working on back then," Haley said.

"Oh? What's that?"

"It was for a psychologist," she said. "I can't remember her name right now, but the gist of the matter was that she had some kind of an impromptu conversation with some man who wasn't a formal client. She took him to be a killer. Apparently he had a certain MO that she recognized. Anyway, since the man asked her questions that could possibly be viewed as the type of thing a patient might ask a psychologist, she wanted a legal opinion on whether the conversation was covered by the physician-patient privilege. Renee had me do the research and we concluded that the privilege in fact attached, meaning she couldn't give the information to the police."

Austin nodded.

"You're talking about Dr. Beverly Twenhofel," he said.

"Exactly, that's her," she said. "I can't help but wonder if Renee's disappearance is somehow tied to that case."

Austin took a swig of the nonalcoholic beer.

"The same thought came to me at one point, namely Renee's working on a case potentially involving a killer, and then she ends up missing. But I don't see a connection for two reasons. First, the guy—whoever he is—wouldn't even know that our client had approached us for a legal opinion. So there's no reason Renee would have been on his radar screen. Second, if the guy did feel threatened, say because he sensed that someone believed he was a killer, he would have gone after Dr. Twenhofel, and not us. That never happened. She's alive and well and hasn't been threatened or harassed in any way."

Haley hadn't been privy to that.

Obviously Austin was way ahead of her.

"Well," she said, "that's the only thing that I know of, sort of offbeat, that might somehow explain something."

He nodded.

"It was a good thought," he said. "But unlikely."

THEN SHE RAN HER OTHER THEORY BY HIM, the theory that maybe Renee hadn't actually been abducted in the parking lot of The Fort at all, but had in fact been abducted somewhere else earlier. Then they dropped her car off in the parking lot to make it look like she'd been abducted there.

Again, he didn't seem overly impressed.

"We had, and still do have, the best private investigators in the state working on the case," he said. "I'm sure they considered that theory. In fact, I'm almost positive they have. I remember talking to them at one point about the fact that Renee gassed up near her house about twenty minutes before she was supposed to arrive at The Fort. It was about a twenty-minute drive there, which meant she was on her way. So if she wasn't taken in the parking lot, she somehow had to be pulled over before she got there. I don't see how that could happen. As I recall, her spare tire was in good condition, meaning she hadn't pulled over with a flat."

He shrugged.

"I'm not saying you're wrong," he said. "I'm only saying that it doesn't seem to fit the facts."

"I didn't know all those facts," she said.

"No way you would have," he added. "But your theories are impressive, especially for someone who just started thinking about it. I can tell we made the right decision hiring you."

"I hope so."

"I already know it," he said. "You're going to be a partner some day. I can tell."

Chapter Six

Day One – September 5
Monday Evening

WHEN JACK DEGAN WOKE FROM HIS NAP, the room was dark and it took him a few moments to remember he was in a sleazy Pueblo hotel. He wandered into the bathroom, took a long piss, then recalled getting the tattoo this afternoon and flicked the lights on to have a look.

It wrapped around his right arm, above the bicep.

"Good job Mia Avila," he said.

Between that and the scar on his face he looked downright dangerous.

Maybe he needed another one now.

On the other arm.

Something different though.

He took a swig of Jack Daniels and then headed for the shower, getting it as hot as he could stand it. When he came out he felt like a new man, a man with a full night ahead of him. He slipped into jeans and a black muscle shirt and then headed down the rickety hotel stairs. He drove around downtown Pueblo until he spotted a bar with thirty or forty Harleys out front, then parked his beat-up Chevy a block down the street and doubled back on foot.

The place was packed, dark, loud and rowdy.

Nice.

Red vinyl booths lined the left wall, and a long bar ran down the right. In the back, by the restrooms, were a couple of pool tables and a small dance floor, with a handful of drunks twirling around with no sense of coordination or timing.

There had to be over two hundred people in there.

And they weren't just drinking.

They were either shit-faced or on their way.

Tattoos were everywhere.

Plenty of women too.

Perfect.

He found a space at the bar big enough to squeeze into, ordered a Bud Light and then looked around for backup prey, just in case Mia Avila turned out to be problematic.

At least half the women were dogs.

Bow-wow.

Worse than dogs, not even worth a bone.

Two nice ones, though—both heavily tattooed and wearing muscle shirts—were playing pool in the back. He wandered in that direction, leaned against the wall and watched 'em without being too conspicuous.

They would work just fine.

Either of 'em.

He walked over and set two quarters on the table. "I got the winner," he told them.

"That'll be me," one of them said.

"My ass," the other one said.

Five minutes later he was up, racked 'em and let the woman break. Two stripes went in.

"You can still take solids if you want," he said.

She laughed, then walked over and leaned in.

"Are you interested in a little side bet?"

He cocked his head.

"What'd you have in mind?"

"The loser buys beer."

That sounded good.

"Fine, but now you got me motivated," he warned.

She ran a finger down his face.

Along the scar.

And laughed.

"It won't matter," she said. "I'm still going to kick your ass."

"Start kicking."

She was about twenty-seven, five-feet-three with jet-black hair, the same color as his, in fact. It hung loose and she constantly tossed her head to get it out of her face.

Very sexy.

Her name was Martina.

She won the first game.

And the second.

Then Degan had to piss like crazy and headed to the men's room while she racked 'em up.

A MAN WEARING A LEATHER VEST with no shirt underneath walked into the restroom just before Degan did. The guy walked past three empty urinals and into the stall, then left the door halfway open and started pissing.

Degan could tell that the jerk was pissing all over the toilet seat.

When the guy came out Degan looked inside and checked.

Sure enough, the seat was still down.

Covered with piss.

Nor had the guy flushed. Degan flashed back to a time last year when he had to crap like crazy and had to wipe someone else's piss off the seat.

"Goddamn pig," Degan muttered under his breath.

The man looked at him.

"You got a problem, buddy?"

Degan stared back at him. "Maybe I do."

The biker paused, as if deciding.

Then he had a knife in his hands and said, "You little bitch."

Degan punched, hard and fast, going for the nose and getting it. Blood splattered from the guy's face. Then Degan hit him in the stomach, below the ribs, as hard as he could. The guy immediately doubled up and fell to the floor. Degan grabbed him by the hair and dragged him over to the toilet.

Then shoved his face in it.

And held him there while he struggled.

After a long time, Degan pulled the guy's head out, let him catch his breath, and then shoved his face back in.

The asshole kicked but it did no good.

"Now you wish you flushed."

Then Degan kicked him in the balls, pulled his head out and threw him on the floor.

TWO MINUTES LATER HE WAS RUNNING down the street with three bikers chasing him.

Gunfire erupted.

The windshield of a car next to him exploded.

He zigzagged and ran even faster.

AFTER HE LOST THEM HE CIRCLED BACK TO THE BAR and hid behind a pickup truck across the street. When they returned he memorized their faces. Then headed back to the hotel.

When he got there he knocked on the door next to his.

A woman opened it.

Not exactly a prom queen but not the opposite either. Her short punked-out blond hair reeked of pot. For some reason he liked her right away.

"You still open for business?" he asked.

She grabbed his shirt and pulled him inside.

"You look dangerous," she said. "That gets me hot."

Chapter Seven

Day Two – September 6
Tuesday Morning

COVENTRY GOT UP EARLY Tuesday morning, with Tianca Holland already in his thoughts. He threw on sweatpants and jogged out the front door well before the crack of dawn, letting his legs stretch and his lungs burn, while he flashed back to being in bed with her yesterday.

He could have taken her if he wanted.

She had him in bed for a reason and it wasn't just to watch the DVD. They could have done that in the study. Or not done it at all.

"You definitely have some willpower," he told himself. "Maybe too much."

Even though September had just started, and Indian summer hadn't yet begun, the mornings were already getting a chill.

Perfect for jogging.

He did three miles at a pretty good clip and then finished the workout with several sets of pushups and sit-ups in his front yard. Forty-five minutes later he was at his desk downtown, the first person to work, trying to get organized while the coffee pot fired up.

He drank the entire pot and was just starting to make the second one when Shalifa Netherwood showed up.

"I checked the Internet to exhaustion last night," she said. "Someone as rich as Tianca Holland ought to be showing up all over the place. But Google acts like she doesn't even exist."

"That's interesting."

Shalifa couldn't wait for the pot to fill so she pulled it out, stuck her cup under the coffee stream, and then switched back after it filled, never spilling a drop.

"Very impressive," Coventry said. "But can you do it behind your back?"

He then did it.

Behind his back.

Spilling coffee all over the place.

"Tell me again why I work with you?"

He smiled, mopping the counter with paper towels.

"Because you have to."

She looked doubtful. "That couldn't be enough. There must be more."

Then Coventry said something he didn't expect.

"I might have to take myself off the Tianca Holland case," he said.

"Why?"

"I think I'm more interested in sleeping with her than finding out if she's a murderer," he said.

Shalifa rolled her eyes.

"Even if you took yourself off, you still couldn't sleep with her," she said.

That was true.

"Such a dilemma," he said.

"Here's what you do," she said. "A, don't sleep with her.

And B, put the little fellow back in his cage and then find out if she's a murderer like the city's paying you to do."

"You're right."

"And C," she added, "don't always look so surprised when I'm right."

He chuckled, then put on a serious face: "What do you mean, *little fellow*?"

She sipped coffee.

"You're not black, are you?"

"No."

"Okay then."

He laughed, then surprised himself again, and told her about the bedroom incident yesterday.

She frowned as she listened.

"Tianca Holland has motive. And unless and until we can better pinpoint when Angela Pfeiffer disappeared, she also has opportunity. Now she's got you off balance with this bed thing. My question is whether she's doing it on purpose."

IT WAS SHORTLY AFTER NINE O'CLOCK when Coventry realized he had done something really stupid.

"I left my mug down by the railroad tracks yesterday," he told Shalifa.

"The one we got you when you got promoted?"

He nodded.

"I'm going to ride down and get it. You want to tag along?"

A half hour later they were back at the scene where Angela Pfeiffer's body had been found. The mug was still there, sitting on the top of the concrete retaining wall.

But now Coventry had another problem.

The first pot of coffee suddenly wanted out.

Now.

Not in two minutes.

Right now.

He looked around for the best spot, decided it was behind a rusted 55-gallon drum, and told Shalifa to look the other way for a few moments.

"Unbelievable," she said. "How is it that you haven't been fired yet?"

He laughed.

"I have no idea," he said.

He looked around, saw no one, then pulled the so-called little fellow out and went for it. That felt so incredibly good. He aimed at a small rock, going for accuracy, hitting it pretty damn good even if he had to say so himself. By the time he finished, the rock was much more exposed.

Except it didn't quite look like a rock any more.

He zipped up and then bent down and looked at it.

It looked like a finger.

He found a stick and moved the dirt away.

And uncovered a hand.

A hand that appeared to be attached to a body.

Chapter Eight

Day Two – September 6
Tuesday

HALEY WILDE PARKED HER CAR—a faded Honda Accord with a dented front fender—in a lot on the east side of Broadway. The law firm was a six-block hike from there but the rates were cheaper. She wore the second of the five outfits she bought on Saturday. Sooner or later people would notice that her wardrobe wasn't exactly overabundant, but with over a hundred thousand dollars owing in student loans she could only afford what she could afford.

It was ironic, actually—an attorney at one of Denver's most prestigious law firms who would be dirt poor for at least three years.

Probably four.

Maybe forever.

She got to the office by 7:30, wanting to make a good impression, and started billing right away. However, Renee Rand's disappearance, and probable death, pulled at her.

Shortly before lunch she went to the dead files storage room and pulled the Dr. Beverly Twenhofel case, knowing she was probably overstepping her boundaries and hoping against hope that no one saw her so she didn't have to come up with some lamebrain explanation.

"Leave it to you to get fired on the second day of work," she told herself.

Renee Rand, Esq.'s handwritten notes were in the file.

Beautiful.

Unfortunately, Renee had either never been told, or had never written down, the name of the so-called patient, the one who Dr. Twenhofel believed to be a killer.

The guy's name was nowhere in the file.

Damn it.

A dead end.

She slipped the folder back exactly where she found it and then returned to her office.

No one saw her.

AT NOON, SHE EXPECTED SOMEONE TO DROP BY and invite her to lunch, but no one did. So she pulled out her brown bag and worked the Internet as she ate at her desk, using every search engine she could think of to see what it had on Renee Rand. By the end of the hour she found six or seven newspaper articles about her disappearance.

None of them were particularly helpful though.

Another dead end.

At 1:00 she went back on the clock.

And worked her ass off until six.

Then she hoofed it to her car and fought traffic until she got home.

THAT EVENING, AFTER SUPPER, SHE DROVE to The Fort. It turned out to be a restaurant south of Morrison, smack dab at the base of the foothills in Jefferson County, surrounded by undeveloped land. She sensed that it might have started out as a getaway estate for someone rich.

She understood now how someone could be abducted in the parking lot without anyone noticing.

She went home and turned on the Fitness Channel for background noise as she went over her outstanding bills. Lots of them were overdue but she just didn't have the funds in hand right now.

A new cell phone bill arrived today.

So she paid last month's.

That brought her checking account balance down to $82.00.

Then she straightened up the apartment and went to bed.

The upstairs neighbors had their music on again. The bass pushed through the walls and straight into her brain. She pulled the pillow over her head and closed her eyes. It did no good, and the more she thought about how rude they were, the more awake she got.

So she drove down to 24-Hour Fitness to exhaust herself on the treadmill.

Chapter Nine

Day Two – September 6
Tuesday Morning

UNDER A CLOUDLESS COLORADO SKY, Jack Degan drove west through Clear Creek Canyon, one of his all-time favorite places in the world. Sheer rock walls rose straight up on both sides, leaving just enough room at the bottom for the twisty two-lane road and the river, which frothed with white foam as it pounded over boulders.

Seriously stunning.

He used to tube those icy waters back when he was a kid, almost drowning himself more times than he could count. That was back in the days when asshole landowners strung barbwire across the river to keep kayaks and tubes off.

Degan got tangled up in some of that barbwire once.

Got eight stitches in his face and almost lost an eye.

He paid a special little visit to the landowner two nights later.

Word got around.

Most of the barbwire on the river came down after that.

He passed through the first tunnel, then the second, where the road cut through the mountains. Now the tunnels were lighted, unlike years ago when all they had were signs that warned drivers to Turn Headlights On. When he came to Highway 119 he took it, deeper into the mountains, past Black Hawk for about five miles, where he turned onto a gravel road that followed a string of short telephone poles.

At the end of that road he came to a cabin.

A beat-up pickup sat out front.

A detached garage squatted to the left.

He stopped, killed the engine, walked to the door and knocked.

A TEENAGER ANSWERED, about seventeen, with shaggy brown hair, dressed in total black with spiked hair. Degan expected someone older and a lot more normal.

"You the guy who wants to see the place?" the kid asked.

"That's me."

"My dad couldn't make it," the kid said.

"Fine," Degan said. "No problem."

"Go ahead and look around."

The place had a large central room with a vaulted ceiling, really nice, actually, and two separate bedrooms. The water came from a well but the electricity was public. The garage was empty and spacious with a dirt floor. You could spill a lot of blood in there, clean it up easily, and no one would ever be the wiser.

Best of all there were no other structures in sight.

No one would hear screaming.

But just to be sure he asked the kid. "No neighbors, huh?"

The kid shrugged. "I've never seen any houses anywhere around here."

"How big is your property?"

The kid wrinkled his forehead. "I think it's a hundred acres, or two hundred, something like that. My dad would know."

Degan nodded.

Good enough.

He'd scout around later, just to be sure no one else was around. But at least for now the place seemed perfect. "Okay," he said. "I'll take it until the end of the month. Five hundred, right?"

The kid shrugged.

"Whatever my dad told you."

"He told me five hundred plus a thousand security deposit." He handed the kid fifteen hundred-dollar bills.

Done deal.

AFTER THE KID LEFT, DEGAN GOT ALL THE STUFF from the trunk of his car and brought it into the bedroom—cameras, tripods, monitors, sheets, cuffs, blindfolds, ropes, chains, locks, and all the rest of it, including the all-important DVD recorder.

Then he scouted the surrounding area.

There were no other houses around.

Very nice.

Pine trees perfumed the air. Green lichen covered boulders that jutted out of the earth, some as big as trucks. The aspen trees were just starting to get a yellow hue.

Just for grins, he jogged all the way down to Highway 119, and then walked back up, enjoying a perfect day.

Then he locked up, stopped at Black Hawk and played blackjack for a couple of hours, stuffed his face at the casino buffet, and then headed back to his Denver apartment.

HE ALMOST PULLED INTO THE PARKING LOT when he spotted four skuzzy bikers hanging around. They looked like they'd been there for a while. He drove past too fast to see their faces but knew they were the jerks from Pueblo, the three assholes who chased him down the street, plus someone else.

Probably the guy Degan stuffed in the toilet.

Shit.

How'd they track him?

They must have seen his license plate number.

The little bastards.

So, they want to play?

They want to play so bad that they came all the way up here to Denver?

Fine.

He can play too.

Chapter Ten

Day Two – September 6
Tuesday

THE HAND IN THE DIRT turned out to be connected to a body, as Bryson Coventry suspected; a woman's body to be precise. He watched as the Crime Unit unburied it scoop-by-scoop, careful to not overlook any foreign materials or evidence. The grave was shallow, not much more than six inches, just like Angela Pfeifer's. The state of decomposition of the two victims was also similar. The graves were no more than a hundred feet apart.

Finally, just like Angela Pfeifer, this woman was naked.

But whereas Angela Pfeifer had been stabbed repeatedly, there wasn't a single mark on this woman.

"Whoever killed this one killed the other one," Coventry said. "They were obviously both buried the same night. That pretty much eliminates Tianca Holland as a suspect."

"Unless this is another one of her past lovers," Shalifa added.

He chuckled.

"Right, except for that," he said.

"Or unless this is Angela's new lover."

"Right, that too."

"Or unless this one was a witness."

"Okay, that too."

"Or unless this one is a decoy," Shalifa added.

He raised an eyebrow.

"What do you mean by that?"

"You know," she said. "You kill the one you want, and then a stranger too, to make it look like someone else did it."

Coventry wasn't persuaded.

"I'm sure there are situations where that's happened," he said. "But you'd have to be awfully cold-blooded. Tianca doesn't even come close to anything like that."

"Yeah, well . . ."

"If I really stretch my imagination, I can *maybe* see her killing Angela," Coventry said, interrupting her. "I have to admit, I never put too much stock in the fact that she threatened the woman's life. Those were nothing more than heat of passion words said during a fight. I say stuff like that two or three times a day but hardly ever actually kill anyone."

Shalifa kicked the dirt.

"I'd agree," she said, "if there was nothing more. But we still have the repeated stabbing."

Coventry knew what she meant.

The stabbing was an act of passion.

The hallmark of someone close to the victim.

"It's curious that this second woman was killed in a different manner," he said. "It'll be interesting to find out the cause of death. In any event, it sort of blows your decoy theory out of the water. If I was going to kill someone, and then a stranger too to make it look like someone else did it, I'd kill them both the same way."

Shalifa shrugged.

"Maybe," she said. "But then again, maybe you do it different, so no one thinks it a decoy."

Coventry chuckled.

"I'm never going to win an argument with you, am I?"

She put her arm around his shoulders.

"That doesn't mean you should stop trying," she said. Then she chuckled, as if she just heard a joke.

"What?" he asked, curious.

"You know you're going to be getting calls by the end of the day."

"About what?"

"From other police departments," she said, "wanting you to come out with that divining rod of yours to help find where the bodies are buried."

He laughed.

"Hopefully," he said, "that was a once-in-a-lifetime deal."

"You never know," Shalifa said. "You may have a gift. It would give you a chance to use that thing for good, instead of evil, for a change."

He laughed.

"You're too much."

IRONICALLY, HE DID HAVE TO USE IT AGAIN, plus he needed more coffee in the gut. So he told Shalifa he'd be back in ten minutes and drove to the 7-Eleven on Broadway, almost getting run over by some idiot in a Hummer talking on a cell phone.

He used the facilities first.

Then found the coffee.

Of course he didn't have a single one of his thermoses with

him, because that would make his life too easy, so he bought yet another one, poured five French Vanilla creamers into it and then topped it off with piping hot caffeine. "Love Shack" played from hidden speakers.

On the way back to the scene, Shalifa's comment—that the second woman may have been a witness—nagged him.

That would explain the different causes of death.

Tianca *might* be capable of that, if she felt trapped enough.

Chapter Eleven

Day Three – September 7
Wednesday Noon

HALEY WILDE COULDN'T SHAKE THE FEELING that Renee Rand's disappearance was somehow connected to the Beverly Twenhofel file. The thought tugged at her so much that, when her lunch hour rolled around, she trotted the six blocks to her car and sped over to the psychologist's Cherry Creek office.

Hoping to get whatever information she could.

Maybe even the killer's name.

Dr. Twenhofel was just about to walk out the door when Haley entered her office, out of breath after having to park more than three blocks away and then power-walk over.

"I'm here about Renee Rand," Haley said.

The woman—an elegant lady about fifty—studied her.

"Renee Rand the attorney?"

"Yes."

She looked at her watch.

Haley sensed that she was already late for an appointment.

But they ended up in her office, anyway, a comfortable cozy space with lots of cherry wood, plants and texture. Haley explained her theory that Dr. Twenhofel's so-called patient was somehow connected to Renee's disappearance. The woman listened patiently and said, "So what is it exactly that you want from me?"

Good question.

Haley bit her lower lip.

"I don't know," she said. "A name, I guess."

The woman retreated in thought and then said, "I don't see how there could be a connection, personally. If the guy felt threatened, he would go after me. That hasn't happened. Plus he wouldn't even know that Renee was involved in providing a legal opinion. Renee wasn't the kind of person who would do anything stupid like try to hunt him down on the side or anything. Not to mention that I'm not sure that I even told her the guy's name."

The woman looked at her watch again.

Then back at Haley.

"Your desire to help Renee is admirable," she said. "But you're pointed in the wrong direction."

"If that's the case, what harm would it do for you to tell me the guy's name? Maybe he called her or something. If we find his name written down in Renee's day-timer or phone messages or something, we'd have a connection."

The woman shook her head.

"Here's the problem," she said. "First of all, I'm not good with names and don't even remember it at this point. Second of all, even if I did, I wouldn't tell you because you'd end up doing something to get yourself on his radar screen. I'm not going to let that happen."

The woman stood up and looked at her watch.

"Like I said," she added, "your desire to help Renee is admirable. But my advice to you is drop it."

Chapter Twelve

Day Three – September 7
Wednesday Morning

AFTER SPENDING THE NIGHT AT THE CABIN, Jack Degan came out of the mountains Wednesday morning to see if the bikers had broken into his apartment.

They had.

The place was a disaster.

It smelled like urine.

They'd pissed all over the carpet and furniture and walls.

Black magic marker on the living room wall said, "Dead man." The TV was shattered. In the kitchen, the refrigerator door was open. Food had been thrown everywhere.

He went into the bedroom, slid the bed over, and pulled up the carpeting to see if they'd stumbled across his secret money compartment.

They hadn't.

"Dumb shits," he said, smiling.

He pulled a pillowcase off a pillow, stuffed the money inside, and tied a knot in the end. Then he grabbed the clothes that hadn't been ruined, stuffed them in another pillowcase, walked down to his car, threw everything in the trunk and drove off.

HE STOPPED AT STARBUCKS AND GOT A COFFEE TO GO, then headed over to I-25 and pointed the rusty front end of the Chevy towards Pueblo. When he got into town two and a half hours later, he went to his old hotel and knocked on the hooker's door, the one who had given him such a good blowjob Monday night.

Gretchen.

Wearing pajamas and no makeup, she now looked even more average than before, and the five extra pounds now showed as ten. He didn't care.

She answered, groggy.

Looking like she just got dragged out of hibernation.

"Hi," he said. "Gretchen? Right?"

She studied him, confused, not quite placing him.

"Monday night," he said. "I had the room next to yours."

She smiled and opened the door.

"I remember you," she said. "You were nice. Come on in."

He sat on the bed while she disappeared into the bathroom. The shower turned on and he could hear her adjusting the temperature. Then the curtain pulled back and she stepped in. Ten minutes later she was out and toweled off.

Looking very nice, actually.

She walked over, pushed him onto his back and straddled him. Then reached under his shirt and played with his nipples.

"So what's your pleasure?"

"How much for the whole day?" he asked.

She looked stunned.

And stopped.

"You want me for the whole day?"

"Yep. Until midnight."

She thought about it and he could tell she was trying to figure out how much she'd make otherwise, it being a Wednesday.

She shrugged.

"I don't know. Three hundred?"

He chuckled.

"How about a thousand?" he said.

"A thousand dollars?"

"Right. Upfront."

"You got it."

She unzipped his pants but he grabbed her hand.

"Part of it might be a little dangerous," he said.

She didn't care.

"And I call the shots, all day long," he said.

"Fine."

He zipped up his pants, then pulled ten hundred-dollar bills out of his wallet and handed them over.

"Let's start with getting some breakfast," he said. "I'm starved."

She looked confused.

"Are you hungry?" he asked.

She nodded.

Then ran her index finger down the scar on his face.

"No one has ever taken me out to eat before," she said. "Not on the clock, anyway."

Chapter Thirteen

Day Three – September 7
Wednesday Morning

BRYSON COVENTRY PARKED HIS PICKUP on Tianca Holland's cobblestone driveway, killed the engine and walked past the water feature. It looked to be an authentic Italian fountain with nude women pouring water out of jugs, very tastefully done. The smell of fresh cut grass perfumed the air. Flowers colored the grounds, clumped in groups like throw-pillows that had been tossed exactly where they should be.

The place oozed money at every turn.

How much, he couldn't even imagine.

He rang the bell and when Tianca answered, she hugged him. Not sideways, like a friend, but straight on, pressing her breasts into his chest. Coventry saw it coming and did nothing to stop it.

She wore a white T-shirt that barely covered her ass. He couldn't tell if she wore a bra or panties.

"You're in a good mood," he said.

"I was wondering when you'd come back."

Coventry chuckled.

"Why, did you miss me?"

She walked as he followed, then turned and said, "How could I miss you? I didn't even throw anything at you."

He laughed.

"A sense of humor," he said. "I like that."

They ended up outside at the pool. She dangled her perfectly-tanned legs in the water while he sat near the edge, staying high and dry, holding a piping hot fresh cup of coffee. The Colorado sun brought the autumn air to the exact right temperature.

Coventry took his sport coat off and threw it on a chaise lounge.

"So are you here to interrogate me or screw me?" she asked.

"I ONLY HAVE A LICENSE FOR ONE OF THOSE," he said.

"The second I hope."

He shook his head and then got serious. "Just out of curiosity, do you know anyone named Tonya Obenchain? She's a real estate agent."

She didn't answer.

Instead she slipped off the edge of the pool and splashed into the water.

The T-shirt floated up around her.

It became immediately apparent that she wore no bra or panties.

Just the T.

She kicked out, then swam back and folded her arms on the edge of the tile.

"No, I don't. Why?"

He swallowed.

"We came across her body yesterday," he said. "About a

hundred feet from where we found Angela Pfeiffer. She was buried about six inches under, the same as Angela."

"You're kidding."

No he wasn't.

Tianca dunked under the water and kicked off the side of the pool, getting halfway across before she surfaced. There she went into a perfect overhand stroke. At the other end she stopped, took her T-shirt off and threw it onto the concrete.

Then she swam back, pulled herself out of the water and sat on the edge of the pool next to Coventry.

She turned her face to the sun and closed her eyes.

She didn't have a hair on her body.

Not anywhere.

THEN SHE LOOKED AT HIM. "I didn't kill Angela and I sure as hell didn't kill any real estate agents, either."

"I'm not saying you did," Coventry said. He didn't exactly know how to ease into the next question, so he just asked it. "Just to be clear, you and Tonya Obenchain were never, you know . . ."

"What? Lovers?"

"Right, that."

Tianca laughed.

"Women aren't like men, Coventry," she said. "We remember the names of the people we sleep with. So I can definitely say no, we weren't. Besides, real estate agents are boring. I like dangerous people. Bad boys and bad girls." She ran a finger down Coventry's chest. "People like you."

"Me? I'm not dangerous."

She looked him in the eyes.

"You're a guy on the edge, Coventry, and you know it. You won't end up boring me. That's why we're going to be lovers."

Coventry was about to say something but she stood up, walked over to the chaise lounge, laid down on her stomach and stretched out.

"You got me all stressed out," she said. "Now you owe me a backrub."

He knew he shouldn't.

But couldn't resist.

He walked over, put his hands on her shoulders and kneaded her muscles.

"I love it when I'm right," she said.

"Just don't spread it around," he said.

"Give me a full body message and I won't."

He worked his hands lower down her back.

Not knowing where he would stop.

Chapter Fourteen

Day Three – September 7
Wednesday Afternoon

WHEN A WELL-DRESSED WOMAN walked into Haley Wilde's office mid-afternoon and closed the door behind her, Haley knew that something was going on and it wasn't going to be pretty.

"I'm Jacqueline Moore," the woman said, extending her hand. "I was in your seat twenty-one years ago. Welcome to our humble abode."

Haley swallowed.

Jacqueline Moore, Esq.

Nickname Cruella de Ville.

Haley had heard the rumors.

None of them were particularly good.

"We're both busy, so I'm going to get right to the point," the woman said, sitting in one of the two chairs in front of Haley's desk. She looked to be about forty-five with perfectly manicured hair and nails, the kind of person who could walk into any boardroom or highbrow party and chat it up with the best of them.

Her outfit was expensive and her jewelry large.

No wedding ring.

"One of the bad things about my particular job," she said, "is being responsible to set course corrections when they're needed. Some people will tell you I thrive on it. I don't and that's the truth. But someone has to be the mouthpiece for the firm's policies, and we decided long ago that if only a few people did it, they'd in effect serve as the lightning rods for any negative feelings that might arise." She paused. "But hopefully there won't be any of those."

Haley remembered the balance in her checkbook.

$82.00.

No matter what happened, she'd have to be polite.

The woman patted Haley's hand. "This is just a small matter," Jacqueline said. "Hardly anything, really. It's come to our attention that you've contacted one of the firm's clients, namely Dr. Beverly Twenhofel. Is that true?"

Haley nodded.

So that's what this was about.

"Yes."

"Apparently in connection with some type of investigation you're conducting into the disappearance of Renee Rand. Is that true also?"

Haley nodded.

"I'm just trying to figure a few things out."

"I understand." Jacqueline looked sympathetic. "Renee's a wonderful person," she said. "We all miss her and we all want her back. But the police are working on it. And the firm has hired two top-notch investigators who are also working on it. What we can't have is individual attorneys running around trying to solve the case. It makes the firm look amateurish. It makes us look like we're not focused on legal matters. Do you see where I'm going with this?"

Haley nodded.

She did indeed.

Jacqueline stood up, smiled and walked to the door.

"Your heart's in the right place," she said. "It's good to have you with the firm."

Then she was gone.

Haley's hands trembled and she gripped them together to make them stop.

But it didn't work.

Chapter Fifteen

Day Three – September 7
Wednesday

JACK DEGAN DIDN'T INTEND TO DEVELOP FEELINGS for the whore—Gretchen—but did, and that screwed everything up. His initial plan was to have her go to the bar this evening, come on to one of the bikers, and then lure him into the back alley for a blowjob. Then Degan would pop out of the shadows and give the asshole a lesson he'd never forget.

The problem is that the scumbags would figure out what happened, afterwards.

Then go after the woman.

She wouldn't be hard to find, not in a town this small.

This morning, when he first hired her, he didn't give a shit what happened to her.

Now, unfortunately, he did.

So he had to regroup and figure out how to get one of the bikers separated from the pack.

After lunch at Wendy's, Gretchen asked, "What now?"

Degan thought about it.

The sky above was clear.

The temperature was absolutely perfect.

"Let's take a hike somewhere," he said.

She beamed.

"I know the perfect place."

THEY ENDED UP AT THE PUEBLO RESERVOIR, which looked like a mini Lake Powell. Gretchen knew a trail that descended into the back of a canyon. They hiked down—well over a mile from the car—found the place deserted and went skinny-dipping.

The rocks baked the water and kept it surprisingly warm, especially in the shallow spots.

Degan felt the need to show off and swam across the canyon, about a hundred yards, as fast as his overhand stroke would take him.

When he got back Gretchen was impressed.

"You look like Tarzan," she said.

He beat his chest and did his best Tarzan yell.

A lizard darted by and Degan chased it. It took a full three or four minutes, but he finally caught it. Holding it by the tail, he walked towards Gretchen swinging it back and forth.

"Got a friend for you," he said.

She screamed and jumped in the water.

"Don't you dare!"

He tossed the lizard on a bush and jumped in after her.

Then it was time to make love. Right there in the water. They both knew it.

Neither hesitated.

This time, unlike Monday night, she kissed him.

Long and deep.

And he kissed her back.

AFTERWARDS THEY DRESSED AND SAT IN THE SUN. Degan's thoughts returned to the bikers.

"I have some scumbags after me," he said. Then he told her the story of what happened in the bar Monday night and how his apartment had been trashed yesterday.

"I heard about the bar," she said.

"You did?"

She nodded.

"The word's out that one of them got beat up in the bathroom."

"Really?"

She nodded.

"I know that jerk," she said.

"You do?"

"Yep. They call him Two-Bits, but his real name's John Sinclair. I know his three friends, too. They're all first-degree assholes. They gang-raped me one night, the little pricks. One of them paid money for it, but the other three jumped in and took me for free. To me, that's rape, not to mention that my ass bled for a week."

Degan felt his jaw muscles tighten.

"Do you know where they live?"

She nodded.

"Yeah, why?"

Chapter Sixteen

Day Three – September 7
Wednesday Afternoon

COVENTRY WADDED UP A PIECE OF PAPER and tossed it up in the air, trying to get it to land in the middle of the snake plant. It hit one of the outer edges and bounced onto the floor. Then his cell phone rang. He couldn't find it at first but followed the sound to his left pants pocket.

He answered just as Shalifa Netherwood pulled up a seat in front of his desk, wearing a nice pants outfit with a matching jacket, one he had never seen before. She looked exceptionally good and he glanced at her as if to say, "Just give me a second."

"Coventry," he said.

"Mr. Coventry?" The voice belonged to a woman, a crying woman. He sat up and concentrated.

"Yes, this is me."

"Mr. Coventry, this is Marilyn Black."

Marilyn Black.

He didn't recognize the name.

"You gave me your card once," the woman said. "You said you'd help me."

Still no memory.

"Calm down," he said. "Tell me what's going on."

"I met you down on Colfax," she said, "when you were asking us questions about Paradise. You gave me your card and said I could call you if I ever needed help."

Still nothing.

Then he suddenly remembered.

She was one of the hookers from the Rainbird Bar, a young woman, probably no more than twenty or twenty-one, with needle marks in her arm. Coventry interviewed her in connection with the murder of Paradise—a hooker who ended up with a six-inch knife in her eye. He told her to get off the drugs and get off the street and get her life back on track. He said he'd help, if she ever needed it.

He gave her his card and even wrote his home phone number on the back.

"I remember you now," he said. "How can I help?"

She cried. "Can you come and get me?"

He got directions.

"I'll be there in fifteen minutes. Just hold on."

STANDING UP, HE LOOKED AT SHALIFA. "I have to run," he said. "But here's what I need you to do. First, get a cadaver dog down at the railroad tracks. If there are any more bodies buried around there I want to know about it now rather than later. Do that ASAP. It's starting to cloud up and I'm afraid it's going to rain."

She nodded.

"I was thinking the same thing," she said.

"You're always a step ahead of me," he said. "Then, in your spare time . . ."

She laughed.

". . . we need to start getting as much background information as we can on Angela Pfeifer and Tonya Obenchain. Somehow they're both connected to the person who killed them and we need to find out what that connection is. Let's start by getting lists of their friends, work, schools, clubs, vacations, hobbies and whatever else you can think of where they might have overlapped, either with each other or with the same man."

TEN SECONDS LATER HE TROTTED PAST THE ELEVATORS, ran down the three flights of stairs to the parking garage, and squealed out in his truck. He found Marilyn Black on Colfax, sitting on the sidewalk under a payphone, shaking and disoriented.

He double-parked the Tundra in the street and ran over.

Then he picked her up and put her in the vehicle.

"I'm taking you to the emergency room," he said.

She looked at him.

Then closed her eyes and slumped over.

He stepped on the gas.

A half block later a man stood in the street, waiting to cross. Coventry recognized him as one of the local drug pushers. Maybe even the one who'd been supplying Marilyn Black. He pointed the truck at him and stepped on the gas even harder.

The man jumped out of the way at the last second.

Then gave Coventry the finger.

Chapter Seventeen

Day Three – September 7
Wednesday Evening

As the day progressed, Haley Wilde found herself more and more concerned about the visit this afternoon from senior partner Jacqueline Moore. She kept her lowly associate ass in her chair until six o'clock and then uneventfully walked out of the office and drove home.

She immediately drank a glass of wine.

Then poured another and sipped it as a Lean Pocket heated in the microwave. She ended up on the couch watching the news and trying to figure out if she had already slid too far down a slippery slope.

She couldn't afford to get fired.

Not if she wanted to continue eating.

She paced, then stopped at the window and looked out. A dark sky threatened rain. She wouldn't be surprised if it poured like a madman in the next ten minutes.

The news caught her attention.

The body of a woman named Tonya Obenchain had been discovered yesterday buried in a shallow grave not more than a hundred feet from the grave of Angela Pfeiffer, who was discovered Sunday afternoon by a homeless man passing through the area. Both women disappeared earlier this spring. It was too early to tell if the same person killed both women but police weren't ruling out any theories at this point.

Interesting.

The two dead women both disappeared earlier this spring.

That's when Renee Rand vanished too.

She set the wine down, fired up the computer and printed out all the newspaper articles she could find on Tonya Obenchain and Angela Pfeiffer.

Not only did both women disappear earlier this spring, they actually disappeared in early April.

Even more interesting, Renee Rand disappeared at that same time.

The conclusion was inescapable.

Whoever abducted and killed the two women in the news also abducted Renee Rand.

And no doubt killed her too.

Renee's body must be buried somewhere near the other two.

Haley grabbed a light jacket and headed to the door.

"Screw you, Jacqueline Moore," she said, racing down the stairs.

WHEN SHE ARRIVED AT THE OLD RAILROAD SPUR no one was there. Two areas were staked off with yellow crime-scene tape. No doubt the locations of the graves. She stopped the Accord and killed the engine.

A heavy rain fell out of the sky.

Pounding on the roof of her car.

She searched around in the back seat to see if her umbrella

was there by chance. It wasn't so she put the jacket over her head and stepped outside.

The weather accosted her immediately.

Heavy but warm.

She could already tell that she'd be totally soaked in just a few minutes. So she decided to just give into it now and threw the jacket on the hood of the car.

Her hair immediately matted down and water ran into her eyes.

She took a Kleenex out of her pants pocket and wiped mascara off.

Now what?

She walked over to one of the gravesites. It was only about eighteen inches deep and filling with water. She checked the other one.

Same thing.

If Renee was buried here somewhere, Haley doubted that it would be too close to the existing graves, otherwise the police would have stumbled on it. It would be better to search farther out. She walked down the tracks for more than two hundred yards, looking in both directions for anything that suggested digging—less weeds, a raised area, whatever.

She saw nothing of interest.

She came back to where the graves were and then walked down the tracks in the other direction.

Again nothing.

This would be harder than she thought.

But Renee was here somewhere.

She knew it.

SHE SET UP AN IMAGINARY GRID AND WALKED IT, step by step. The rain never let up, not a bit. If anything, it got stronger. Her tennis shoes were caked with mud.

Slippery mud at that.

She fell and ended up with an ass full of it.

Then fell again.

And again.

Now she had mud all over her arms.

And in her hair.

"Goddamn rain."

Her legs ached and her eyelids were raw from rubbing the rain out of her eyes. She'd been at it for what seemed like forever when she finally finished the grid.

Still nothing.

"Shit."

Enough.

She went back to the car and rested against it, wondering what to do. If she got in this muddy, she'd ruin the interior, or at least end up having to clean it for an hour.

No thanks, either way.

Maybe she should just take her jeans off and throw them in the trunk. The evening was getting on, darker by the second. There was no one around. It was doubtful that anyone would see her. But still, she wasn't wearing panties, and the thought of being bare-ass naked out here in the middle of nowhere creeped her out.

Then she remembered the gravesites, filling with water.

She headed over to the nearest one and found it half filled.

She stepped over the yellow tape and waded into the pool of water. Then she leaned backwards and put her hands down, like a crab, and wiggled her ass back and forth in the water.

She felt the mud coming off.

Good.

This was working just fine.

She wiggled more.

Her left hand suddenly sank down.

Twelve inches or more, almost up to her elbow.

As if she had slipped into a shaft.

Her fingers felt something weird.

Soft.

Silky.

Definitely not dirt.

She pulled herself up, turned around, kneeled down and then dug. In a few minutes she found the silky stuff again. She tugged at it and found it still firm, but on the verge of breaking loose. She dug even more, scooping out mud and throwing it over the side of the hole.

This time when she grabbed the silky stuff something gave way and pulled up. She fell backwards on her ass with a splash, still gripping whatever it was that she had found.

She studied it—something about the size of a small basketball—and then dunked it in the water and swished it around.

When she pulled it up she was holding a head.

Renee Rand's head.

Chapter Eighteen

Day Three – September 7
Wednesday Night

After dark, Jack Degan drove around Pueblo with Gretchen seated next to him, her leg pressed against his. Country-western played on the radio. She showed him where each of the bikers lived. Degan wasn't sure yet whether he'd kill them, screw them up or just leave them alone.

Maybe he'd let Gretchen decide.

"Do you want them dead or just messed up?" he asked.

She pondered it.

"Dead," she said. "I've pictured it in my mind a hundred times. I don't know if that's such a good idea, though."

Degan considered the pros and cons both ways.

"It probably isn't," he said. "At least not right off the bat. But if we don't kill them, they can't know you're involved."

She exhaled and fidgeted in the seat.

"I'm not afraid of them," she said.

"Well you should be. Which one do you hate the most?"

She answered immediately.

"Two Bits," she said. "The guy you flushed."

"Fine. We'll start with him."

THEY PARKED DOWN THE STREET from Two-Bits' crappy little rental house and drank Jack Daniels from Degan's flask in the dark as they waited for the asshole to return home.

Lightning crackled in the distance and then it rained.

Gretchen ran her finger down the scar on Degan's face.

"So how'd you get this?" she asked.

He shrugged.

"Hell if I know," he said.

She kissed it.

"I like it," she said.

He chuckled.

"Good, because I don't think it's going to wash off or anything." He played with her hair. "What about you? You got any scars?"

"I'm not telling," she said. "You have to check for yourself."

"Careful," he said. "I will."

She unbuttoned her blouse.

"Do it then."

He laughed.

"It's too dark," he said. "I can't see anything."

She took his hand and put it on her breast.

"Just feel for them, then."

Not more than ten seconds later a headlight came down the street, jiggling and bobbing, unmistakably a motorcycle. Then the deep roar of the engine cut through the rain.

"Company," Degan said.

DEGAN WAITED UNTIL THE ASSHOLE KILLED THE ENGINE

and stepped off the bike. Then he walked out of the shadows and cut the jerk off before he reached the front door.

"You pissed all over my carpet," Degan said. "That wasn't very nice."

The biker tried to focus.

Too drunk to place him.

Then the confusion dropped off his face and he charged.

Even in the rain he smelled like alcohol and smoke.

Degan punched him in the face repeatedly until he fell to the ground. Then he straddled him and punched him another ten times, until his knuckles bled. The man withered under him, hardly able to even moan.

"This is your only warning," Degan said. "Tell your friends too."

He was standing up when a figure appeared.

Gretchen.

Carrying a rock in her right hand, the size of a softball.

She brought it down on the biker's head as hard as she could.

The guy's skull cracked.

Then he gurgled and stopped moving.

"Shit!" Degan said. "What are you doing?"

Gretchen just stood there, frozen.

He looked around.

Then grabbed her by the arm and pulled her towards the car.

"Come on!" he said.

She dropped the rock.

He stopped long enough to pick it up.

Ten miles away, out in the sticks, he threw it out the window.

Chapter Nineteen

Day Four – September 8
Thursday Morning

COVENTRY GOT UP AT HIS USUAL TIME, before dawn, even though he had been up half the night at Marilyn Black's bedside and the other half of the night fishing a head out of the gravesite down by the railroad spur.

Coffee.

He needed coffee.

Lots and lots of coffee.

He also needed a jog in the worst way but was too tired. So instead he showered, popped in his contacts and ate a bowl of cereal in the Tundra as he drove to work. Being the first one there, as usual, he fired up the coffee machine and then headed over to his desk to see what additional work had landed on it while he hadn't been around to fend it off.

He pulled Marilyn Black up on the computer.

She had a couple of prostitution arrests and some minor drug charges but luckily hadn't gotten herself into any major trouble yet.

Maybe she could actually turn her life around.

She must be terribly alone to call Coventry in her hour of

need. He only met her that one time. He needed to find out if she had any friends or relatives. He'd personally spring for the plane ticket if she had somewhere healthy to go.

That wasn't even an issue.

The coffee machine stopped gurgling. Coventry picked yesterday's cup off his desk, found it half filled with cold brown goop, and dumped it in the snake plant on his way over for fresh stuff.

Shalifa Netherwood pushed through the door three minutes later and headed towards the pot. Coventry glanced at the oversized industrial clock on the wall—7:12.

"What are you doing here so early?" he asked.

She rolled her eyes, poured coffee, stirred in cream and then pulled up a seat in front of his desk.

"You don't remember?" she asked.

He didn't.

Then did.

Last night he asked her to come in early.

"Of course I remember," he said. "I'm just messing with you."

She slurped the coffee, getting as much noise out of the act as she could. Then she smiled as if she just heard a joke.

"What?" he asked.

"So, I heard you got some head last night," she said.

He grunted.

"Give me the details," she added.

He told her what he knew so far. Some woman made an anonymous call from a payphone last night and said she found a head in one of the gravesites down by the railroad spur.

She said it belonged to Renee Rand, a lawyer who disappeared in April. Coventry took it for a joke but went down to check just in case.

"Sure enough," he said. "There it was just the way she said."

Shalifa looked puzzled.

"A fresh one?" she asked.

He shook his head.

"No, decomposed. Very decomposed, in fact."

"But the K-9 Unit had the cadaver dogs there all afternoon," she said. "They would have found it."

He nodded. "My guess is the dogs pointed out the grave, but everyone thought they were smelling the old body. No one had any reason to think that there'd be a second body stacked in the same hole."

"So there was, then? A second body?"

He shrugged. "We're not exactly sure yet," he said, "but that's my guess. It was too muddy last night to be messing around, so I had a unit stay there to guard the scene. We should be able to dig today. In fact, we should probably head over there now."

"Let's do it."

Coventry walked over to the coffee pot and refilled for the road. "Prepare to get muddy," he warned her.

She looked at him.

"It's never easy with you, Coventry," she said. "Stuff just finds you. It's like that bird we hit driving back from Santa Fe."

He chuckled, remembering the way it came all the way through the windshield and landed in the back seat, blood and feathers everywhere. He still had a vivid picture of Shalifa picking it up by one foot and tossing it into the brush.

WHEN THEY ARRIVED AT THE OLD RAILROAD SPUR the sun cast long morning shadows and the night chill was lifting. The gravesites still had standing water but only half as much as last night.

"We can probably get going any time," Coventry said.

He called the Crime Unit and the truck pulled up forty-five minutes later with Paul Kubiak at the wheel. He got out, scratched his gut, and frowned.

"Let me see if I got this straight," he told Coventry. "Somewhere, someone's going to work today, and their job is to sit around in a fancy showroom and sell BMWs to smiling rich guys. My job, on the other hand, is to dig a body out of mud."

Coventry nodded.

Then said, "Two bodies."

Kubiak looked confused.

"Two?"

"Well, maybe two," Coventry corrected himself. "We're going to check the other hole too."

"You think . . .?"

Coventry held his hands up in surrender. "I don't know. But we're going to find out. I'm hoping not."

In the first hole they did in fact find a body—a body without a head.

Then they checked the second hole.

And found another body.

The fourth.

A woman.

Her eyes were gouged out.

Kubiak looked at Coventry. "I hate it when you're right."

"Me too," Coventry said.

"Good thing it doesn't happen that often," Kubiak added.

Coventry nodded. "See if you can find her eyes," he said. "If you can't, get some kind of sifter out here and go through every inch of dirt. In fact, do that anyway, for both gravesites. Find whatever it is we haven't found so far."

COVENTRY PULLED SHALIFA TO THE SIDE. "We need to find out who made that call last night. She knows something we don't. Dispatch told me it came from a payphone. What I need you to do is check with them and find out which one, then go down there and see if there are any security cameras around that might help." He raked his fingers through his hair. "That's top priority."

"Okay."

"Even topper than top."

Chapter Twenty

Day Four – September 8
Thursday Morning

ON THURSDAY MORNING, HALEY WILDE'S fourth day of work, every attorney in the firm must have found out she existed, because they paraded through her door with big smiles on their faces and dropped files on her desk.

"It's called getting rid of your dogs," Christina Huynh warned. "Everyone's dumping their crap on you, either because the client's a no-pay or a slow-pay, or because they finally figured out the case is a loser. The end result is that you'll work tons of hours but won't bring any money through the door. That's not good. No matter what anyone tells you, this firm is driven by the bottom line, so the sooner you learn to say no the better off you're going to be."

More work landed on her desk.

More dogs.

Dogs with fleas.

She didn't say no though, not wanting to burn bridges. So instead she smiled and said thanks for the work.

Then Christina walked in shortly before noon. "Want to get some lunch?"

Haley couldn't afford it.

Not with only $82 in her account.

But couldn't afford to not have friends, either.

"Great," she said.

THEY MILLED THROUGH THE CROWD down the 16th Street Mall under a perfect Colorado sky and ended up at the Hard Rock Café, eating salads at the bar.

"So what's the scoop with Jacqueline Moore?" Haley asked at one point.

"Cruella?" Christina asked. "Don't even think anything bad about her. She has radar. And definitely don't cross swords with her. She'll gut you like a fish."

Haley frowned.

"I may have already done that."

"Already?" Christina said, slapping Haley on the back. "Congratulations girl, that's a new law firm record."

"Lucky me."

"Why, what'd you do?"

Haley explained about how she contacted Dr. Beverly Twenhofel and then got a tongue lashing from Moore, after which Christina said, "Yeah, you're on her short list all right. If I were you I'd snuggle up to Austin Gray. He's the only known antidote to Cruella."

Haley chewed.

"What's the scoop with him?"

"Austin?"

"Yeah."

"He's a good guy."

"He seems like a good guy," she said. "He took me to lunch

and told me his door's always open."

"It is," Christina agreed.

"Really?"

She nodded.

"Yeah, you'd think it's just empty bullshit, but it isn't," Christina said. "I had a case during my first year here, where I didn't get our expert disclosed in time. The other side got anal about it and convinced the judge to exclude his testimony. We lost the case and the client ended up paying about fifty grand, when we should have had a defense verdict."

"Ouch," Haley said.

"Major ouch," Christina agreed. "Anyway, there was some talk in the halls as to whether I had what it takes to be here. Austin stepped in and brought that to a screeching halt. Even more than that, he paid the client a chunk of change out of his own wallet."

"Damn."

Christina nodded.

"I'd be washing dishes right now if it wasn't for him."

THE TV MONITORS OVER THE BAR interrupted the current programming with a newsbreak. Two more bodies had been discovered at the abandoned railroad spur north of town, bringing the total now to four. Footage of the Crime Unit working the scene filled the screen, and then switched over to reporter Jena Vernon interviewing a man.

The detective in charge, apparently.

Haley had seen him before somewhere.

He had one of those faces you don't forget.

"We're very interested in talking to the person who called us last night," Coventry said. Looking straight into the camera, he added, "If you're that person please call us as soon as possible."

Haley dropped her fork.

"What?" Christina asked.

She tried to not appear shaken. "Nothing, just clumsy. Scary stuff, all those bodies."

Christina made a disgusted face. "There's no shortage of sickos in the world, that's for sure." She wiped her mouth and added, "I love that guy's eyes."

Haley studied them.

"They're two different colors," she said.

"I know," Christina said. "He should be in that Right Said Fred song, *I'm too sexy for my eyes, too sexy for my eyes, that's no lie.*"

Haley laughed.

But stayed focused on the news update to see if they mentioned that one of the new bodies was Renee Rand's. They didn't, probably because they still needed to verify it conclusively.

So, who was the fourth victim?

No doubt someone who also disappeared in early April. With a little work on the Internet, Haley should be able to figure it out in short order.

She paid for lunch, for the both of them.

$22.00 including the tip.

Meaning $60.00 left.

Chapter Twenty-One

Day Four – September 8
Thursday Morning

JACK DEGAN WAS PISSED that Gretchen smashed in the dumb-ass biker's skull, not really needing to be connected to too many things like that right now. "I didn't know I was going to do it until I did it," she apologized. Then, to make up for it, she gave him a long, slow blowjob.

They hid out all night in the canyon at the Pueblo Reservoir.

Now, as the morning sun rose with a warm orange glow over the rocky ridge, Degan's anger waned and they laughed about it.

"He did deserve it," he noted.

Gretchen locked her arm through his as they hiked back to the car. "Screw him," she said. "Now what?"

Good question.

One he'd been wrestling with all night.

"The biggest liability is my car," he said, "in case anyone saw it parked in the area. I doubt that anyone got a license plate number, but they might have a general description. So I need to get it out of Pueblo, starting now."

She squeezed his arm.

"Take me with you."

He shook his head.

"You can't break your routine," he said. "That'll draw attention. You need to get back to your hotel room and turn tricks like nothing happened. What's today? Thursday?"

"Yeah."

"Do you have some Thursday regulars?"

"There's this one guy . . ."

Degan cut her off. "You need to be there then," he said. "But here's the most important thing. Don't tell a single person about last night, ever. Do you understand?"

She did.

He stopped, grabbed her arms and made her look in his eyes. "Tell me."

"I won't tell anyone."

"Ever."

"Ever."

He found no lies and continued walking.

When they got to the car, they drove north on I-25 for fifteen miles, until they came to a rest stop. Degan pulled in and killed the engine. An identical rest stop sat on the other side of the freeway. They used the facilities and then found a shady spot with a picnic table.

"Here's the plan," he said. "Be sure there are no cops around, then go over to that other rest stop and get a trucker to give you a ride back to town. Then just follow your normal routine."

Her forehead wrinkled.

"What about you?" she asked.

He laughed. "Me? I'll be fine."

"No, I mean, when will I see you again?"

He thought about it and said, "I got some stuff going on, but

I'll be back as soon as I can, probably within a week, two weeks max. Be at the hotel where I can find you."

She squeezed his hand.

"Do you promise you'll come?"

"Yes I promise," he said, and meant it. "As soon as I can." He gave her his cell phone number and said, "That's for emergencies only. If you have to call, do it from a payphone, preferably one with no security cameras around."

A pack of Harleys—ten or more—flew past the rest stop, heading north towards Denver with a serious twist on the throttle. No biker-bitch passengers meant they were on a mission—probably headed to Degan's.

He and Gretchen held each other for a long time and then parted.

HE DROVE NORTH ON I-25, taking more hits of Jack than he should, keeping an eye in the rearview mirror for bikers or cops.

Shit.

Now everything was screwed up.

One of the main goals of coming to Pueblo, namely nabbing Mia Avila—the tattoo woman who inked the warrior band on his arm—had slipped away. Still, he and Gretchen now had a history, and he wouldn't trade that for six miles of women, tattooed or otherwise.

He flicked the radio stations.

Trying to shake his brain away from the fact that Gretchen would be sucking other men until he got back.

Maybe he should turn around before it was too late.

An exit popped up and he pulled off. A gas station appeared and he instinctively checked the gauge, surprised to find he was riding on fumes. "Damn you're an ass." He pulled in, filled up with 87 and then went inside to pay.

A toothless old lady worked the register with agonizing slowness while truckers three deep bit their lips and tried their best to not jump over the counter and rip her arms off.

Degan stepped to the end of the line and shifted from foot to foot, watching the old woman's every move. A cheap black-and-white TV monitor in the corner caught his eye. A newscast reported that the number of bodies found at the old railroad spur north of Denver now numbered four.

Who could possibly give a shit about something so trivial?

"Hey! Hurry it up, will you?" he said.

The tucker in front of him turned, as if ready to get in Degan's face, but looked in his eyes and didn't say anything.

The gas bill was $36.50.

Degan stepped to the front of the line, threw two wadded-up twenties on the counter and said, "There, you happy?"

Then stormed out.

SOMEONE MUMBLED SOMETHING BEHIND HIS BACK. He walked back in and looked everyone in the eyes, one by one. No one made a sound.

"That's what I thought," he said.

Then left.

Chapter Twenty-Two

Day Four – September 8
Thursday

BRYSON COVENTRY WAS STILL WORKING the crime scene at the railroad spur when Tianca Holland called. "I saw the news," she said, "about finding two more bodies. So I'm ready to accept your apology for thinking I was involved with any of it."

Coventry chuckled.

"Who is this?"

"Not funny," she said. "Come over tonight. I have something to show you." She hung up before he could say anything.

Shalifa Netherwood showed up a few minutes later, walking towards him with a Cheshire Cat grin on her face. "Good news," she said, handing him three pieces of paper—black-and-white printouts of a young woman talking on a payphone. "That's your anonymous caller."

"You sure?"

"Positive," she said. "This is definitely the phone used for the call, and the time on the security camera tape exactly matches the time of the call, from start to end. Plus she looks stressed."

Coventry was impressed.

"Good work," he said. "I suppose now you think I owe you lunch or something."

She punched him in the arm.

"Lunch? Dinner at a minimum," she said. "Got some more news for you too. The head definitely belongs to Renee Rand, like our caller-friend said."

"Any word yet who the other one is? The one without the eyes?"

"Nada."

Coventry studied the caller's face again.

"Let's get a press conference set up ASAP," he said. "I want her photo on the five o'clock news. She's up to her eyeballs in this and I want to know how."

Shalifa shook her head.

"If all I'm getting out of this is a lunch . . ."

"You're also being paid, don't forget."

"Right, but I would be extra motivated if there was a dinner involved."

Coventry held his hands up in surrender.

"Okay," he said. "Fine. But this is blackmail, for the record."

She smiled. "Black female, actually. I choose the restaurant."

Ouch.

"Just be sure they have a two-for-one special." He looked at his watch for the first time in hours: 3:25. Shit. "I got to run," he said over his shoulder. "Be back in an hour."

Then he headed over to see how Marilyn Black was coming along. It was turning out that she was more alone in the world than he first thought. Her father skipped out when she was just a baby. Marilyn ran away from home when she was fifteen and had been on the streets ever since.

When he walked into her room she was asleep.

He held her hand for a half hour and then told the orderly, "Be sure she knows I was here."

On his way back to the railroad spur, Coventry called Leanne Sanders, Ph.D., the FBI profiler who proved to be so invaluable on both the David Hallenbeck and Nathan Wickersham cases. She was a Supervisory Special Agent assigned to the National Center for the Analysis of Violent Crime (NCAVC) at Quantico, Virginia. Luckily he actually got her on the line. As usual, she listened patiently as he explained the situation.

"The thing that puzzles me the most is the four different methods of murder," he said, referring to stabbing, beheading, suffocation and slitting of the throat. "Oh," he added, "I almost forgot to tell you, the last one we found—the one with the slit throat—had her eyes gouged out too. We haven't found them yet. The guy ate them for all we know."

She asked a number of questions.

The ages of the victims.

Physical descriptions.

Similarities.

"This is a tough one," she said. "Given the widely divergent causes of death, I'm leaning towards multiple murderers, maybe a cult of some kind, or a gang initiation. But I'm also not inclined yet to totally rule out one murderer—maybe someone with multiple personalities, or one personality but multiple fantasies." She cleared her throat and added, "Looks like you're going to be all over the news again."

Unfortunately that was true.

"It's already getting big," he said. "And they don't even know yet that a head was cut off and that eyes were gouged out."

"That'll leak out," she said.

"Probably," he agreed.

"I haven't seen an agency yet that can keep that level of noise under wraps, including my own," she said.

As soon as he hung up Shalifa called.

"Where are you?" She sounded panicked. "You said you'd be back in an hour."

"En route."

"Well hurry up, the press is already here."

Chapter Twenty-Three

Day Four – September 8
Thursday Evening

Haley Wilde was already in her pajamas when someone knocked at the door. Through the peephole she saw a stranger, a man, about fifty with glasses. With hesitation she opened the door as far as the chain would allow.

"The firm needs you at a meeting, right now," the man said. "I have a limousine waiting."

"Right now?"

"Yes."

"Hold on."

She checked outside and saw a limousine in the parking lot.

"Give me ten minutes," she said.

"I'll be in the car."

She dressed and threw on a face while a feeling of nausea grew in her stomach. The two glasses of wine might be on her breath so she gargled as long as she could with mouthwash.

Thirty minutes later she was at the firm, sitting in one of the conference rooms with Austin Gray, Jacqueline Moore and another attorney she hadn't met before named Derek Bennett.

Jacqueline Moore took the lead in what appeared to be more

of an interrogation than a meeting. "You're all over the news, you know that, right?"

The words shocked her.

"No. What are you talking about?"

They powered up the flat-panel TV on the wall and played a videotape of the evening news for her. A detective by the name of Bryson Coventry wanted to talk to the woman in the photograph in connection with the case involving the four bodies found at the railroad spur. If anyone knew who the woman was they should call the number at the bottom of the screen.

Shit.

She looked at everyone.

"I had no idea," she said.

The looks on their faces indicated they didn't care.

"So what's going on?" the woman asked.

Haley put a confused look on her face. "I don't know."

The woman slammed her hand on the table. "We don't have time for bullshit!"

A pencil bounced, rolled, and fell to the floor.

"You're dragging the law firm into something negative and we've struggled too hard and too long to get blindsided by something like this. So you can either tell us what this is all about or you can march down to your office right now and clean it out."

IN SPITE OF HERSELF, HALEY STOOD UP. "Who in the hell do you think you're talking to?" She walked to the door and then turned around. "As far as the job goes, shove it up your ass. No one talks to me like that."

"Haley! Wait a minute!"

The words came from Austin Gray, chasing her down the hall.

She was in no mood.

She opened the door to the stairwell and bounded down, taking two steps at a time, while he called for her to come back.

Chapter Twenty-Four

Day Four – September 8
Thursday

When Jack Degan got back to Denver he parked a couple of blocks away from the apartment and then walked back through the field behind the building to see if any bikers were hanging around. Good thing, too. A few of the scumbags were milling in the parking lot and several more buzzed the neighborhood.

They better be careful.

The assholes.

They think they're all macho when they're in a pack. Get them alone, though, and they were nothing. In fact, he had half a mind to pick one of them off from the herd right now, just to show them who they were messing with.

Instead, he drove over to Avis, rented a van and spent the next two hours driving back to Pueblo. When he got in town it took all his strength to not knock on Gretchen's door and screw her silly.

She couldn't know he was in town, though.

It would be better that way.

Against his better judgment he drove by the dead biker's

house, just to see what was going on, if anything. The body was gone and the place was deserted. Whatever investigation had taken place was already over.

Then he swung by the tattoo shop.

Good.

The woman—Mia Avila—seemed to be alone.

He parked in front of the building, killed the engine and walked in.

SHE LOOKED JUST AS GOOD AS HE REMEMBERED, with those big eyes and that thick brown hair pulled into a ponytail. Ample breasts filled a flimsy white tank top, seriously sexy. When she smiled he just about melted. She would definitely do.

"Hey there," she said, recognizing him. "Nick? Right?"

"Very good," he said, remembering he had given her a fake name.

"Back for the other arm?"

"Actually, something better than that," he said, pulling out his wallet and laying twenty hundred-dollar bills on the counter. "How would you like to earn that today?"

She counted it.

"That's two thousand dollars," she said.

He nodded.

"That it is."

"So what's on your mind?"

"I have a friend up in Denver," he said. "The guy's got more money than God. I showed him my tattoo and he went nuts. He wants one just like it. He wants you to do it."

"Me?"

"Yep."

"Fine, tell him to come in."

Degan shuffled. "Well, there's this one small problem," he said. "This guy doesn't have time to be driving down here so he wants you to come to Denver. That's what the money's for."

She pondered it.

And looked interested.

"When?" she asked.

"Now, if possible," Degan said. "I'll drive you up and bring you back. He's got someone delivering some tattoo equipment so you don't need to worry about that. Just bring the pattern and your hands."

She picked up a pencil and twisted it in her fingers.

"You can bring your other body parts too," he added.

She laughed, and said, "Men."

Then set the pencil down.

"Okay," she said. "Let me put this money in the safe first."

She disappeared to the back, packed a bag with latex gloves and other small items, grabbed a bottle of water, flipped the window sign to Closed, turned off the lights and locked the door.

"You're going to make his day," Degan said.

"I need to be back by seven," she said.

DEGAN LOVED THE ARID LANDSCAPE on the stretch of not-much-but-road heading north out of Pueblo. Civilization hadn't cluttered it up yet and, because there were hardly any trees, you could see the sagebrush-covered hills roll all the way to the mountains. Mia talked her head off as they drove, telling Degan story after story in that bubbly optimistic voice of hers, taking small sips of water every few minutes.

He didn't mind the chatter.

She was bubble-gum for the brain.

It was almost a shame about what was going to happen to her.

She didn't deserve it.

But who did?

They stopped at a rest area after they passed Monument Hill. He spiked her water while she used the facilities. By the time they reached Denver she was asleep.

When they pulled up to the cabin, the beautifully desolate cabin, she was still out cold.

He carried her inside, chained her to the bed, played with her hair for a few moments, and pictured her dead.

Chapter Twenty-Five

Day Four – September 8
Thursday Evening

Bryson Coventry worked his ass off all day until eight o'clock. He felt like a three-legged, broke-dick dog that someone had entered into a horse race, but wasn't too tired to walk down the stairs to the parking garage and point the Tundra towards Tianca Holland's house.

Come over tonight. I have something to show you.

That's what she said this morning and the words hadn't left him all day.

He pretty much dismissed her as a viable suspect in the murder of Angela Pfeiffer as soon as they found the second body. Now, with four, he couldn't picture her involved even in his wildest scenarios. And he certainly couldn't get a mental image of her cutting someone's head off with a hacksaw, or gouging someone's eyes out.

Men use hacksaws.

Not women like Tianca.

When he arrived, Tianca answered the door wearing only a thin long-sleeve white blouse with rolled-up cuffs, barely long enough to cover the top of her thighs. She must have just showered because her hair hung wet. An expensive fragrance floated around her. When she hugged him he hugged her back.

"I didn't know if you'd come," she said.

"How could I not?"

Two steps into the atrium he found what she wanted to show him. The four pieces of modern art that had been on the walls were gone. In their stead hung four of Coventry's paintings.

"You like them?" she asked. "Apparently they're done by some local guy."

Coventry chuckled and walked over to the closest one, a twelve-by-sixteen landscape, looking up a hill into a clump of Ponderosa pines, backlit by an early morning sky. "I painted that one at Lair of the Bear," he said. "I remember the wind kicking up halfway through it and almost driving me nuts."

"So it's plein air then?"

He nodded.

"Right. I'm not good enough for fancy air. Look right here," he said, indicating.

She obliged.

He pointed out a small bug imbedded in the paint.

"There's your proof," he said.

"Very impressive, a painting with protein. You don't charge extra for those, I hope," she said.

He nodded. "Afraid so. Five bucks each." He studied the background and found another one. "To support my coffee addiction. How'd you find out that I paint?"

"I know lots of stuff about you." She linked her arm through his and led him off. "Come on."

THEY ENDED UP TAKING A WALK through the neighborhood, carrying plastic glasses of wine, as a bright orange Colorado sunset hung over the mountains. Coventry had a few questions to ask and knew if he didn't get to them soon he never would. "Just out of curiosity, where do you get your legal work done?"

"I stay away from lawyers for the most part."

"Smart move," Coventry said. "Have you ever used Hart, Sanders & Day for anything?"

She nodded.

"A minor matter, a couple of years back." Coventry tried to not appear surprised. He didn't really expect to find a connection. "Why? Are you going to pump them for secrets about me?"

"Maybe," he said. "Do you happen to know Renee Rand, of that firm?"

"Not that I recall—I basically only dealt with one of the senior partners, Jacqueline Moore. Why?"

He swallowed.

"She's one of the bodies we came across," he said. "Actually, we found her buried under Angela Pfeiffer."

She stopped and studied his face.

"You found her *under* Angela?"

He nodded.

She looked confused.

"That is so freaky."

He agreed.

"So you only dealt with that other lawyer, what's her name?"

"Jacqueline Moore," she said.

"Right, Jacqueline Moore."

"Even that was fairly brief," she said. "She has a pretty abrasive personality."

"Is that the only connection you have to Renee Rand that you can think of?"

"Right," she said. "Except I wouldn't call it a connection."

Coventry sipped the wine.

The sunset, so spectacular just a few minutes ago, was already loosing its intensity.

"How about Catherine Carmichael?" he asked. "Do you know her or have you ever heard of her?"

"No."

"She was also found at the site," Coventry said.

"The only one I know is Angela," she said.

"Okay."

In another ten minutes it would be dark. Up ahead a sprinkler oscillated, shooting onto the sidewalk at the end of every arc. Coventry paused while Tianca ran through it. "Come on," she said. "You can do it."

So he did.

When he caught up, he had one more question. "I don't suppose that you or Angela were ever part of any cult or gang or anything like that," he said.

She gave him a startled look.

"Coventry, you come up with the weirdest questions, I swear," she said. "No we weren't. Now I have a question for you."

He raised an eyebrow.

"And what might that be?"

She stopped and put her arms around his neck.

"When we get back to my place, are you going to screw me silly, or what?"

"To be honest," he said, "it's about the only thing I've been thinking about all day. But I can't."

She made a face.

"You're such a tease," she said.

He got serious.

"Believe me, it's worse for me than you."

She slapped his ass.

"I doubt that," she said.

When they got back to her house she uncorked another bottle of wine and they sat in front of the fireplace and talked until midnight. Then Coventry retreated to the spare bedroom and tossed for ten minutes before falling asleep.

Chapter Twenty-Six

Day Five – September 9
Friday Morning

AFTER A FITFUL NIGHT OF TWISTING AND SHIFTING, Haley Wilde woke early Friday morning to a cold and cloudy dawn. She didn't have a job but she did have her dignity. Who would hire her now, though, after being fired on her fourth day of work?

No one, that's who.

Still, she wouldn't take back her words last night even if she could. Maybe she didn't have a paycheck or a career, but at least she could look in the mirror without disgusting herself.

She showered and ate cereal.

Then she headed to Einstein Bros and drank coffee alone at a table as she pondered her options. She remembered turning off her cell phone last night, pulled it out of her purse and powered it up.

She had a half-dozen voice messages.

All from Austin Gray.

"We need to talk."

As soon as she erased the last message the phone rang. When she answered Austin Gray's voice came through. Before she could hang up, he said, "First, you're not fired. Second, Jacqueline Moore was way out of bounds. Third, we need to talk and get this straightened out."

She almost powered off but didn't.

"Talk about what?"

"Last night, the future, everything," he said. "Where are you?"

She told him.

"I'll be there in twenty minutes. Don't go anywhere."

She tried to warn him that he was wasting his time but he had already hung up. So instead she got in her car and left.

WHEN SHE GOT HOME SHE CHANGED HER MIND and went back. Austin Gray arrived three minutes later wearing a wool-blend suit worth more than her entire wardrobe.

He hugged her around the shoulders and said, "Give me two minutes, I need coffee or I'm going to be cranky all day." She nodded and felt queasy. Whatever happened in the next ten minutes would be a turning point.

He came back, sat down and took a noisy slurp from the cup.

He looked good.

Powerful.

Yet compassionate.

She wished she had dressed in something other than jeans and a sweatshirt.

"Good stuff," he said.

She muttered something and waited.

"First," he said, "Jacqueline told me to tell you she's sorry. She'll tell you herself when you see her." He lowered his voice.

"Unfortunately, she's a damn fine lawyer—one of the reasons the firm even exists, to be honest with you—but she also has her moments. Between you and me, I'm trying to keep her in the firm but she's making it more and more difficult every day. I don't know what's going to happen, if this keeps up."

Haley sipped her coffee.

"It's more than just her attitude," she said. "I don't understand why I was called into a meeting to begin with. It felt like the KGB had come to get me."

He nodded and understood her viewpoint.

"Outsiders see big law firms as rock-solid institutions that have been there forever and always will be," he said. "In reality we're very fragile. Personalities, egos, money and a million other things take their toll every day. I know, because my primary responsibility as the head of the firm is to keep it healthy, so we can all make a living and pay our bills."

He got a gleam in his eye and stood up.

"Come on," he said. "I want to show you something."

THEY TOOK HIS VEHICLE—a white F-150 pickup that had to be every bit of twenty years old—to an edgy section of Colfax Avenue, not far from Capitol Hill. They parked on the street and walked over to a comic book store sandwiched between a mom-and-pop grocery and a laundromat.

He opened the door for her and they walked in.

The musty smell of aged paper permeated the air.

The man behind the counter looked like a throwback to the '60s, with long thinning gray hair and a goatee. His face exploded into a smile when he saw who walked in.

"I'll be damned," he said, "Austin Gray himself. How long

has it been? A year at least . . ."

"Too long," Austin said. He made introductions and then said, "Mind if I give this pretty lady the tour?"

"Please."

Austin turned to Haley and said, "This is where I had my first law office, right out of law school. I had a desk over there, a table there, and a small bookshelf over there. I lived in the back room, illegally. I used to hang out in the front door and pass my card out to people walking by. I didn't get my first client for six weeks and he stiffed me on the bill. That's the check I have framed in my office by the way."

Austin bought a $50.00 comic, an old Tarzan classic, and they left.

Then they walked down Colfax.

"I love this part of town," he said. "It has an edge to it, it's real. I know every step of the way from the office I just showed you to the one I have now. And I know it's a two-way street. It's my job to be sure the firm doesn't end up back here."

A couple of elderly women walked towards them.

They gave Austin the evil eye.

He chuckled.

"They think you're a hooker and I'm down here picking you up," he said. "Anyway, to get back on track, the meeting last night was my idea. It's still important for us to know how you're connected to all these murders."

Haley felt he deserved to know that much and told him how she connected the fact that Renee Rand disappeared right around the same time as the two women who were found buried at the old railroad spur. She concluded that Renee was a third victim and was probably buried around there as well, so she went down to look.

She told him how she found a head in one of the graves.

"I called the police anonymously," she said, "because I had nothing else to tell them that would be of any help, and I didn't want to get involved because Jacqueline Moore had already warned me to back off."

They walked and talked until Austin understood the events to his satisfaction.

"Here's what we need to do," he said. "First, you come back to work, okay?"

She hesitated.

Then gave in.

"Okay."

"Good," he said. "I'll call that detective and invite him to come down to the firm and talk to you this afternoon. Would that be okay?"

"Sure."

He put his arm around her shoulders and squeezed. "You know," he said, "big law firms are just a slice of life, meaning that things don't always go perfect. We all get our bumps and bruises as time goes on. What I look for in a lawyer is someone who can keep things in perspective and stay in it for the long haul. You're already showing me that you have that quality."

She cocked her head.

"You can stop feeding me bullshit now," she said. "I already said I'm coming back."

He laughed.

"I would," he said, "except I'm not."

Back at his truck she commented, "I always pictured you in a Mercedes."

He patted the hood as they walked past.

"Never forget your roots," he said. "This guy here's my daily reminder. By the way, no one knows what happened last night, except the people who were in the room. It's probably best if it stayed that way."

"I agree."

Chapter Twenty-Seven

Day Five – September 9
Friday Morning

MORNING AT THE CABIN BROKE WITH A CHILLY DAWN, hinting of colder days ahead. Jack Degan removed every last stitch of his lovely captive's clothing, rolled her unconscious body around so he could study her tattoos, and then made sure she was securely chained to the bed. She had a killer physique, he had to admit, in fact sweet enough to make his cock stand up. But he didn't screw her. Instead, he covered her with a blanket, gave her a shot that would keep her out until at least noon, and then checked the equipment.

All was in order.

Then he got in the van and headed down the twisty mountain roads until the flatlands appeared. He worked his way into the Denver skyline and ended up at a Starbucks near Washington Park.

The designated place.

He drank coffee and read the *Westword* until his phone rang.

It was the person he only knew by voice.

Swofford.

"Is everything set?"

He chuckled.

"Of course."

"Okay. Come out the front door and walk west," Swofford said.

Degan stood up, threw the coffee away and pushed through the front door. The day had warmed up considerably. He walked west, holding the phone to his ear.

"I'm walking west," he said.

"I know."

He almost looked around, to find the face behind the mystery voice, but knew better.

"Okay, stop. There's a black trash bag under the blue car to your right."

He bent down and looked.

There it was.

He pulled it out and walked back towards Starbucks.

"I'll let the client know it's a go," Swofford said. "He'll be there about noon, so don't go back."

"Noon?"

"He had to move it up."

"Why?"

"I don't know and I don't care," Swofford said. "Make yourself scarce until I call you. That'll be sometime tomorrow."

"You're kidding," Degan said. "He's going to take that long?"

"Apparently so," Swofford said. "Is that a problem?"

Degan felt the weight of the bag in his hand.

Inside was $75,000 in cash.

His cut.

"No, that's cool," he said. "I've got about four thousand in expenses, by the way. I gave the woman two grand to get her to come to Denver. That was easier than abducting her. Then I got the cabin rental, a van rental, and a bunch of miscellaneous stuff."

"Not a problem," Swofford said. "We have another one in the works, by the way. He has someone specific in mind."

Degan smiled.

A specific target meant more money than a generic one.

$100,000 instead of $75,000.

"Who?"

"I don't know yet."

WITH THE REST OF THE DAY TO KILL, Degan stopped in a small Mexican mom-and-pop restaurant, sat in a red-vinyl booth with his back against the wall where he could see everyone who came and went, and ate a smothered burrito.

The waitress was cute.

So he hung around and drank three or four cups of coffee after she took his plate.

"How'd you get that scar?" she asked.

"Eating an ice cream cone," he said. "It went horribly wrong."

She laughed and said, "Remind me to stay away from ice cream cones."

"Lot's of people don't appreciate how dangerous they are," he said. "Especially those hard sugar cones."

He paid in cash and tipped her a twenty.

Out in the parking lot he heard someone shout behind him.

It was her, running to him, with her white waitress apron flopping up and down.

"You forgot this," she said, handing him a piece of paper.

He looked at it as she turned and ran back.

It had a phone number on it, under her name—Janessa.

He waved to her and shoved it in his pants pocket. Then he drove over to Avis, traded the van for a 4-door Nissan sedan, and headed south on I-25. Two hours later he arrived in Pueblo.

He swung past the dead biker's house just to see if anything had changed. It hadn't. Then he drove past Mia Avila's tattoo shop. There was no activity there either. Everything was exactly as it had been yesterday.

The Closed sign still hung in the door.

The lights were off.

From there he headed over to the hotel, drank a swig of Jack in the parking lot, and walked up the stairs two at a time to surprise Gretchen. Music came from inside the room. The drapes were drawn but he found a slit big enough to peek in, just to be sure she wasn't on her knees giving some asshole a blowjob.

Shit!

Gretchen was sitting on the bed.

Two cops stood in front of her, talking intently, a male and a female.

Degan quietly walked down the stars, jumped in the car and got the hell out of there.

AFTER THE COPS LEFT he parked a block down the road and doubled back on foot. A peek through the curtains showed Gretchen lying face down on the bed.

Alone.

He found the door unlocked and walked in.

She ran to him and he held her tight. "The cops were here," she said.

"I know," Degan said. "What'd they want?"

"They partly wanted to see if I had anything to do with the asshole biker's death," she said. "It's no secret around town, about what they did to me—and what I'd do back, if I ever got the chance. But I played dumb and said I was here turning tricks all night. They believed me, I could tell."

Degan felt the stress melt.

"Good job."

"But they also came to warn me," she said. "Apparently the word's spreading around town that the bikers think I had something to do with it. There's talk that they're going to interrogate me."

"Not on my watch," Degan said.

She hugged him tight.

"Thank God for you," she said. "The cops said I'd probably be better off getting out of town until the whole thing blew over."

Degan agreed.

And kissed her to prove it.

"Pack your suitcase," he said. "I'm taking you to Denver."

She studied his eyes.

"You mean it?"

"Absolutely," he said. "I have money. You won't need to work."

She pulled a suitcase out from under the bed.

Then hesitated.

"The cops asked about you," she said. "Not you by name, but about a tall Indian with a scar on his face."

Degan pulled the curtain an inch to the side and peered out.

No one was there that shouldn't be.

"The bikers figure I did it," he said. "Their buzz has already been picked up by the cops. It's time to get out of this screwed up town once and for all."

She agreed.

"And I'm not ever coming back," she added. "Even if you dump me."

He chuckled.

"That's not going to happen."

Chapter Twenty-Eight

Day Five – September 9
Friday Morning

BRYSON COVENTRY WOKE FROM A DEEP SLEEP when someone straddled him. He opened his eyes to a dim room and found Tianca Holland on top, wearing only a thong. "Come on, sleepy head," she said. He stretched, remembering their conversation last night about getting up early for a jog. It seemed like a good idea then; now, not so much. Tianca bounced up and down. "Come on. You can do it."

He rolled her over and laid on top, pretending to fall back asleep while she struggled under his weight.

He almost took her right then and there.

But knew he couldn't.

Not quite yet.

Five minutes later, a yellow ochre sun rose as they headed out the front door. The grass smelled like dew and a mild chill hung in the air. They ran in the street with Tianca setting a faster pace than Coventry was used to.

"No problem," he said. "We'll go slow if you want."

She sped up.

"No, that's okay," she said. "We can go faster."

He struggled to keep up, concentrating on his breathing.

"That's better," he said.

She took him on a three-mile course and hardly broke a sweat. When they got back he showered, inhaled coffee, slapped her on the ass and headed for the door.

She caught up with him, slapped his ass back, and said, "Don't forget, you're coming over tonight."

He raised an eyebrow.

"I am?"

"Yep. I'm going to cook for you."

Coventry chuckled.

"You know how to cook?"

She laughed.

"I have talents in more than just one room of the house, Coventry."

HE TURNED OUT TO BE THE FIRST ONE TO WORK, as usual, and got the coffee pot gurgling. One of the florescent lights over his desk hummed like a madman so he took it out and swapped it with one from the chief's office.

That was much better.

He dumped a cold half-cup of yesterday's coffee in the snake plant, filled the cup with fresh stuff without rinsing, and then sipped it as he listened to his voice mails. One of them was from CNN who wanted to interview him today on the four-body case. That was fine. The public had a right to know what was going on. He just needed to be careful to not give any secrets away.

Plus, Tianca would be impressed, seeing him on the news.

Shalifa Netherwood showed up around 7:30, wearing a dark-blue skirt with a matching jacket, and walked to the coffee pot. Coventry met her there and held out his cup while she still had the pot in her hand. She filled him up.

"I checked my messages driving in," she said. "If we received any tips on who the 911 caller is, they didn't come to me."

"Me either," Coventry said.

"We got her face in the paper this morning," she added. "Someone will call with her name today, guaranteed. I just hope she doesn't play hide and seek."

THEY ENDED UP AT HIS DESK, he with his feet propped up but pointed away from her so she wouldn't have to look at the bottom of his shoes.

"Okay," he said, thinking out loud. "Let's see where we're at on this. The biggest thing we need to do is find out who victim number four is. She's been haunting me because she's so young, that and the fact that she had her eyes gouged out."

Shalifa frowned.

"Any word yet on whether that happened pre or post-mortem?"

He shook his head.

"Nothing yet," he said. "But if it was pre, I'm going to personally rip the guy's head off and pee in the hole." He wove a pencil in his fingers and snapped it in two. "Same thing goes for Renee Rand's killer. If he took her head off while she was still alive, he's going to wish he hadn't."

She studied him.

"So you're thinking we're dealing with different killers."

That was true.

"Three of the killings are violent," he said, "but in different ways. As to the fourth woman—the one with no obvious signs of trauma—we're still waiting on the cause of death. I already know it's going to be suffocation or poison. Either way, I think we have four different killers."

Shalifa had a serious expression.

"Theoretically, then, Tianca Holland is still a suspect as to Angela Pfeifer."

Coventry dismissed the concept with a facial expression.

"Not really," he said. "She'd never be connected in any way to other killers. She's basically a decent person who just happened to get tangled up in a love life that went south."

"She's partying her way through life, the way I hear it," Shalifa said.

Coventry nodded.

"True to a point," he said. "But there's a lot more to her than that."

"So have you joined the party yet? Fully, I mean?"

"No, but I don't know how much longer I'll be able to hold out, if you want to know the truth," he said. "You're the only one who knows that, by the way."

She shook her head in disapproval.

"Bryson, I'm honestly starting to worry about you," she said. "You never played this fast and loose with the rules before."

That was true.

"Why jeopardize your job or your reputation, is all I'm saying," Shalifa added.

He knew she was right.

But she didn't understand Tianca's power.

Time to change the subject.

"We need to find out who the fourth woman is. My guess is

that she disappeared right around the time of the other three victims, which is the beginning of April. I think if we do a statewide search of missing persons from that timeframe she's going to pop up."

Shalifa agreed.

"I can do that, if you want."

"I want," he said. "You should probably get right on it. We're going to look pretty stupid if CNN figures it out first."

AN HOUR LATER COVENTRY RECEIVED a telephone call from an attorney named Austin Gray. As soon as he hung up he walked over to Shalifa Netherwood and grabbed her by the arm.

"We're taking a field trip," he said.

She stood up and fell into step.

"Where?"

"To interview our 911 caller."

"You found her?"

"More like she found us," he said.

Chapter Twenty-Nine

Day Five – September 9
Friday Morning

HALEY WILDE FOUND TWO NEW FILES on her desk when she arrived at her office—more dogs for the doghouse. She didn't care. The worst day at work was still better than the best day in the unemployment line. She touched base with the lawyers who had dropped them off, calendared the due dates, and then concentrated as much as she could on pounding out assignments.

But she hadn't slept much last night.

Which forced her to shore up with too much coffee this morning.

Plus Renee Rand's death wouldn't leave her alone. She kept getting a mental picture of someone sawing Renee's head off. On top of that, Jacqueline Moore hadn't shown up yet to apologize in person.

She jumped when her phone rang.

Austin Gray's voice came through.

"The cops are on their way over to interview you," he said.

"Okay."

"You sound stressed."

She probably did but said, "I'm fine."

"Why don't you come up to my office? We'll get organized."

When she got to his office, Austin was standing in the doorway talking to Jacqueline Moore. The woman saw her and said, "Sorry about last night. I have some personal stuff going on. I was wrong to unload on you."

Haley said, "No problem."

Jacqueline hugged her around the shoulders and said, "I'm a bitch, but most of the time I'm a nice bitch. Yesterday things got away from me."

"I understand."

"We'll do lunch and I'll tell you some gossip to make up for it," Jacqueline said.

Austin jumped in.

"Not about me, I hope."

Jacqueline rolled her eyes. "*Mostly* about you."

The talk continued but Haley paid only enough attention to react when she needed to. Instead she savored the fact that everything had actually returned to normal. Maybe she really did have a long-term place with the firm after all.

AUSTIN GRAY'S OFFICE TURNED OUT TO BE slightly more than a desk and a credenza. It had a pool table, a wet bar, couches and chairs galore, plants, a treadmill, a fountain and two old pinball machines—all pointed at an incredible view of the Rockies.

"This is just like my office," Haley said.

Austin laughed.

"Now you see why I can't go back to Colfax."

The walls held expensive modern art, except for the wall

behind his desk, which was totally barren except for an old check framed under glass.

"That's the check I told you about," Austin said, "the one that bounced. My reminder of reality."

She looked at it.

$182.53.

"Insufficient Funds" stamped in red ink.

"After getting that check," Austin said, "I spent a lot of time figuring out how to not get another one." He chuckled. "Of course, it did no good. We still take our share of hits."

Five minutes later Austin's personal assistant escorted two people into the room. Haley recognized the man—Bryson Coventry—from the news report, but wasn't prepared for the live version. She took her eyes off him only long enough to glance at the woman, an attractive African American with a powerful body, professionally dressed, about Haley's age.

"Nice digs," Coventry said.

He focused on the pinball machines.

"I used to play a little when I was a kid," he said, looking at Austin Gray. "If you want to make a wager, I'll bet everything I own against everything you own."

Austin grinned.

"I don't own anything," he said. "My bankers do. But I'll bet everything that I owe against everything that you owe."

Coventry walked over to the machine, tested the flippers, and put a ball in play as he talked to Haley.

"So tell me the story," he said. "How'd you find her?"

Haley talked while Coventry and Austin vied for points. "It was no stroke of genius," she said. "I knew the date that Renee Rand disappeared. It was at the top of my mind. When the news report came on about the other two bodies, who disappeared about the same time as Renee, I just put two and two together. It was just a matter of one dot, and another dot, and a straight-line connection."

Then she told him about how she ended up in the water and actually found the head.

"No one knows yet that the head was detached," Coventry said. "We're keeping that close to the vest. Have you told anyone about that?"

She ran through her memory.

"No," she said. "Just Austin."

Coventry nodded.

"Good. I'd appreciate it if you both kept it that way."

Not a problem.

"That's all I know," she added. "It was just a fluke."

Even though the ball was at the top of the board, Coventry took his hands off the flippers and looked at her. "That's not entirely true," he said. "You heard that we found a fourth body too, right?"

She nodded.

That was true.

"And you know her name, don't you?"

She swallowed.

"Well, I did happen to sniff around some news articles on the Internet," she said, "to see if anyone else also disappeared in early April."

"And?"

"A name did come up," she said. "Catherine Carmichael."

Coventry was impressed.

"Bingo," he said. "We haven't confirmed it yet but that's who we think it is too. Again, keep that close to the vest."

After Austin Gray soundly beat Coventry three games in a

row, they ended up on leather couches drinking coffee, where Coventry learned that Renee Rand didn't have an enemy in the world.

"Not even a little tiny one?" Coventry asked.

"If you're looking for tiny stuff that doesn't really count," Austin said, "she did have a minor personality conflict with another lawyer in the firm by the name of Jacqueline Moore."

Haley wasn't sure, but Coventry seemed to react to the name.

"Jacqueline Moore," he repeated.

"But no more so than everyone else," Austin added. "Jacqueline rubs some people the wrong way." He turned to Haley. "Right?"

Haley almost agreed, but decided to be politically correct instead.

"She's not so bad," she said.

Coventry looked at her and frowned.

"In hindsight," he said, "I wish we hadn't put your face on the news. Someone might think you're a witness or a threat." He handed her one of his business cards. "Just keep a lookout. If you hear any strange bumps in the night, give me a call."

He turned to Austin Gray. "I'd like to look through Renee's emails."

Austin put on a face as if he'd love to cooperate, but couldn't. "They'll be lots of attorney-client stuff in there," he said. "I'll tell you what I can do. I'll look through them for you and let you know if anything looks suspicious. I'll do that this afternoon and call you by the end of the day."

Coventry shrugged.

"Okay," he said. "We'll start like that."

Five minutes later, just as they were about to break up, Austin Gray's secretary buzzed on the intercom, apologized for interrupting, and informed Austin that he had an emergency phone call. Austin excused himself, walked over to his desk, picked up the phone and put it to his ear.

As he listened his face grew serious.

He said nothing.

He only listened.

Then, at the end, he said, "I understand," and hung up.

Chapter Thirty

Day Five – September 9
Friday

WHEN THEY GOT TO DENVER FRIDAY AFTERNOON, Jack Degan dropped Gretchen off at his beat-up Chevy and gave her the keys to it, plus two thousand dollars in cash. Her job this afternoon was to find a cheap furnished place to rent for a month and stock it with food, beer and Jack Daniels.

And buy clean sheets too.

Degan hated dirty sheets.

Then, in the rental car, he drove up to the cabin and parked a half mile down the road. He snuck up to the structure on foot and found a car parked in front. After jotting down the license plate number, he crept up to the bedroom window and peeked in.

What he saw almost made him vomit.

He jogged back to the car and snaked down the mountain to Denver. On the way his cell phone rang.

"We got another client," Swofford said.

Degan smiled.

Another client meant another pile of money.

"Details," he said.

"He wants a specific person," Swofford said. "She's a stripper at a club called Cheeks. She goes by the name of Chase but her real name's Samantha Stamp. Are you getting this?"

Cheeks.

Chase.

Samantha Stamp.

"Yeah, I got it," Degan said. "The fee's a hundred for a specific person," he said.

A reminder.

Just to be absolutely sure there was no confusion.

"I know that and the guy's already paid. He's going to call me when he gets to Denver. My suspicion is that we'll need the woman sometime tomorrow or the day after, so you'll want to get it in motion. Don't take her though until I give you the word. The guy wants to be sure he knows when that's going to happen so he can be somewhere public, with an alibi—just in case."

Degan could care less about that.

He already had a plan how to get the woman.

He was more concerned with being sure he didn't have to worry about two live ones at the same time.

"We need to clean out the cabin first," Degan said. "You know I don't like overlap."

"I'll call you tomorrow and let you know when you can go back up," Swofford said. "My guess is it'll be sometime in the morning, before noon. I don't see an overlap problem at this point. Remember to not take the woman until I give the go-ahead. Just scope her out and figure out how to do it, for now."

"Understood."

AS SOON AS HE HUNG UP, THE PHONE RANG AGAIN. This time it was Gretchen, calling from a payphone. "I got us a really cool place," she said.

Excitement oozed from her voice.

Degan smiled, picturing her face.

"It's a house."

She gave him directions and thirty minutes later he pulled into a long gravel drive that dead-ended at a small bungalow in an undeveloped area of Jefferson County, on the west side of Highway 93, between Golden and Boulder. The place must have been a farmhouse at one point, say fifty years ago, given the acreage.

Paint peeled off the sides.

No doubt an old lead-based paint.

A wooden fence lay flat and neglected.

Weeds choked the driveway.

When he stepped out of the car, the air smelled like nature and the Colorado sky was clear and blue. He couldn't hear any traffic at all. The foothills jutted up not more than a couple of miles to the west

He liked the place immediately.

Gretchen bounded out the door and jumped on him, wrapping her legs around his hips.

"Isn't it great!" she said. "I only paid for a month, but we can have it longer if we want."

She grabbed his hand and pulled him towards the front door.

"It's got a huge bed," she said. "And I put fresh sheets on it like you wanted. I've been waiting all day to try it out."

"You mean with me?"

She kissed him.

"Yes, silly, with you. Only with you."

THAT EVENING HE HEADED TO CHEEKS while Gretchen went out to shop for a TV. He told her he was a private investigator and would have to work weird hours. She had no problem with that.

He didn't like lying to her.

But it wasn't as if he had a choice.

Cheeks turned out to be a bustling, high-energy place with lots of grade-B strippers and beer-gut guys. Degan ordered a Bud Light and hung out at the bar until Chase got called to one of the stages—Stage Number Four, apparently—near the back. Men flocked over so fast that Degan was lucky to get a seat.

And no wonder.

Chase was no ordinary stripper.

She had one of the most incredible bodies he had ever seen but, up top, had a very ordinary face. Because of that the guys, apparently, didn't find her intimidating.

She had a sleazy, in-your-face routine.

Not afraid of body contact.

Degan laid a five on the stage and waited for his turn. She responded by straddling his shoulders with her legs and rubbing her crotch in his face.

Not close to his face.

Actually touching.

He tipped her another five then bought her a drink when she came off stage. When she hit him up for a private dance he said, "Sure."

She took him to the back of the club, sat him in a dark booth facing the wall, and let him feel her up.

"Do you ever give any really private dances, off-site?" he

asked.

She ran a finger down his scar.

"Maybe."

Degan pulled two hundred-dollar bills out of his wallet and handed them to her. "There's eight more where that came from," he said. "Are you interested?"

"Very."

She gave him her cell phone number and he told her he'd call her within the next couple of days.

"You won't be sorry," she said. "I don't watch the clock or anything."

Chapter Thirty-One

Day Five – September 9
Friday Afternoon

THE CORONER—A SMALL SERIOUS MAN named Robert Nelson who had a perpetual hint of whiskey on his breath—called Bryson Coventry shortly after two in the afternoon. He confirmed a lot of the puzzle pieces that Coventry already suspected.

The head of body number three did in fact belong to Renee Rand, according to her dental records.

The other Jane Doe, body number four—who Coventry suspected to be a 19-year-old by the name of Catherine Carmichael based on the date of her disappearance—was in fact who he suspected. Again, according to dental records. Her eyes had been gouged out post-mortem, after her throat got slashed.

Body number two—Tonya Obenchain—who showed no exterior signs of trauma, died by suffocation.

Then the coroner dropped a bomb.

"Going back to Renee Rand," Nelson said, "whoever took her head off used some kind of a saw with a jagged blade."

Coventry spun an empty coffee cup around on his desk.

He already knew that.

"A hacksaw?" he asked.

"I don't think so," the coroner said. "The jags appear to be too big. I'm thinking something more in the nature of a wood saw."

"Ouch," Coventry said.

"That word, unfortunately, is probably pretty appropriate," Nelson said.

The man's voice trembled.

Coventry had never heard him like this before and stopped spinning the cup. "What do you mean?"

"What I mean is," Nelson said, "the guy cut her head off while she was still alive."

Coventry stood up.

"Tell me you're screwing with me," he said.

No response.

"Are you serious?"

Nelson confirmed that he was.

Very serious.

"Well, what kind of sick ass does that?"

"I don't know," Nelson said. "But there's more. From what I can tell, the cutting started, stopped, and then started again. A number of times."

Coventry paced.

And felt sweat on his forehead.

"He took his time," the coroner said. "He started on one side of the neck and worked his way in. Then he shifted over to the other side and did the same thing. It seems that each cut only went in a quarter of an inch or so at a time."

Coventry kicked his trash can and sent it rolling across the room.

"Goddamn it!"

"I'm thinking he purposely avoided the front throat area so she wouldn't drown in her own blood," Nelson said. "He also avoided the back spinal area. Maybe because he wanted to watch her kick and didn't want to paralyze her."

Coventry pictured it.

Then noticed that his hands trembled.

"How long did it take?" he asked. "All told?"

"A while," Nelson said. "Even after he hit the aorta and she started bleeding to death."

"Is that how she died then? Bleeding to death?"

"No. She died when he cut through her spinal cord," Nelson said. "If she'd bled to death she wouldn't have had as much blood left as we found."

It was at that moment that Shalifa Netherwood stepped into the room and motioned at him.

"CNN's here," she said. "They're getting set up."

Coventry told Nelson he'd call him back later and hung up. He hadn't taken two steps towards the door when his phone rang. He almost didn't answer it but did.

It turned out to be a nurse from the hospital, Denver Health.

"Marilyn Black is ready to be released," she said. "Short term she's okay. But if she doesn't get into a rehab program ASAP, we're going to be seeing lots more of her—us or the coroner. She got really lucky this time."

Coventry already knew that.

"I'll be down in about a hour to pick her up. Is that okay?"

It was.

THE CNN INTERVIEW TURNED OUT TO BE a lot more brutal than Coventry initially envisioned. The questioning focused on why the other three bodies weren't discovered when the first one was. They also wanted to know if there were any suspects yet—which of course there weren't. Finally, they wanted to know if Coventry had located the person in the photograph that was being broadcast on the local TV stations and in the newspapers. What was her connection to everything?

He was actually glad they asked about that.

It gave him an opportunity to publicly state that they found the woman and determined that she didn't know anything. Hopefully, if any of the killers had perceived her as a threat, they didn't now and would leave her alone.

WHEN THE INTERVIEW ENDED, Paul Kubiak blocked Coventry's path in the hall and brought him to a stop.

"This is your lucky day," Kubiak said, scratching his big old gut.

Coventry looked skeptical.

"If you have good news you'll be the first."

"I got a lead for you on a guy selling a '67 Corvette," Kubiak said. "I'd jump on this one myself, but I'm already tapped out after getting that '63. It's a small-block, but it's a numbers-matching, two-owner car."

"Have you seen it?" Coventry questioned.

Kubiak shook his head.

"Not yet," Kubiak said. "But it's supposed to be primo. Red over black; and the seller's not looking for a lot of money. He's more interested in being sure it gets a good home."

"Wow."

"I'd jump all over it if I was you," Kubiak said.

Coventry looked at his watch.

He was already late picking up Marilyn Black.

"Right now I have to run an errand," he said. "Can we see it this evening?"

"I'll make a call and find out," Kubiak said. "I don't see why not."

"Let me know. If not tonight, then tomorrow. I want to be the first guy there."

"I'll call you."

Before he could get out of the building, Shalifa cornered him. "I'm keeping track of young females disappearing, like you wanted me to," she said. "Apparently a young Hispanic woman disappeared in Pueblo on Thursday, someone named Mia Avila, a 24-year-old. She runs a tattoo shop."

Coventry nodded and headed for the stairwell.

"Pueblo?"

"Right."

"That's a ways off," he noted.

"True."

Hispanic too.

All the victims so far were white.

"Anyone else?" he questioned.

"No."

"Well, just keep her on your radar screen for now," he said. Then he stopped and turned. "Have you talked to the Pueblo PD?"

"No."

He opened the door to the stairwell.

"Why don't you give them a call just for grins and see what they have to say."

"Where are you going?"

He stopped.

"To pick up Marilyn Black from the hospital," he said.

She walked towards him.

"Let me go with you."

"Why?"

"She's going to need a place to stay," Shalifa said. "I was thinking she could stay with me."

Coventry cocked his head.

"I located her mom—in Idaho. With any luck I'm going to put Marilyn Black on a plane. If that fails, you can be Plan B."

Chapter Thirty-Two

Day Six – September 10
Saturday

HALEY WILDE WOKE WELL RESTED on Saturday morning. She yawned, stretched, showered, and counted her lucky stars that she had actually survived a whole week at the law firm.

She studied her face in the mirror as she brushed her teeth.

"Don't screw up again," she said.

"Yes master."

"I mean it."

Knowing she still had a paycheck coming in, she let herself think about the pile of bills. It would be tough going until the end of the month, when she actually got paid, but after that she should be able to make ends meet and actually chip away at the student loans.

Maybe even get an oil change for the little Honda fellow.

She couldn't even remember the last time she did that.

The poor little thing.

Dressed in khakis and a cotton short-sleeve shirt, she headed straight to work, wanting to bill at least six or seven hours today. Almost every associate on her floor had already beaten her in.

Shit.

What a horse race.

She filled a Styrofoam cup with coffee, grabbed a day-old donut out of a Krispy Krème box in the kitchen, and headed to her office. Outside, the day was perfect, sunny and blue. Ordinarily, right about now, she'd be on her bike trying to not kill herself on some insane mountain trail that was never intended for two wheels.

Oh well.

Maybe tomorrow.

She pounded out solid work for more than three hours before her mind wandered to Renee Rand. Deep down she still believed that the legal file Renee was working on for the psychologist—Beverly Twenhofel—was somehow connected. Or, if not connected, at least held some answers.

Should she tell Bryson Coventry about it?

Or more importantly, *could* she?

Probably not.

It was an attorney-client matter.

And one thing beyond all others was certain at this point—if she screwed up again then Jacqueline Moore would bounce her ass so far out of Denver that she'd end up speaking with a New York accent.

"Well you look serious," someone said.

The words startled her so much that she dropped the coffee.

Papers immediately soaked up the liquid and curled.

"Shit!"

The woman in her doorway—Christina Huynh—looked amused and said, "I've done that five million times. It's all part of riding a desk."

Christina held out her hand.

"Come on. I'm here to save you."

THEY ENDED UP ON THE 16TH STREET MALL, buying dollar hotdogs from a street vendor and finding a bench in the sun. Christina wanted to know why Haley's photo had been on the TV, so Haley told her about how she found Renee Rand. But didn't tell her that the head had been severed.

"It always struck me as strange," Christina said, "that someone would take Renee."

"Why?"

"I don't know. She just wasn't *enough* of any one thing to make a stranger pay attention to her," she said. "She wasn't attractive enough, she wasn't weird enough, she wasn't young enough, she just wasn't anything enough. I mean she was a great lawyer and a wonderful person, but to someone who didn't know her, she'd look pretty plain vanilla."

Haley agreed.

"So why her?" Christina asked.

Haley considered it.

"Wrong place wrong time, I guess." A couple of cops on horseback passed by and waved at them. They smiled and waved back. "Was Renee seeing anyone?" Haley asked. "You know, romantically?"

Christina chuckled, as if the concept seemed strange.

"Maybe, but not that I know of. The woman was a workaholic. Much unlike me. Why?"

"When a woman goes missing, nine out of ten times a lover did it," Haley said.

"Right. But in this case, with four bodies, there's obviously something a lot more sinister going on."

When Haley got home later that afternoon, two news crews were waiting for her in the parking lot. They probably thought she had some great big juicy tip for them.

Well too bad, because she didn't.

Something in her gut told her to turn around and walk away before they spotted her. She had nothing to say and didn't want to contradict Bryson Coventry by accident. But another part of her said to talk to them.

Just to reinforce that she didn't know anything.

Just in case Bryson Coventry was right, and someone out there perceived her to be a threat.

So she walked over.

Nonchalantly.

They recognized her and got the cameras rolling.

She stopped and smiled.

"Do you have any idea why anyone would trash your apartment?"

What?

The smile fell off her face and she looked up at her door.

"Were they trying to find something?"

It was open.

"What does this have to do with the four killings?"

A policeman was inside her apartment, talking to someone.

Shit!

She ran in that direction.

"Is someone after you?"

"Is this a warning of some kind?"

"What do you know about the four killings?"

"Why was Bryson Coventry trying to find you?"

She stopped just as she reached the bottom of the stairs.

Then turned and faced them.

"I don't know anything about anything," she said. "Anyone who thinks differently is wrong. That's the honest-to-God truth."

Then she ran up the stairs.

Chapter Thirty-Three

Day Six – September 10
Saturday Noon

JACK DEGAN LIKED THE MONEY but he didn't like the cleanup. In fact, sometimes he wondered if it was even worth it. Like right now, for example, as he drove up to the cabin.

This was the sick part.

And he never knew what to expect.

All he could hope for is that things hadn't gotten too bloody.

He arrived at the cabin shortly before noon, saw that the car that had been there yesterday was now gone, and pulled in front of the structure as the tires kicked up a cloud of dust. The radio played "Heart of Stone," which he hadn't heard in years. He left the engine running until it ended, watching a bluebird bounce up and down on the branch of a lodgepole pine.

Then he took a swig of Jack and stepped out.

The sky above him was just about perfect—blue, sunny, warm and inviting. A thick pine fragrance filled the air. He stood still and listened.

No sounds came from anywhere.

Not from inside the house.

Not from the gravel road behind him.

Not from anywhere.

Good.

He walked to the front door, found it locked as it should be, and used his key to get in. He located the body in the bedroom, posed in a spread-eagle position on the bed, covered by a white sheet. He checked the DVD recorder and confirmed that the client had removed his souvenir copy of the snuff.

He couldn't see any blood on the sheet and pulled it off.

The woman's eyes were closed.

He saw no visible evidence of trauma or blood.

Excellent.

This would be a piece-of-cake.

He felt for her pulse and found none.

Her body was still warm.

She couldn't have been dead more than an hour or two.

He sat on the edge of the bed and ran a hand up and down her body, tracing her tattoos. She didn't move. He felt his cock swell and pushed it down, but the pressure only made it stand up more. Maybe the woman needed one final act of love to send her off. He checked his wallet to see if he had a condom.

He did.

So he put it on and mounted her.

She was tight.

He took his time.

Working up to the verge of a climax and then backing off.

Two times.

Then three.

Then four.

Finally he couldn't stand it any more and thrust like a rock star.

"Yeah baby!"

"How's that feel?"

"Good, huh?"

"You like it."

"You like it."

"You like it."

Then he exploded in her.

Drenched in sweat and exhausted, he collapsed on her and didn't move. Staying inside her. Then he closed his eyes just to rest them for a second.

At some point later he felt movement.

Very minor.

Barely perceptible.

When he opened his eyes the woman was staring at him.

Chapter Thirty-Four

Day Six – September 10
Saturday

IN TIANCA'S SPARE BEDROOM, Bryson Coventry twisted and tossed in bed half the night, going back and forth on whether he should buy the Corvette. The seller liked him and offered a good deal last night, a steal-of-a-deal in fact; but stressed he could only hold it until noon today. Lots of other people were calling and wanting to see it. The car was everything Kubiak described, namely a primo representative of classic American muscle. But, even at a good price, it was still a pretty penny. To get it in his garage would take every bit of his savings plus a small loan.

But it was so damn beautiful.

Not to mention a sound investment.

It would never go south in value.

He already pictured himself driving it on Sunday afternoons with the top down and the Beach Boys blasting.

"Just get it," he told himself.

Too excited to sleep any longer, he crawled out of bed, peeked in on a still-sleeping Tianca, and then took a jog, thinking it over one last time before he committed. When he got back to the house he called the seller and left a message that he'd take the car and would be over before noon with the money.

There.

Done.

He hit the shower and got his mind back on the case. The four murders were connected. If he could crack one then the others would follow. But which one was the weakest link?

Probably Renee Rand.

That killer was the most extreme and would probably stand out the most. Plus the law firm was eager to help. She was also the one who cried out the most for justice. No one should have their head cut off, especially while they were alive.

He toweled off and found Tianca in the kitchen, firing up the coffee and wearing a short pink nightie. Every time he saw her he was shocked at how beautiful she was.

"Morning, wet-head," she said. "So did you decide to get it, or what?"

He nodded.

"Yep—guilty of stupidity."

"I knew you would."

He chuckled.

"Even I didn't know I would until thirty minutes ago."

"I knew last night," she said.

"Meaning what? That you know me . . ."

". . . better than you know yourself?"

He shook his head.

Beaten.

They picked the car up shortly before noon. Coventry gave the seller two checks and told him not to cash the second one until Tuesday. The seller trusted him, gave him the keys and a bill of sale, and said, "Remember. None of us really ever owns a car like this. We just save it for the next guy."

Coventry drove it back to Tianca's, parked it in the driveway and drooled on it for over an hour while Tianca washed her Lotus. Then she said, "Why don't you pull it in the garage? We'll get in the back and you can feel me up."

LATER THAT AFTERNOON, COVENTRY LEFT the Corvette in Tianca's garage and took the Tundra home to get a jump on all the dreaded, time-wasting tasks that came with being alive—clothes washing, house cleaning, food shopping, bill paying, checkbook balancing and a thousand other little things that were already long overdue.

He was halfway through food shopping at the King Soopers in Green Mountain, trying to not buy too much junk food, when his cell phone rang. A female's voice came through. "This is Haley Wilde, the attorney. You said I should call you if anything happened."

She sounded panicked.

He listened patiently, hung up and then walked over to a young lady stocking the shelves with cans of corn. "See that cart over there?" he said, pointing. "That's mine but I have to leave. There's some frozen stuff in there that someone's going to need to put back. I'm really sorry about this."

He kicked himself in the ass all the way over to Haley's apartment.

He was to blame.

He should have never put her face on the news.

He had turned her into a target.

Chapter Thirty-Five

Day Six – September 10
Saturday Afternoon

HALEY WILDE SAT BEHIND THE WHEEL of her parked car, still trying to determine who or why anyone would trash her apartment, when Bryson Coventry raced into the parking lot and slammed his pickup to a stop.

Even from this distance he looked tense.

By the time she walked over and got his attention, he couldn't apologize fast enough. "This is all my fault," he said.

She disagreed.

"I turned you into a target," he added.

She grabbed his hand. "I've been thinking about this," she said. "If it's somehow connected to Renee Rand or the other dead women, then we have fresh clues inside my apartment. Right?"

He agreed and wondered why he hadn't thought of that himself.

Before she could say another word, he bounded up the stairs two at a time and got all the local cops out of the apartment before they contaminated the scene to death.

Then he shut the door and walked back down, already

punching numbers on his cell phone. As he waited for an answer, he told Haley, "The Lakewood PD gave me permission to bring the Denver Crime Unit down to process the scene."

Fifteen minutes later the Crime Unit showed up, with a beer-belly man behind the wheel.

"That's Paul Kubiak," Coventry told Haley.

"I find you a primo 1967 Corvette," Kubiak said getting out, "and this is how you repay me? Making me work on a Saturday?"

Coventry chuckled.

"I was going to call you," he said. "I bought it."

Kubiak looked flabbergasted.

"You did?"

"Just picked it up a couple of hours ago," Coventry added.

Kubiak shook his head in wonder.

"I'll be damned. I didn't think you'd do it."

"I shouldn't have. It took all my money and then some," Coventry said.

"Do what I do," Kubiak said. "Get a cardboard sign—*Need Money, Did Something Stupid.* Just stay off my corner."

Then they turned their attention to the job at hand. Coventry wanted it processed as if it was a homicide scene, not a B&E. If someone left a fingerprint, a hair, or dropped his wallet by mistake, Coventry wanted Kubiak to find it.

HALEY WILDE WATCHED FROM A DISTANCE, talking to the renters who had wandered over to see what all the commotion was about. All the fuss made her knees weak.

She didn't know where she'd sleep tonight.

Not here, though.

She went over to her car, sat behind the wheel and called Austin Gray to let him know that she'd be showing up on the news again. She didn't want him to get blindsided by it.

"I'm coming over," he said.

"Austin, really, you don't have to. I'm fine."

"I'll see you in about twenty minutes."

When he arrived he had a proposition for her. "This is somehow tied to the four dead women, especially if you're correct that nothing was taken. Here's what I think we should do. We should send you to the firm's D.C. office until all this blows over. The firm will pick up all the expenses—air, lodging, meals, the whole thing. You need to get acquainted with the people out there sooner or later anyway, so it might as well be now. Then, when this blows over, we'll bring you back to Denver."

She thought about it.

"What if it doesn't blow over?"

He cocked his head.

"Everything blows over sooner or later. The main thing is your safety. Tonight, tomorrow, and the next day."

She almost agreed, but then shocked herself.

"Thanks but no," she said. "I'm not going to give in to intimidation."

Chapter Thirty-Six

Day Six – September 10
Saturday

WITH THE TATTOO WOMAN MIA AVILA HOGTIED on the bed, terribly and disgustingly alive, Jack Degan took a hit from the flask and watched his copy of the DVD—the secret copy no one ever knew about, the one transmitted to a second recorder located in the garage. It convinced him that the client fully intended to kill the woman and thought he had.

Degan felt better knowing that.

If the asshole had chickened out, and intentionally left him with a live mess to dispose of, Degan wouldn't have had much of a sense of humor about the whole thing.

He didn't mind abducting the women.

And he didn't mind that they died.

He didn't even mind *how* they died.

Quick.

Slow.

Clean.

Messy.

Whatever.

But he had absolutely no respect for little spineless twits who didn't have the balls to carry through with what they started. That had happened twice before. Afterwards, Degan hunted them both down and taught them a little lesson, about how gutless little toads didn't deserve to breathe the same air as him any more. They didn't even know who he was until their last ten seconds of life when he told them. Without being fully vested they couldn't continue to live, plain and simple. Because otherwise they might end up with buyer's remorse and feel the need to go to the cops.

The assholes.

This case was different, however.

Nothing more than an innocent mistake.

No need to hunt the guy down.

HE GOT THE CALL HE WAS WAITING FOR mid-afternoon, from Swofford, and explained that the tattoo woman had been left alive, unintentionally, according to his best guess. Swofford paused and then said, "I see three options. You can kill her, or I can call the client and see if he wants to come back and finish up, or you can offer the woman to the next client as a freebie."

Degan chewed on it.

"When's the next client coming?" he asked.

"He flies in Monday night, then he'll drive up to the cabin Tuesday morning, so you need to have the stripper in place by then at the latest. He wants to be sure she's snatched before he gets to Denver. Is all that doable?"

"I'm pretty sure," he said.

"Handle the tattoo woman any way you want. Just be sure you have the stripper at the cabin by Monday evening. This guy isn't the kind of person I want to screw around with."

"No problem."

AFTER HE HUNG UP, DEGAN WENT INTO THE BEDROOM to check on his little catch, Mia Avila. Lying there, naked and hog-tied, she looked incredibly vulnerable. He played with her hair.

She made wonderful little noises through her gag.

"So, what should I do with you? Kill you myself or save you for the next guy?"

Either way, he should definitely have a little fun first.

He turned her on her back and played with her nipples, then ran an index finger up and down her incredibly smooth stomach.

"Feels good, doesn't it?"

Chapter Thirty-Seven

Day Seven – September 11
Sunday

ON SUNDAY MORNING, COVENTRY WANTED TO take Tianca for a ride in the '67, maybe up to Red Rocks or old town Morrison, somewhere in that geography, where the mountains were big and the traffic lights were few. Stop for a cup of coffee somewhere. But he knew deep down that he wouldn't be able to relax and enjoy it.

Not with so much going on.

So instead he got up early, showered in the guest bathroom so he wouldn't wake Tianca, left her a note that he was reserving her for this evening, and headed to the office. He hadn't been there more than ten minutes when Barb Winters, the dispatcher, a woman with new breast implants and a new wardrobe, called.

"Got a body for you," she said. "And it's not mine."

Coventry frowned.

"Where?"

"Way out east, past Monaco."

Coventry knew the area well and pulled up an image of meticulously restored tutor mansions sitting on tree-lined boulevards, the home of Denver's rich, powerful and elite.

"Kate Katona's on call and she's taking it," Winters added. "She just wanted me to let you know about it in case you were in the mood to drive out there and bring her a cup of coffee."

Fifteen minutes later Coventry arrived at the scene with a thermos of coffee and two Styrofoam cups.

The house turned out to be a brick castle, well guarded by a designer wrought-iron fence, with a long cobblestone driveway that ended at a six-car garage.

Money.

Money.

Money.

Some people had too much of it.

He slipped on gloves, checked in with the scribe and walked into the house. In the lobby he found a huge oil painting, almost three-feet square. He'd never seen it before but immediately recognized it as a Delano. The work, titled "Navajo Boy," depicted an Indian boy of ten or eleven, wearing a red shirt and red bandanna, walking with a heavily packed and very tired mule in a desert setting. A panting dog followed.

Coventry got up close and studied the brushwork.

Many of the strokes were thick and bold, with heavy paint, obviously applied when the painting was almost complete. They were the kind of strokes that took guts, because they had to be laid on perfectly the first time, otherwise they'd ruin the painting.

"Good for you," Coventry said.

He found Kate Katona in the bedroom with the body of a man who had been shot in the face and didn't have much of it left.

"Lovely," he said. "Who is he?"

Katona jumped and said, "Don't sneak up on me like that." She wore black pants, tennis shoes and a dark blue blouse that did nothing to show off the world-class chest beneath. "His name's Brad Ripley," she said. "Apparently some kind of high roller with a propensity for coke and women."

She pointed to a plastic bag of white powder on the nightstand.

Coventry bent down and examined it.

It looked like cocaine all right.

A lot of cocaine in fact.

"So someone shot him and didn't take the coke?" he questioned. "What's wrong with that picture?"

Katona nodded.

"That's the same weird thought I had," she said. "Nor did they take his Rolex or the wallet in his back pocket with over five grand in it."

Coventry felt his curiosity perk.

"So, we're either dealing with a very bad thief, or something else altogether," he said.

Katona cocked her head.

"I'd say it's a hate thing," she said. "Someone didn't want to see his face anymore."

Coventry agreed.

"Make a list of his enemies," he said. "Your killer's somewhere on that piece of paper." He took one more look at the hole where the man's face used to be, and then headed for the door. "I'm around as a backup if you need me. Otherwise, run with it."

Chapter Thirty-Eight

Day Seven – September 11
Sunday Morning

HALEY WILDE ROLLED OVER IN BED and almost continued sleeping when she realized that everything was a little off—the feel of the pillow, the smell of the air, the texture of the sounds. She opened her eyes, found herself in a strange dark room, and bolted upright as her heart pounded.

Where was she?

She held her breath, listening for danger, but detected none. Then she remembered Austin Gray insisting that she be somewhere safe last night and checking her into the Adams Mark Hotel in downtown Denver.

Another room connected to hers.

In that room was a man named Larry Speaker, a professional bodyguard and part-time black-belt instructor, packing a SIG .45 and a Concealed Weapon Permit.

She got out of bed, checked the connecting door and found it just as she had left it before going to bed last night—closed but unlocked.

She opened it as quietly as she could and peeked into the other room. She found her protector, Speaker, curled up on his side under a white blanket, breathing deep and heavy.

Okay.

She had survived the night.

But what about two months from now, when the bodyguards and hiding places were long gone?

The clock said 5:30 a.m.

She dressed without making a noise and went down to the hotel's fitness center. One other person was there, a middle aged bald man walking on a treadmill and watching an early morning news program on the monitor. He smiled and said hello when she walked in, but she could tell he wouldn't be hitting on her.

She worked the weights for thirty minutes and then spun the stationary bike until her legs burned.

When she got back to her room, Speaker was there, pacing, dressed and stressed, talking frantically into a cell phone. When she stepped into the room he said, "Goddamn it! Don't ever do that again without leaving a note."

She felt like shit.

He was absolutely right.

"Sorry," she said. "I guess I wasn't thinking."

He must have read something in her voice because he immediately softened and said, "Don't worry about it. I'm just glad you're okay."

"Sorry," she said again.

He nodded.

"No problem."

SHE SHOWERED, PACKED, PUT A NOTE on the nightstand, and then quietly slipped out of the room. The note said: *Larry. Thanks for protecting me last night. Sorry again for the brain-fart.*

She headed back to her apartment but found yellow crime tape on the door and didn't know whether she should enter even though it was her place. She decided she probably shouldn't and drove to Einstein's for coffee and a bagel instead.

Then her cell phone rang.

Christina Huygh's voice came though.

"Are you still alive?"

Haley grunted.

"As far as I can tell. Why? Do you have your eye on my office?"

"God, no. Your office sucks."

Twenty minutes later Christina showed up, waved, got in line to buy a coffee and then joined her. She wore tennis shoes and a short white skirt that emphasized smooth golden legs.

"I've been thinking about what you asked me," Christina said, slurping at the cup.

"What's that?"

"About whether Renee Rand had a lover," she said.

"Meaning what? She did?"

"No," she said, pushing her glasses up. "But a thought came to the surface while I was trying to go to sleep last night. I saw Renee once, at a restaurant, having lunch with Austin Gray. I was going to go over and say hello but their body language told me they wanted to be alone, so I stayed back."

Haley considered it.

And didn't find it particularly compelling.

"Probably discussing a case," she said.

"Could be," Christina said. "But I didn't get that impression. They were in this real private booth, way in the back of the restaurant. I didn't see any briefcases or papers with them. And Renee had this look on her face as if she was about to slip under the table and give him a blowjob."

Haley laughed.

"Renee never struck me as the blowjob type."

"Maybe, but she had the blowjob look," Christina said.

Haley cocked her head.

"There's a look for that?" she asked.

Christina nodded.

"Show me," Haley said.

Christina paused at first and then put on her best blowjob face.

Haley couldn't help but laugh.

Then Christina got serious and said, "I have an idea."

Chapter Thirty-Nine

Day Seven – September 11
Sunday Morning

Jack Degan stayed at the cabin Saturday night, mounting Mia Avila before he went to sleep, and once again in the middle of the night. She didn't mean anything to him, emotionally that is. Gretchen—who thought he was on an all-night stakeout on an important case—was still the one.

In fact, he even thought of her when he came.

He slept late Sunday morning, having downed a little more Jack than he probably should have. Then he finally crawled out of bed, threw water on his face, dressed and jogged all the way down to Highway 119 and back.

Pine scent hung thick in the air.

The early autumn Colorado sky didn't have a single cloud.

There wasn't a wisp of wind.

The temperature was nice.

By the time he got back he was wide awake, energetic and very glad to be alive.

When he walked into the bedroom, Mia Avila watched

his every move.

"Do you want a shower?" he asked.

She nodded.

And mumbled as if asking him to remove the gag.

He did and she immediately gulped for air.

"Don't say a goddamn word," he said. "Otherwise it goes back on."

She stared at him, sizing him up, not daring to utter a single syllable. He warmed the shower, untied her, and then marched her in. He let her close the curtain but stayed in the room. She didn't come out until the hot water turned to warm water and the warm water turned to cold water. Then she turned the faucet off and opened the curtain just a touch, enough to stick her head out.

"Can I have a towel?" she asked.

Degan threw her one. She dried off behind the curtain, wrapped it around her body and then stayed there.

"Get out here," Degan said.

She pulled the curtain open, sized him up, and must have decided that he wasn't playing around, because she stepped out. Her hair dripped on the floor.

Suddenly Degan felt hungry.

"You want some breakfast?" he asked.

She nodded. "That would be nice."

He sat her in one of the orange vinyl chairs at the kitchen table and said, "Put your hands on top of your head and leave them there."

She hesitated, but then complied.

He kept a good eye on her, made two bowls of cereal, carried them over and put one in front of her. She started to bring her hands down and he said, "Not yet."

She kept them up.

The towel unwrapped and fell into her lap.

She knew better than to reach down.

He got the coffee pot started then sat down and told her she could eat now.

She brought her hands down and immediately covered up.

"Don't even think about trying anything," he warned.

"I won't."

She devoured the cereal so fast that he realized just how long it had been since she last ate. He fixed her another bowl and watched her.

"Just let me go and none of this ever happened," she said. "I won't tell a soul. Not a single soul. I promise."

Degan chuckled.

How many times had he heard that before?

"Oh, really?" he said.

"I promise," she said. Her voice took on an animated tone, as if she believed she could actually talk her way out of it. Degan played along, asking her the details of how they would work things out, and how he could be sure she wouldn't ever tell anyone.

Then she said something he didn't expect.

"If you don't let me go they'll find you sooner or later," she said. "I put the two thousand dollars in the safe, with a note that it's from you." He must have reacted to the words, because she seemed to brighten. "Your fingerprints are all over the money."

He stood up, put his hands in the middle of the table and leaned towards her.

"What does the note say, exactly?"

"*Money from Nick Evans for Denver tattoo.* The police will eventually figure out that I left the shop with you and never came back."

Then he remembered telling her that was his name.

Good thing, too, in hindsight.

He eased back in his chair.

"That's not my real name," he said.

The smug look fell off her face.

But then she said, "It doesn't matter. The name's in the logbook. So is the name of the woman I was tattooing when you came in. When the police ask her about Nick Evans, she's going to describe you."

Degan stood up, his heart pounding.

She was right.

"Then they'll ask around town, or get a composite sketch on the TV," she added. "Someone will end up calling in with your real name."

Shit!

She was right again.

The guy at the hotel might pick up the phone.

Or someone from a gas station.

Damn it.

A surveillance camera might have even picked him up somewhere.

He slammed his hand on the table—so hard that her cereal bounced up and fell in her lap. Then he grabbed her hair and yanked her out of the chair.

"You goddamn bitch!"

Chapter Forty

Day Seven – September 11
Sunday Afternoon

BRAD RIPLEY'S SHOT FACE stayed in Bryson Coventry's mind on the drive back to the office, but soon faded as he drank coffee and delved into the reports that Shalifa Netherwood had put together on the four victims.

The central theme appeared to be that there was no theme.

If there was any connection between the four women—other than the fact they all disappeared at about the same time and ended up buried in the same place—it wasn't popping out in neon lights.

Other than those two facts, the women had no obvious overlap.

He took a sip of coffee, found he had let it cool too much, and swallowed what was in his mouth but dumped the rest in the snake plant.

Then walked over to the pot for a refill.

Come on.

Think.

But instead of coming up with some brilliant theory he stared out the window aimlessly, across the street to the houses that had been turned into cartoon-colored bail bond dens. A couple of small boys raced down the sidewalk on bicycles, peddling as fast as they could, a reminder of how innocent we all start out. How does someone go from that to sawing someone's head off?

The oversized industrial clock on the wall said 3:52.

Probably time to head home since his brain had pretty much turned to mush at this point anyway. Or, to be more precise, head to Tianca's house and take her for a ride in the '67.

Then his cell phone rang.

Kate Katona.

She sounded as if she had just stepped out of a plane crash. "Bryson! I need you over here, right away."

"Here, where?"

"Oh, sorry. I'm still at the crime scene. Brad Ripley's. The guy who got shot in the face."

"Why? What's going on?"

"Just come over," she said. "You have to see this for yourself."

WHEN HE ARRIVED AT THE VICTIM'S HOUSE he put on his gloves, registered with the scribe and found Kate Katona in the media room.

She seemed to be equal parts excitement and stress.

"Sit down and watch," she said. "I have to warn you, though, this is graphic."

He sat down on a leather couch and faced a flat-panel television while Katona got a DVD playing. Within ten seconds he moved to the edge of the seat, leaned forward and watched, with his elbows resting on his knees and his fingers laced together. For some reason the day's coffee suddenly kicked in and twitched his nervous system.

"It's almost two hours long," she said.

He stared at the screen.

Already committed to watching every single goddamn second.

The film was obviously homemade, but of very high quality. In it, a man wearing jeans, a black sweatshirt and a black mask toyed with a tightly bound woman.

He cut her clothes off with a knife until she was totally naked.

Then played with her.

Coventry recognized the woman.

Tonya Obenchain.

The real estate agent.

Body No. 2 at the railroad spur, the one who got suffocated.

He looked at Katona.

"Does this go all the way to the end?"

"I'm afraid so."

HE FAST-FORWARDED THROUGH THE WHOLE THING and then called Dr. Leanne Sanders, the FBI profiler. "Leanne," he said. "It's me, your favorite pain in the ass."

"Bryson? Is that you?"

"Afraid so," he said.

"It's Sunday, man. Don't you ever give it a rest?"

She had a point.

He hadn't even painted a landscape in over three months.

Not even a little two-hour piece.

"Never mind that," he said. "I have a snuff film I need you

to take a look at. The perpetrator's wearing a mask but we're pretty sure it's a guy named Brad Ripley, who coincidentally just got his face shot in. The main thing I need right now is a confirmation that Ripley's the guy in the film."

"Are you telling me you have an honest-to-God snuff film?"

"That's what I'm telling you."

"Lucky you, the whole thing on film."

"This is part of the four body case," he said. "The one CNN's been chatting up."

"Interesting," she said. "Okay, here's what we're going to need on our end. The guy's wearing clothes in the film, I assume. Look around the house, find 'em and bag 'em. If the film's good enough quality . . ."

". . . It is . . ."

". . . we'll be able to match them to the ones in the film based on stitching and dye markings and stuff like that. Also, see if you can find other film with him in it so we can compare body posture and movements. We'll need the guy's exact height and weight too. Any idea when the film was made?"

"Early April is my guess," Coventry said.

"That's five months ago. Ask around with neighbors etcetera just to see if the guy's body has changed significantly in that time period, you know, if he went on a diet or pigged out or anything like that."

"Done," Coventry said. "By the way, did I say thanks?"

She laughed.

"No."

"Well remind me to."

She chuckled. "I'll add it to the list."

Chapter Forty-One

Day Seven – September 11
Sunday Afternoon

TECHNICALLY THEY WEREN'T BREAKING into the law firm, since they worked there, but Haley Wilde felt like a criminal nonetheless. She and Christina Huygh entered on the 44th Floor, since that's where their offices were, and then walked up to the 45th Floor where the dead files room was located.

No one seemed to be around.

Still, they walked down the hall cautiously.

Watching for office lights.

Listening for even the slightest whisper of a sound.

They made it all the way to dead files room, closed the door quietly and turned the lights on. Thousands of neatly labeled legal boxes sat on metal racks.

"The mother lode," Christina said.

It didn't take them long to find the box containing Renee Rand's law firm items. Using a ladder, they pulled it off a shelf near the ceiling and muscled it down to the floor.

"Heavy sucker," Haley said.

Inside, among other things, they found Renee's Weekly Planners going all the way back to her first year with the firm. They pulled out the one from this year. On the exterior they found a yellow post-it: "Copy given to investigators 4/6—JAM."

"JAM means Jacqueline A. Moore," Christina said.

They opened it to early April, when Renee disappeared, and worked their way back in time. It turned out that Renee kept a hodgepodge of handwritten information in the book, including appointments, phone numbers, client-billing start and stop times, things to-do, and whatever else that needed to be jotted down for whatever reason.

Christina laughed.

"What?" Haley asked, curious.

"I'll look for the entry that says, *Screwed Austin Gray silly this afternoon*, and you look for the one that says, *Christina Huygh is the best associate attorney I've ever seen. That girl should get a raise.*"

Haley smiled.

"Deal," she said. "I'll also look for the one that says, *If I ever turn up dead, Jacqueline Moore did it.*"

Unfortunately, they found nothing of use.

Then they got to February 18. "This is weird," Haley said. "It's a Monday and Renee has no billing recorded for a period of three hours."

Christina studied it.

"It's over the lunch hour," she said. "And look, she drove to Grand Junction later that afternoon, for a trial starting Tuesday. So she was probably packing or doing errands or something."

"Or," Haley said, "she knows she's not going to see Austin Gray that evening, since she'll be out of town, and they decide to grab a quickie at the no-tell motel."

Christina laughed.

Then suddenly grew quiet.

Voices came down the hallway.

THEY FROZE, PERFECTLY STILL. As the voices grew louder Haley recognized them. The female voice belonged to Jacqueline Moore. The other one belonged to Derek Bennett, the senior attorney who was in the meeting with Austin Gray and Jacqueline Moore on Thursday night, when they summoned Haley to the firm in a limo and interrogated her about why she was on the news.

She pulled up a picture of him.

Forty-something.

Slightly pot-marked.

Eyes too far apart.

Thinning hair.

Tall and muscular.

As the voices approached, Haley began to make out strings of words.

"A person's dead and we're in it up to our asses, is what I'm saying," the female said.

"And like I keep saying, there's nothing we can do about it now, so let's just move on," the male said.

Then the voices disappeared down the hall.

Chapter Forty-Two

Day Eight – September 12
Monday

ON THE CAR SEAT NEXT TO JACK DEGAN sat the keys to Mia Avila's tattoo shop, Degan's knife and a half-empty flask of Jack. Normally the Colorado topography on the drive to Pueblo excited him. This afternoon, however, he could only think about getting the two thousand dollars and the note out of the bitch's safe and then getting the hell out of that damn town once and for all.

Getting the keys to the shop was easy. They were in the woman's purse. Getting her to tell him the combination to the safe, however, required more than a little persuasion.

But he was a good persuader when he needed to be.

A very good persuader.

Right now the little bitch was drugged and tightly secured to the bed. He almost killed her as soon as she gave him the combination but at the last second he stopped himself, just in case she was screwing with him and gave him the wrong numbers.

He'd need her alive, if that happened.

SWINGING BY THE FARMHOUSE to tell Gretchen he'd be tied up with work today had been a good idea. She'd started to get lonely—horny, too. He took care of both those needs in style and promised he'd be back this evening. In the meantime, he gave her some more money to buy more things that she'd thought of for the house.

He could still smell her on his skin.

He pulled into Pueblo mid-afternoon. In a perfect world he'd wait until dark. But he needed to get this done fast so he had enough day left to get the stripper, Chase, up to the cabin for tomorrow's client.

Not to mention having to kill Mia Avila.

HE SWUNG PAST THE TATTOO SHOP and found everything exactly as it had been before. He expected yellow crime-scene tape on the front door but found none. Good. He parked the beat-up Chevy two blocks down the street and doubled back on foot, wearing a dark blue sweatshirt with the hood over his head.

He slipped on latex gloves, entered through the back door and locked it behind him.

Not a sound came from anywhere.

The only break to the silence came from the movement of air in and out of his lungs.

Perfect.

He found the safe exactly where the bitch said it would be, in the corner of the back room under a white sheet. It turned out to be a freestanding unit, not bolted to the floor, about four feet high and big enough to hold a good-sized dog. It looked to be at least fifty years old. He pictured it starting life in an old western saloon.

Now to open it and then get the hell out of Dodge.

He pulled the combination out of his wallet and set it on top of the safe.

27-42-61.

He dialed it, being careful to land exactly on the numbers.

It didn't work.

Shit.

He tried it again.

It didn't work again.

What the hell?

Sweat beaded on his forehead and he wiped it off with the back of his sleeve.

This time he tried going to the left first, LRL instead of RLR.

Again nothing.

"Bitch!"

He tried it a dozen more times, varying the number of passes, but couldn't get the little asshole to open.

Goddamn it!

It took him over three hours to get here.

For nothing.

The little bitch would pay for this.

Big time.

She wants to play games?

Well he can play games too.

He picked it up to get a feel for the weight. Using a bear hug he got it off the ground, but barely. It had to be every bit of two hundred pounds, which would have been manageable if the damn thing wasn't so bulky and awkward. Even if he waited until dark and pulled the Chevy up to the back door, he wasn't sure if he'd be able to muscle it into the trunk.

Or whether it would fit.

He kicked it.

So hard that a tingle shot all the way up his leg.

"You little bitch!"

HE COVERED IT BACK UP WITH THE SHEET, opened the rear door a slit, peeked outside, saw nothing, stepped outside and then locked up.

The sun beat down and he knew he looked suspicious with the hood over his head but left it there anyway. He got to the street without encountering anyone and then walked towards the Chevy.

Then he saw something.

A Harley sat in front of the car.

A biker with greasy black hair stood behind the vehicle, by the license plate, talking into a cell phone and making animated gestures.

Shit!

Degan backed up and hid behind a pickup truck.

Almost immediately a deep-throated rumble came from a distant street. Several bikes were coming this way.

Degan headed away from his car, walking as inconspicuously as he could. By the time he turned down a side street, three more Harleys had pulled up to his car.

Chapter Forty-Three

Day Eight – September 12
Monday Morning

WITH AN EARLY MORNING JOG UNDER HIS BELT, and a bowl of vitamin-packed cereal in his gut, Bryson Coventry got to the office by seven, already fine-tuning a mental checklist of the things he wanted to get done today. He was almost positive that Brad Ripley was the man in Tonya Obenchain's snuff film, meaning that one of the four murders was solved. The big question now is whether Ripley killed the other three women as well.

Yesterday, Coventry and Kate Katona spent hour after hour tearing Ripley's house apart, looking for other films. By the time Coventry felt fairly comfortable that there weren't any more he was astonished to find that it was almost midnight.

"Sorry Kate," he said, looking at his watch. "It looks like I worked you to death today."

She cocked her head.

"Are you sorry enough that I should sleep in tomorrow?"

He grunted.

"Actually, I was hoping you'd come in early. Say 7:15."

She actually rolled into the office at 7:14, gave him a dirty look and walked over to the coffee machine. "Here's the problem, Bryson," she said. "You love Monday mornings. Sane people, like me for instance, don't."

Actually, she spoke the truth.

Monday mornings meant five uninterrupted days of hunting.

He held a white bag up and dangled it. "Donuts," he said. "White cake with chocolate frosting."

She pulled one out, took a bite, and said, "No thanks, I'm on a diet."

Two minutes later Shalifa Netherwood showed up, said hello to Katona, ignored Coventry, and headed straight for the coffee.

"You look like I feel," Katona told her.

"We need a nicer boss," Shalifa said, giving Coventry a sideways look. "Someone who respects our First Amendment right to sleep."

THEY ENDED UP HUDDLED AT COVENTRY'S DESK, the only ones in the room, pounding down coffee and coming up with a game plan.

Then they split up.

Thirty minutes later Coventry walked down 17th Street in the heart of Denver's financial district, holding a Styrofoam cup now empty of coffee. The city bustled around him, smelling like tar and perfume. He swung into an Einstein Bros, stood in a short line, handed the cup to the guy behind the counter and asked for a refill.

"This isn't our cup," the guy said.

"Yeah, I know," Coventry said. "But I really need coffee."

"Do you need it enough to pay for it?"

He shrugged and pulled out his badge.

"Einstein was my great grandfather," he said. "He'd want me

to have the coffee for free."

The guy smiled and filled the cup.

"You should have told me right off the bat you were related."

Coventry nodded.

"Sorry," he said. "I thought the resemblance was obvious. Thanks a lot. I appreciate it."

He threw a five-dollar bill into the tip jar and walked out.

Ten minutes later he entered the lobby of the Cash Register Building on Lincoln Street, paused briefly to see if he was in the mood to get jammed into an elevator, determined he wasn't and opened the door to the stairwell. Seventeen stories later, with burning thighs, he entered the clean-lined contemporary lobby of Brad Ripley Concepts, a space replete with floor-to-ceiling glass, stainless steel, eclectic textures, and splashes of color.

A young blond sat behind the reception desk.

She fluffed her hair as he walked over.

"You're the guy from the news," she said. "The detective working on the four women who got killed down by the railroad tracks."

"Guilty," Coventry admitted. "What's your name?"

"Tammy."

"Well, Tammy, let me tell you why I'm here."

Then he told her, as gently as he could, that her boss was dead. Someone shot him in the face.

HE FOUND THE KITCHEN, FILLED UP WITH COFFEE, then went into Ripley's office and closed the door while the news of the man's death ricocheted through the halls. The name of Ripley's snuff victim—Tonya Obenchain—didn't seem to exist anywhere in Ripley' s office.

It wasn't in his Rolodex.

Or day planner.

Or computer.

Or emails.

Or anywhere else.

Meaning what? That Ripley chose the woman out of the blue as a random encounter? That she just happened to be at the wrong place at the wrong time?

Wait.

This is interesting.

His day planer has the word SAVE written in red ink on April 3 and April 4. Tonya Obenchain disappeared on April 3. *That's when you killed her, you little shit.*

He walked around the floor until he found the receptionist, Tammy, and asked her to come down to Ripley's office. Then he shut the door behind them.

"You want to be my deputy?" he asked.

She looked at him weird.

"What does that mean?"

"It means you help me, but you don't tell anyone what we're doing or talking about."

She looked stressed, but intrigued.

"Sure," she said. "Why not?"

Coventry smiled.

"Good," he said. "Now, just suppose for a minute that Brad Ripley had a dark side. A very dark side that he wanted to keep secret. Where around here would I find it?"

Chapter Forty-Four

Day Eight – September 12
Monday

HALEY WILDE CRANKED OUT BILLABLE HOURS Monday morning, intentionally not doing anything that could get her in trouble, except for calling Bryson Coventry to set up a meeting.

He suggested lunch.

And said he'd pay.

"It'll give me a chance to dispel those nasty rumors that I'm the cheapest guy on the face of the earth," he added. Someone in the background said, *Those aren't rumors, Coventry. They're etched-in-stone facts.*

He suggested Wong's, a Chinese place on Court Street, because he solved most of his cases using their fortune cookies.

She got there first, shortly before noon, and claimed a booth with her back to the wall and a good view of the entrance. Coventry showed up a few moments later, wearing jeans, a gray cotton shirt and a sport coat. An elderly waitress hugged him as he looked around. He spotted Haley and, as he walked over, she decided that he was close enough to her in age, if he decided to make a move.

"You're still alive," he said, slipping into the booth. "I like that."

He looked good.

Really good.

Magazine cover good.

"That's the first thing I check every morning when I wake up," she said.

He grunted and picked up the menu.

"Anything you want, up to three dollars," he said. She must have had a look on her face because he grinned and said, "Okay, four."

They ordered.

Then he somehow got her to tell him her life story.

Halfway through the meal she decided it was time to get to why she called the meeting. "I have to tell you what I'm going to tell you because you need to know," she said. "But no one can know that I told you. If the word gets out, I'll lose my job."

Coventry was okay with that.

"I think two of the lawyers in my firm might be mixed up in Renee Rand's death."

He raised an eyebrow.

"Who?"

"They're both senior partners," she said. "One is a woman by the name of Jacqueline Moore. The other is a man named Derek Bennett." Then she told him about the conversation she overheard in the hallway yesterday.

He seemed interested, but not as much as she expected.

"I'm working another angle," he said. "Between you and me, we're pretty sure we know who killed one of the four women, namely Tonya Obenchain. What we're trying to figure out now is if he killed the other three as well."

She stopped chewing and studied him.

"That's not public knowledge," he emphasized. "So keep it that way."

She promised.

"If you give me his name I can snoop around the firm," she said. "See if he has any connections to Renee or the other two lawyers I just told you about."

Coventry hesitated, then leaned across the table and whispered in her ear: "Brad Ripley."

Then he got a call.

He listened intently, wrinkled his brow, and stood up. "I have to run," he said. Then, over his shoulder, "Sorry."

After Coventry left, Haley realized he hadn't paid the bill.

She checked her purse and found four dollars.

Shit.

Now what?

Two minutes later, just as she was about to flag down the waitress and explain the situation, Coventry ran back in and put a twenty on the table. "Sorry about that. I have no idea where my mind is half the time."

Chapter Forty-Five

Day Eight – September 12
Monday

WITH HIS CAR SURROUNDED BY BIKERS, Jack Degan walked through the side streets of downtown Pueblo, hugging the buildings and keeping a good lookout for alleys and doorways in case Harleys rumbled up the street.

He was six or seven blocks away when he realized he made a huge mistake. Because of all the frustration trying to open the goddamn tattoo woman's safe, he completely forgot to grab the logbook.

He immediately turned around and headed back.

Shit.

It would have only taken him three seconds to pick it up.

Now he had to go all the way back.

Dodge the asshole bikers.

Risk being seen by some busybody with a cell phone.

He kicked a pop can lying on the sidewalk. It turned out to still be half full and drenched his sock with sticky syrup.

Goddamn it!

He managed to get back into the tattoo shop without incident, then stayed low and crept to the front window and looked down the street.

Oh, man!

The bikers were still there, about six or seven of them. Worse, someone was hooking the car up to a tow truck. Degan hugged the floor for ten minutes or longer and then looked out the corner of the window as the truck went by. Faded white lettering on the door said, "Bob's Recovery and Repo Service."

"Screw you Bob," Degan said under his breath.

Two bikers followed the tow truck.

The remaining assholes split into two groups and headed off in separate directions.

No doubt to scout for Degan.

He found the logbook and checked for the name of the woman who had been in the shop the same day as him, getting the tattoo on her breast. She was Isella Ramirez. Then he shoved the book under his sweatshirt, checked the back of the building, saw no one, and left.

TWO CABS SAT IN FRONT OF THE DOWNTOWN MARRIOTT. Degan got in the front one and told the driver to take him to wherever it was that the used car lots clustered together. Five minutes later he got dropped off on Main Street, about a mile north of town. At a place called Harvey's Quality Cars and Trucks, he bought the cheapest car on the lot—a rusty 1979 Ford Granada—under a false name for $450 cash, and then headed north on I-25.

Mia Avila was going to be sorry for sending him on this wild goose chase.

Very sorry.

On the way back he stopped at a payphone and called Chase,

the stripper. "Have you got some time for me today?"

"You're going to give me another eight hundred, right?"

"Absolutely. That's the deal. I have it right here in my hand."

"Then I got all the time in the world, sweetie. I just have to get my ass to the club by seven—eight at the latest."

Chapter Forty-Six

Day Eight – September 12
Monday Afternoon

BRYSON COVENTRY SHOWED UP TEN MINUTES LATE to the one o'clock meeting, apologized, sat down, then stood up and walked out. He returned a heartbeat later, this time holding a cup of coffee, which he set on the table.

His favorite piece of furniture.

Stained, beat-up and scratched to the point of no return. He looked at it and said, "You could live for a week, just off the stuff in this wood." Then he got serious. "Okay. Where we at?"

Shalifa Netherwood went first. "We now have in hand all of Brad Ripley's phone records, going back a full year. We have records for his home phone, cell phone and business phone. There isn't a single call to, or from, the phones of any of the four victims."

Coventry frowned.

"Are you sure?"

"Unfortunately, yes," she said.

"You cross-referenced to *all* the victim's phones, meaning home, office, cell, whatever?"

Yes she had.

"And still no connection to anyone, not even Tonya Obenchain?"

"Nope."

"Well that's not good," he said. "So you worked hard all morning, just to give me bad news."

She grunted.

"It's what I do."

Coventry turned his attention to Kate Katona. "Give me something good and you win," Coventry said.

"I've run a pretty solid background check on Ripley," she said. "So far, nothing of interest has popped out. And I can't find any social, economic or other connection between him and any of the four victims. No common friends, jobs, clubs, or anything. None of Tonya Obenchain's family or friends recognize Ripley's name or face."

Coventry looked at the coffee and then took a sip.

"If I didn't know better," he said, "based on what you've said so far, I'd probably conclude that Tonya Obenchain was just a random, spur-of-the-moment pick."

Shalifa raised an eyebrow.

"Meaning what? That you do know better?"

Coventry nodded.

"We found a day planner at his office," he said. "He had April 3rd and 4th set aside to SAVE, in red ink. Tonya disappeared on April 3rd. But more interesting is the fact that the only other red ink notation occurs on March 15th. My guess is that both entries were made at the same time, meaning on March 15th. So in mid-March he knew he was going to kill her on April 3rd or 4th."

Shalifa cocked her head.

"I think you might be going a tad too far," she said. "That

doesn't necessarily mean he knew he was going to kill *her.* It could just mean he knew he was going to kill someone."

Coventry understood her reasoning but didn't buy it.

"I really don't see him planning a future date for a random target," he said. "But I do see him planning a future date for a specific target."

"Possibly," Shalifa said. "But maybe his specific target petered out for some reason and he went to Plan B."

Coventry hadn't thought of that.

She was right.

"Either way," he said, "we need to recreate March 15th in the life of Brad Ripley, which is the day he knew he would kill someone two weeks later. If we have multiple killers, they obviously coordinated and communicated with each other. It looks like one of those communications took place on March 15th. So I want to know the details about every phone call he made or received on that day. I want to know everyone he met with and everywhere he went that day."

He combed his hair back with his fingers and read the discouragement on their faces.

"I know," he said. "We're looking at tough, tedious work."

AFTER THE MEETING BROKE UP he went straight to the restroom. He was standing at the urinal when his cell phone rang and he wasn't sure whether to answer it or not.

He did.

The voice of FBI profiler Leanne Sanders came through. "We're about 99 percent sure at this point that the guy in your snuff film is who you thought, Brad Ripley, based on body size and posture. We'll know 100 percent after we get his clothes."

"Thanks," he said. "I appreciate you getting to it so fast."

She hesitated and then said, "Where are you right now?"

He shook his head.

"You don't want to know."

"Are you taking a piss?"

"Maybe."

"This is so gross," she said. "You have me in one hand and Mister Happy in the other. I feel downright violated."

THEN, BEFORE HE COULD ZIP UP, the phone rang again. This time is was the coroner, Robert Nelson. "I looked at that film, like you wanted," he said. "I don't think the guy in that film killed Catherine Carmichael or Angela Pfeifer. As to the other woman, I don't know one way or the other."

"Why not Catherine Carmichael or Angela Pfeifer?"

"Well," Nelson said, "unless I'm totally reading things wrong, the guy in the film is left-handed. The slit on Catherine Carmichael's throat appears to be from someone who's right-handed. So do the stab wounds to Angela Pfeifer."

"What makes you think he's left-handed?"

"That just seems to be his dominant hand," Nelson said. "But you should be able to ask a few people who knew him and confirm it fairly easily, one way or the other."

That was true.

But if Nelson was correct, then they were definitely dealing with more than one killer. Meaning that Renee Rand's killer was still on the loose. Which also meant that Haley Wilde was still in potential danger.

Chapter Forty-Seven

Day Eight – September 12
Monday

HALEY WILDE FELT PRETTY GOOD following her lunch meeting with Coventry, until he called later and told her he had a solid reason to believe that Brad Ripley didn't kill Renee Rand after all, meaning she should continue to take every safety precaution.

"Gee, you really know how to cheer a girl up," she said.

But he didn't lose his serious edge.

"Where are you sleeping tonight?"

"At Christina Huygh's house."

"Give me the address." She did. "That's actually not far from my place. I'll try to drive by a couple of times."

"Stop in if you do."

She worked her little billable ass off all afternoon, intent on having the right numbers at the end of the month. Then Christina walked in shortly before five and closed the door.

"So what's the plan?"

"The plan's changing," Haley said. "Earlier today I thought it would be best to snoop around and find out if this Brad Ripley guy had any connection to Renee Rand, or Derek Bennett or

Cruella. But now Coventry is thinking that Ripley isn't Renee's killer." She twirled a pencil in her fingers. "So instead I'm thinking we should focus on Derek Bennett."

"Focus how?"

Haley shrugged.

"I don't know. Maybe we start in his office, tonight after everyone leaves."

Christina put her hand up.

"That's too risky."

"Not really," Haley said. "I'll go inside with my cell phone set on vibrate. You stand lookout down the hall and call me if anyone's coming."

Christina didn't seem impressed.

"Bad idea," she said. "It's too risky. And if he actually is involved in Renee's death somehow, he's not exactly going to draft a memo about it and leave it sitting on his desk."

Haley considered it.

Christina was probably right.

"So we need to look outside the office, is what you're saying."

"I don't know what I'm saying."

"Like a good old-fashioned stakeout or something," she added.

DEREK BENNETT LIVED in a Greenwood Village mansion and drove a silver BMW flagship. That night, after dark, Haley and Christina parked down the street from his house, not really expecting anything to happen.

But it did.

Bennett pulled out shortly after eight-thirty and they followed.

"We're officially crazy at this point," Christina said.

"You watch," Haley said. "He's going to lead us straight to more bodies."

"Yeah, ours."

Bennett wound his way to I-25, headed north, drove all the way through Denver and out the other side, and finally exited at 56th Avenue. A mile or so later he pulled into an industrial park. Haley continued down the road and then circled back.

"There it is," Christina said, pointing.

Sure enough, Bennett's BMW was parked in front of a detached brick building, in the company of eight or ten other vehicles. They killed the lights and drove past. The only signage consisted of small white lettering on the door.

Tops & Bottoms.

"What the hell is this?"

Haley backed into a dark deserted area about fifty yards away and killed the engine. Then she pulled out her cell phone, called information to get the number for Tops & Bottoms, and dialed.

She got a recording.

A sexy female voice.

She listened and then looked at Christina. "The best I can tell, it's some kind of a dungeon."

Christina slapped the car seat.

"Do you mean to tell me that Derek Bennett, senior partner in our prestigious law firm, is in that building over there, even as we speak, chained naked to a cross and getting his cock whipped by some lady?"

Haley grunted.

"No more visuals, please," she said. "Or it could be the other way around. He might be a top, working some woman over. Or a guy, even."

They waited.

Just to see how long he stayed.

It turned out to be an hour.

"The old Richard's got to be hurting a truckload," Christina said.

"All red and irritated," Haley said.

"Wondering what it ever did to justify all this."

After Derek Bennett pulled his BMW into the night and disappeared, Haley started the engine and pointed the Honda towards the street, but instead swung into a parking space in front of Tops & Bottoms at the last second.

"I'm going in," she said.

Christina unbuckled her seatbelt. "Then I'm coming with you."

"No," Haley said. "That'll look too suspicious, like we're cops or something. Just wait here."

THE DOOR OPENED INTO A SMALL WAITING ROOM with barren white walls, no chairs or furniture, a red door, and a sign that stated this is not a place of prostitution and that it is against the law to solicit a sexual act. Haley hadn't been in the room more than ten seconds when the red door opened and a woman walked in.

She was strikingly beautiful, young—younger even than Haley—and wore her breasts falling out. She looked Haley up and down, then hugged her and said, "I'm Jasmine. We don't get many women."

Haley shifted from one foot to the other, nervous.

"I'm Haley. I'm not sure you have me yet," she said. "I just stopped in to get more information."

"Have you visited our website?"

"No. I didn't even know you had one."

Jasmine turned, opened the red door with one hand and grabbed Haley's hand with the other.

"Follow me," she said.

They entered a hallway and walked past several doors, each painted in a different cartoon color. Haley felt weird, holding a woman's hand, but didn't pull away. They entered the room with the green door. And Jasmine said, "This is our green room."

It was a well-equipped dungeon with a hospital smell.

"It's fully soundproof and totally private," Jasmine said. "Are you a top or a bottom?"

Haley knew she better have an answer.

And quick.

The thought of surrendering control to a stranger terrified her.

"A top," she said.

Jasmine smiled. "No problem. We have three subs working tonight. None of them have any problem surrendering to a woman. I think you'd especially like Antoinette. She'll do bondage, light spanking, cum control, obedience training, submissive wrestling, and just about anything else you might have in mind."

Haley pictured it.

"The room's totally soundproof," Jasmine added. "And totally private. There are no cameras or anything like that. Whatever happens in here is between you and your sub. The rate is a hundred dollars an hour for the room, which goes to the house. The girls work for tips. The minimum tip rate is a hundred an hour. So, would you like to meet some of the girls?"

Haley nodded.

"Sure. Why not?"

Chapter Forty-Eight

Day Eight – September 12
Monday Afternoon

ON THE WAY BACK TO DENVER, JACK DEGAN swung by the stripper's apartment. She scrunched her face as she looked at the Granada and almost didn't get in, but changed her mind when he handed her the remaining eight hundred dollars.

"Nice ride," she said, sliding over on the bench seat until she was next to him.

"My Porsche is in the shop."

Her face brightened.

"You have a Porsche?"

"A 911 Turbo," he said, which was true. That, his house on the beach, and his whole other existence was in Malibu, all under his real name, Jack Brentwood.

"Red, I hope."

"That's the only color," he said. "If it ain't red, it's dead."

She rubbed her hand on his thigh. "Do you want to know what I have in store for you, for paying me so well?"

He pulled into traffic.

"Sure, why not?"

She moved her hand to his cock.

"Okay," she said. "But don't come before we get there."

HE DRUGGED HER ON THE WAY TO THE CABIN, then carried her into the second bedroom, stripped her down to her thong and secured her spread-eagled to the bed, double checking the knots to be absolutely sure there was no way she could escape.

THEN HE WALKED INTO MIA AVILA'S ROOM, carrying the logbook that he got from her tattoo shop, and bitch-slapped her across the face before she could make a sound.

"You screwed with me," he said. "That was a very wrong career move."

She mumbled something through the gag.

He could pry the safe combination out of her but he really didn't care about it anymore. He already had the logbook, which was the main thing. Without that, the police wouldn't be smart enough to tie him to the other woman getting the tattoo, Isella Ramirez. And without her, they wouldn't get a description of him.

Plus he'd had enough of that stupid town.

It stunk.

It stunk with biker heat.

It stunk with cop heat.

Better to just stay away.

His phone rang and Swofford's voice came through.

"How you coming on that stripper?"

"Done deal," he said. "She's already at the destination."

"Good. What'd you decide to do with the other woman?"

"She ended up pissing me off, so I've got something special

planned for her. Something slow."

"As long as she doesn't turn into a problem."

"She won't," he said.

Chapter Forty-Nine

Day Eight – September 12
Monday Evening

BRYSON COVENTRY HAD BEEN THE ONLY ONE in homicide for some time now. When the windows turned black and started to reflect the florescent ceiling lights, and he had to fight to stay focused, he knew the useful part of the day had come to an end.

So he headed to Tianca's.

She fed him.

Then they ended up in the garage, sitting in the '67 Vette in the dark, drinking Bud Light from the bottle.

"Heaven," he said.

"Rough day?"

"Not really," he said. "A rough day is when I'm the victim and someone else is doing the investigation."

She laughed.

Headlights came up the street and swept a pattern of light across the garage walls. Then they disappeared and everything returned to black. Coventry held his hand up in front of his face and couldn't see it.

"Dark," he said.

"Sort of weird," she said.

He agreed.

"Good weird, though."

Halfway through the second round he told her about the day.

"This Brad Ripley guy is getting more and more interesting," he said. "It turns out that the woman he killed, Tonya Obenchain, the real estate agent, disappeared between two house showings, sometime between one and three in the afternoon. Today we found out that Ripley was in a meeting during that time period, all afternoon in fact."

"So he's not the one who abducted her?"

"Apparently not," Coventry said. "But he's the one who killed her, the one in the snuff film."

"So two people are involved? Is that what you're saying?"

Coventry nodded.

Even though she couldn't possibly see him in the dark.

"At least two," he said. "We found out some other stuff too. He set the whole thing in motion on March 15th. On the 18th, he withdrew a hundred and fifty thousand from his bank."

"So that's connected to the killing?"

Coventry didn't know.

"It could have been for coke, or gambling debts, or who knows what. All we know is we can't trace it. Then," he added, "we found out that he flew to Vegas in July. He stayed for almost two weeks and lost a boatload of money. A Titanic full. He ended up cashing out of a lot of stocks to pay casinos. I'm talking millions."

"I hate that place," she said. "They ought to just wipe it off the face of the earth. All it does is fill people full of false sunshine and then suck their money away."

Coventry took a long drink of beer.

He didn't agree, at least not totally.

But didn't feel like getting into it.

"Anyway," he said, "the gambling problem might be connected to the hole in his face. Maybe he did something stupid like go to some after-hours place to win money to pay back the casinos. Then he lost there too and couldn't pay up."

"Do people actually still do that?" she asked. "I mean, rough people up over gambling debts? I thought those days were all in the past."

Coventry sighed.

"Money's a motivator," he said. "Always was, always will be. Anyway, I was hoping Ripley would be nothing more than a two-hour puzzle, but he's turning more and more into a two-story question mark."

She played with his hair.

"Maybe you need some stress relief," she said.

Then his cell phone rang.

Chapter Fifty

Day Nine – September 13
Tuesday Noon

The Mountainside Trailer Park, no doubt once a quiet place nestled in the foothills of unincorporated Jefferson County between Golden and Lakewood, now sat in close proximity to no less than three interstate systems. Haley Wilde eased her Honda through the narrow lanes until she found the trailer she was looking for—Number 65. A vehicle occupied the one and only parking space for the unit, so she parked near the main office and headed back on foot, solidly overdressed in her attorney attire. She had no idea how anyone could actually sleep around here with all the freeway noise. Several large Cottonwoods shaded the park, still green but with hints of autumn yellow.

She knocked on the door.

Then felt movement inside and saw the curtains move.

A woman opened the door.

She looked to be about twenty-eight and, without makeup, could hardly be described as stunning. Still, she was pretty, and had high cheekbones and classic lines. She probably scrubbed up pretty good.

"Are you Sarah Maine?" Haley asked.

The woman nodded, then looked past Haley to see if anyone else was with her.

"Yeah. Are you a cop?"

Haley laughed.

"Me?"

The woman was clearly serious.

"Not hardly," Haley said. Then she held up a picture of Derek Bennett, a printout from the firm's website. "Do you know this man?"

She said nothing.

But the expression on her face said it all.

"Why?"

"I need to ask you a few questions about him," Haley said. "You're not in any kind of trouble or anything. I'm just trying to help a friend."

The woman almost opened the door, but then said, "My place is a mess."

Haley shrugged.

"I don't care about that."

"Wait here. Let me put my shoes on."

THEY ENDED UP WALKING DOWN A TRAIL that started at the far end of the trailer park and headed into the foothills. Haley did her best to keep dust from kicking onto her shoes and nylons. On the way, she explained that she suspected Derek Bennett of being involved in a murder.

"Me and a friend followed him last night," she said, "to Tops & Bottoms. We stayed in the parking lot until he came out, then I went inside to see what the place was about while my friend waited outside in the car. She spotted you coming out about five minutes after Bennett left. She said you looked stressed. We figured that you were the one he had the session with."

"We can't talk about our customers," Sarah said.

Haley nodded.

"Of course not," she said, "as a general rule. But this is entirely between you and me."

Something caught her eye.

A coyote.

About fifty yards off, loping through the field.

With two more following.

"Coyotes," she said.

"They're all over," Sarah said. "They won't hurt you."

"So what kind of sessions do you do with Bennett?"

The woman looked hesitant, deciding whether to talk or not, then said, "I get a thousand an hour. You see the way I live. I can't afford to lose that money."

"Honest," Haley said, "this doesn't go anywhere beyond me. Believe me, I'm no stranger to money problems."

Suddenly the coyotes barked and yelped.

Now they were scrambling, chasing something in the rabbitbrush.

"Found some lunch," Sarah said. She looked at Haley. "Derek Bennett's a mean son-of-a-bitch. I don't like serving him, even at a thousand an hour, but I have a sister with some medical problems. That's where all the money goes."

Then she described Bennett's routine.

Haley pictured it, biting her lower lip so hard that she almost drew blood.

The money wasn't enough.

"Did he ever talk about killing anyone?"

"No."

"Are you sure?"

"I'm pretty sure," Sarah said.

"What's that mean?—you're *pretty* sure."

She shrugged. "He calls me a little bitch-whore and tells me I'm getting what I deserve. I mean he's intense. In my opinion he's the kind of guy who could kill someone in a heartbeat, so long as he could justify it in his own mind. Somehow he justifies what he does to me. He doesn't even see me as a real human being."

"You're just his little bitch-whore."

"Exactly."

"What about the name Renee Rand? Did he ever mention that name to you?"

Sarah wrinkled her forehead, going deep.

"The name seems familiar for some reason but I can't place the context."

"She was one of the four women found dead at the railroad spur."

Sarah looked confused.

"I don't know anything about that."

"Her name's been in the news," Haley added.

"I don't watch the news."

When they got back to the trailer park, they hugged and Haley thanked the woman for talking. "And like I said, this is just between you and me. I understand money problems." Sarah looked doubtful so Haley added, "See that Honda over there? That's mine."

The woman grinned.

"I'm glad you said that. Now I feel better."

THE MEETING TOOK LONGER than Haley planned. By the time she arrived back at the law firm her entire lunch hour was gone and then some.

Christina spotted her almost immediately, slipped into her office and closed the door.

"Well?" she asked.

"I'll give you the details later," Haley said. "But it's worse than I thought. We need to get into Bennett's office and have a look around."

She sensed that Christina was going to say no, it was too risky. But instead she said, "Okay."

"Tonight," Haley added.

"Fine."

"Cruella's too."

Christina looked confused.

"But if Bennett killed Renee, how could Jacqueline Moore possibly be involved?"

Haley shrugged.

"I don't know. All we know for sure is that she is. Maybe she found out about it and is helping him cover it up. Or maybe she put him up to it in the first place. Remember, she and Renee had a personality conflict. All I know for sure at this point is that we need to find out."

"Maybe we should just go to the police and tell them what we have," Christina said.

"No," Haley said. "They don't have the kind of access we do. For better or worse this is on our shoulders. Or my shoulders, at least."

"Our shoulders," Christina said.

Haley studied her.

"Maybe it's time for you to back out," she said. "You've been here a while and actually have something to lose."

Christina shook her head.

"I need to know where I'm working," she said. "And whether I want to bother building my career here."

Haley nodded.

"Okay. Tonight then."

Chapter Fifty-One

Day Nine – September 13
Tuesday Morning

STILL 95 PERCENT ASLEEP, JACK DEGAN twisted from his left side to his right, sending a stiff but short ripple through the mattress. When the ripple didn't ricochet back he opened his eyes, just a slit. He was in the bed at the farmhouse and recalled drinking too much JD last night and screwing Gretchen like a rock star before passing out. He'd woken up three or four times during the night to piss, and each time Gretchen had been lying next to him, motionless and breathing deep and heavy.

But now she wasn't.

Then he heard noises from the kitchen and remembered that she wanted to get up early and make him pancakes for breakfast.

He rolled onto his back and put his hands under his head.

Dawn had broken, but not by much.

Gretchen sang.

Too low and off key for him to figure out the song.

"What are you singing?" he shouted.

She walked in wearing only a T-shirt, straddled him and pinned his arms above his head.

Then kissed him.

"Are you hungry?"

"Yeah. What were you singing?"

"La Isle Bonita."

"Never heard of it. Sing it to me."

She pinned his arms tighter. "No. I'm too embarrassed."

"I'm not going to let you go until you do," he said.

She moved her weight higher on his chest.

"Not let me go? I'm the one who has you, in case you haven't noticed."

He flipped her, then straddled her and pinned her arms over her head.

"Now who has who?"

"That's not the question," she said.

"Oh?"

"The question is who's going to turn the pancakes over before they burn?"

"Tricky," he said. "Very tricky."

He brought her hands together, clamped them in his left hand and then reached down with his right and tickled her armpits until she went nuts and begged for mercy. Then he released her and headed for the shower.

Then, shit!

He suddenly remembered Mia Avila, outside in the Granada, under a blanket on the floor of the back seat, drugged and chained to the seat brackets. He couldn't leave her at the cabin last night, not with the client coming in to do Chase.

He threw on a pair of jeans and stepped out to check on her.

There she was.

Exactly as he left her last night.

"Good girl," he said, and then headed back inside for a shower.

Gretchen slapped his ass as he walked by. "I'm the dessert," she said, "In case you're interested."

"Oh, I'm interested all right."

HE GOT THE WATER AS HOT AS HE COULD and then stepped inside and lathered up. Today would be busy. He'd have to clean the cabin and dispose of the stripper's body after the client left, for starters. He also needed to kill Mia Avila sometime today and get rid of her remains.

When he got out of the shower, the farmhouse smelled like pancakes—buttery, delicious pancakes. He dressed in the bedroom and shouted into the kitchen, "God, that smells good. I'm starved."

No response.

"Gretchen? You there?"

Nothing.

Weird.

He walked into the kitchen.

She wasn't there.

"Gretchen?"

Silence.

He stepped out the front door and couldn't believe his eyes. Gretchen stood next to the Granada, with the door open, looking into the back seat.

At Mia Avila.

She turned and stared as he walked towards her.

Then she ran.

Chapter Fifty-Two

Day Nine – September 13
Tuesday Morning

BRYSON COVENTRY MET WITH SHALIFA Netherwood late Tuesday morning. She had run down all the phone calls that Brad Ripley made on March 15th. In fact, she personally called every number and talked to the person Ripley had talked to. She asked them what they talked about and took careful notes.

Everything was legit and unremarkable.

Only one call remained unexplained.

It came to Ripley's cell from a payphone on the south side of Denver and lasted four minutes. There was no way to track it. Even if it turned out to be within view of a security camera, the tape would have long been recycled at this point.

"Drive out there and check it anyway," Coventry said. "You never know."

She frowned.

"That seems thin," she said.

Coventry cocked his head and asked, "When did that call come in?"

She checked her notes.

"12:49."

"Ripley used two different colored pens in his day planner that day," he said. "Some of the stuff happened in the morning. That was in black ink. More stuff happened in the afternoon, also in black ink. The red ink comes in the middle of the day, the same time of day as the call from the payphone. So run that call to ground, and then to underground if you have to. Whoever's on the other end of the line is our connection."

She said, "I'll check his credit card statement from that day too to see if he went to lunch anywhere and happened to end up paying, just in case the communication was in person."

"Good idea," he said. "You're welcome."

"Welcome for what?"

"For giving you so much job security."

She grunted. "As if I need any more of *that*."

TEN MINUTES LATER HIS PHONE RANG. He recognized the caller's name—Tammy—but didn't remember from where. Then she reminded him and he pulled up a mental picture of Brad Ripley's blond receptionist.

"Remember when you deputized me and asked where we could find a dark secret, if Mr. Ripley had one?"

Yes he did.

She hadn't had any brilliant ideas at the time.

"Well," she said, "I've been snooping around in his office and found a wall safe."

Coventry stood up and almost fell over the snake plant.

"Go on," he said.

"I also found the combination," she said.

"How?" he asked.

"He has a bunch of passwords for various things," she said.

"I know what some of them are. Then I found a list of passwords in his computer for various things, including something called Wall Unit. I figured out that the computer passwords have two random numbers, then the real password in reverse numerical order, followed by three random numbers. So I was able to work backwards from that to figure out the right number for the safe. When I tried it, it actually opened."

Coventry cocked his head.

"You have to come and work for me," he said. "That's all there is to it."

Twenty minutes later he arrived at Brad Ripley's office. No one besides Tammy had reported to work. She opened the safe and pulled the door open.

A pile of hundred dollar bills lay in plain view.

"I haven't touched anything," she told him. "Just in case it turns out to be evidence or something."

Coventry put on latex gloves and looked at her.

"You could have taken the money," he said. "No one would have known."

She diverted her eyes.

"I would have."

He nodded and made a mental note that she needed the money now more than ever, being suddenly unemployed.

"There aren't many like you left."

The money turned out to be just short of twenty-five thousand dollars. Also, inside, he found a number of keys, insurance policies, a bag of cocaine, and a variety of other equally uninteresting things.

He also found an envelope.

Inside were eight or ten photographs. They had been taken at night without a flash. They were dark and vague but still clear enough to show a vehicle parked in front of a rickety wooden building. They were taken from slightly different angles, but mostly from the side view. All were shot from a distance.

Coventry laid them out on Ripley's desk and looked at them as a group.

Then he pointed to one of them and said, "It's a BMW. You can see just a bit of the front end in this picture. See the double ovals?" She looked. "Does Ripley have a BMW?"

"I don't think so," she said. "I think he has a black Mercedes."

Coventry focused on the photographs.

"This car's either white or silver," he said.

She agreed.

"Do you know anyone who has a white or silver BMW?"

"No. Not really."

"How about this building? Do you recognize it?"

"No."

"It looks abandoned," Coventry said.

"It looks creepy," she said. "You'd never catch me there in a thousand years."

Coventry understood.

"It looks like something out of a slasher movie," she added.

Chapter Fifty-Three

Day Nine – September 13
Tuesday Evening

Haley Wilde left work shortly after five, saying goodbye to lots of people so it was clearly on the record. Then she came back about seven-thirty. Christina Huygh, who never left, met her at the door and let her in. That way neither of their keycards would show up as being used for an after-hours entry. They weren't positive but were pretty sure that keycards were tracked in a computer or security system.

"Everyone's gone on this floor," Christina told her.

"Good."

"You nervous?"

"Scared shitless."

"Me too."

Haley held up a flashlight. "Brought this," she said.

"You're such an organized little criminal."

They had already planned it. Christina would hang out in the dead files room with the door open. She'd have a box down and one of her old cases on the floor. If anyone asked, she'd say she was pulling some research out of it to use in a current case. No one would suspect a thing. She'd have her cell phone already set to Haley's number. If she heard anything, she'd call. Haley would have the phone in her pants pocket, set to vibrate, and immediately turn the flashlight off and hide.

They walked up to the 45th Floor.

Derek Bennett's office sat near the end of the hall with the rest of the rainmakers.

"So have you figured out what you're looking for?" Christina asked.

"No."

"That'll make it harder to find."

"Considerably."

THEY FOUND THE HALLWAY DESERTED. None of the attorneys locked their office doors at night. In fact, most didn't even shut them. Derek Bennett was no exception.

Haley walked in and turned the flashlight on.

Her heart pounded and her mind raced.

Okay.

You're in.

Now get your ass moving.

She checked the filing cabinets first, looking for a folder on Renee Rand, or the killings at the railroad spur, or Tops & Bottoms, or anything else out of the ordinary.

Nothing of interest surfaced.

Everything appeared to be related to clients.

She checked his voice messages, being careful to not delete any.

Nothing unusual.

Did she dare fire up his computer?

Not yet.

Exhaust everything else first.

His credenza drawers held a lot of personal crap, phone books, office supplies, and other junk. Quite normal. Except the last drawer she checked.

There she found a gun.

She carefully picked it up with two fingers. She didn't know anything about guns but the insignia indicated it was a Springfield 9mm. She memorized the shape and put it back.

Then her phone vibrated.

Shit!

SHE TURNED OFF THE FLASHLIGHT, jumped with giant but very quiet hops to the coat closet, got in and shut the door, setting metal hangers in motion. She reached up and steadied them. Not more than a heartbeat later the lights went on.

Someone walked over to the desk and sat down.

She opened her mouth and breathed as slow and shallow as she could.

Frozen in place.

Someone grunted.

A man's voice.

She pictured Bennett at his desk, getting ready to do who knows what for who knows how long.

Goddamn it.

If he found her, there was absolutely no explanation that would work. She would be history at the firm. Nor would any other firm have her after the word got out about what a sneaky little bitch she was.

Then his computer came on.

Damn it!

He was going to be there for a while.

SHE STOOD THERE, MOTIONLESS.

Second after second.

Minute after minute.

For a long time.

Fifteen minutes, at least.

Then thirty.

Bennett was doing something at his desk, possibly getting ready for a trial or a meeting tomorrow. Maybe looking at Internet porn. Who knows?

Come on!

Just finish and leave!

Then Bennett's phone rang. He picked it up, said "Bennett," and then listened without talking. After a while he said, "Yeah, I saw the newspaper article. It's sitting right here on my desk. The dumb bitch. I agree, it's reaching critical mass . . ."

Suddenly someone entered the room.

"KNOCK KNOCK." Haley recognized the voice as Christina's. "Hey, Derek. I'm really sorry to bother you, but I did something stupid."

"What's that?"

"I left my car lights on all day."

He chuckled.

"That'll wear your battery down."

"Yeah, I just found that out."

"Have you got jumper cables?"

"No."

He stood up. "Well I do. Let's see if we can get you back on the road."

AFTER CHRISTINA THE GENIUS GOT BENNETT out of there, Haley waited until the coast was clear and then slipped out of the closet. She walked directly over to his desk and found the newspaper article sitting on top of his briefcase.

It was a *New York Times* article from this morning about a woman named Rebecca Yates who walked in front of a bus in Times Square yesterday. Witnesses reported that she appeared to do it on purpose. "Suicide by bus," they were saying. There were high-society rumors that she had been despondent since her husband, Robert Yates, and their daughter, Amanda Yates, were murdered two months ago.

There were still no suspects in that case.

Haley turned off the flashlight and listened for sounds.

There were none.

Okay leave.

Now.

Right this second.

Chapter Fifty-Four

Day Nine – September 13
Tuesday Morning

GRETCHEN RAN FROM THE GRANADA, and from the body on the floor of the back seat, as fast as she could, down the long gravel driveway towards the country road. She sprinted straight towards the sun, which just now broke over the horizon.

Degan chased.

He wore no shoes.

Almost every step landed on a rock or pebble that shot a pain up his leg and straight into his brain.

"Gretchen! Come back here!"

She turned as she ran and looked over her shoulder, to see if he was closing the gap.

He wasn't.

"Gretchen! Let me explain!"

She kept running.

Degan slowed down, knowing he'd never catch her without shoes, and then stopped. The wind immediately went out of his lungs. He doubled over and put his hands on his knees to steady himself, breathing deeply.

"Don't do this," he shouted.

She kept running.

HE WALKED BACK TO THE FARMHOUSE, pulled socks onto his bloody feet, threw on tennis shoes, and grabbed the keys to the Granada. By now Gretchen would be at the main road trying to flag down a car.

He needed to get the hell out of there.

Or get to her before anyone else did.

Suddenly the door opened and she walked in.

"It isn't what you think," he said.

They went outside and sat on the front steps. Degan squinted to keep the sun out of his eyes.

"Part of my P.I. work sometimes involves capture," Degan said. "It's no different that what the police do or what a bounty hunter does. The only difference is it's private in nature. The woman in the car is married to a very wealthy man in Los Angeles. She walked out and took a lot of money and diamonds with her. More than her share. The man wants his share back. Then she's free to go. That's all there is to it."

"Why doesn't he just report it to the police?"

Good question.

"Let's just say he has to keep it under the radar screen."

"Meaning what?"

"Meaning there are illegalities involved." He reached down, picked up a rock and threw it at a crumpled pop can, missing by a mile. "I get paid well. In fact, I was waiting to surprise you with this later, but I have a nice house in Malibu."

She studied his face.

Trying to determine if he was bullshitting her.

"Malibu, California?"

He nodded.

"I want you to come out there with me."

"You're kidding."

"I'm not kidding," he said. "All I have to do, first, is drop this woman off with a guy who does the transportation. He's the one who's going to take her back to L.A. I don't like that part of the business and never have. He's supposed to be here today or tomorrow. Once I hand her over we're free to leave."

"I've never seen the ocean."

He pictured it.

"It's so beautiful you're not even going to believe it," he said, which was true. "We're going to get you a whole new wardrobe, some nice jewelry, a car, the whole bit. You'll never have to work another day in your life."

Water formed in her eyes.

"Why would you do that?"

He shrugged.

"I don't know. There's just something about you."

"You too." She kissed him and then said, "I wasn't going to turn you in or anything. I was just scared."

"I know. We're going to take long walks on the beach."

Chapter Fifty-Five

Day Nine – September 13
Tuesday

ON THE WAY BACK TO HEADQUARTERS from Brad Ripley's office, Bryson Coventry realized that he hadn't done anything formal for Paul Kubiak for giving him the lead on the '67 Vette. So he made a pit stop on the way.

Thirty minutes later, with a cup of coffee in hand, he hiked up to the sixth floor and handed Kubiak a coffee-table book on Corvettes. "For the lead," he said. "It's got a picture of a yellow '63 split-window, exactly like yours."

Kubiak thumbed through until he found it.

"Way cool."

Then Coventry handed him the pictures, sealed in individual evidence bags. "This relates to the four-body case at the railroad spur," he said. "We found these photos in Brad Ripley's safe."

Kubiak look confused.

"Brad Ripley's the guy in the snuff film, who killed Tonya Obenchain."

"Right. Okay, I'm with you now."

"I think the building in these photos is the place where the women were killed. Also, if I'm right, then whoever owns this

BMW is involved. The car doesn't belong to Ripley. We already checked. I need you to enhance the crap out of these little fellows."

Kubiak studied the pictures and didn't seem enthusiastic.

"They're pretty dark and grainy," he observed.

That was true.

"I want to find that building and be walking around inside it by the end of the day," he said.

Kubiak scratched his oversized gut.

"It looks abandoned. As far as the vehicle goes, we don't have much of an angle on the license plate number," he observed. "It's definitely a BMW though."

Coventry agreed. "I need the model, year and color."

SHALIFA NETHERWOOD SHOWED UP mid-afternoon and plopped down in the chair in front of Coventry's desk. "The phone's a dead end," she said, referring to the public phone that someone used on March 15th to place a four-minute call to Brad Ripley.

"You drove out there?"

"I did. The phone itself is located at a gas station on County Line Road. The security cameras don't shine on it. And even if they did, the tapes have already been recycled about two thousand times."

Coventry frowned.

"Thanks for trying," he said. "I wouldn't have been able to sleep without running it to ground."

Then she smiled like the Cheshire Cat.

"What?" he asked.

"Well, just because your idea is a dead end doesn't mean that mine is."

He thought about it.

But couldn't remember what her idea was.

There were too many ideas floating around to keep track of.

That was the problem with this whole case.

"It turned out that Brad Ripley's credit card statements show a March 15th purchase at the Cheesecake Factory," she said.

Now Coventry remembered.

Brad Ripley's connection to someone on March 15th might have been live, over lunch, rather than by phone.

He nodded, impressed.

"Okay," he said. "Run with it."

She beamed and stood up.

"Whoa," he said. "Sit back down. First I need to fill you in on Brad Ripley's safe."

LATER, UP ON THE SIXTH FLOOR, Paul Kubiak beamed as he handed Coventry printouts of the photos in an enhanced state. Coventry shook his head in disbelief.

"It almost looks like day," he said.

"You got to love technology," Kubiak said.

Coventry had never seen this particular building—old, boarded up, long and low with several doors. It reminded him of a small manufacturing facility.

"What is it?" he asked.

"I can't find any markings or signage on it," Kubiak said. "It was used to make something or store something, is my best guess."

"What about the BMW?"

"That was easy," Kubiak said. "Last year's model, a 5-Series.

The color has some fancy name but it's basically silver."

Coventry shuffled through the printouts again.

"Can you bring the building up on the monitor?"

He could.

And pulled it up on a 30" flat-panel screen.

Electronically it was brighter and clearer but still didn't give up any secrets.

"So how do I find this place?" Coventry asked.

Kubiak cocked his head.

"Find the BMW," he said. "Then do something to make it go back there. And follow it when it does."

Coventry laughed.

"Do you have any simpler ideas?"

He didn't.

"I'm a complicated man," he said.

Chapter Fifty-Six

Day Nine – September 13
Tuesday Evening

HALEY AND CHRISTINA SAT AT THE BAR in a half-filled tavern near Larimer Square, drinking white wine too fast and bowing to the Luck Gods for letting them get out of the law firm alive and undetected. The crowd seemed like young professionals, dressed for success, taking a mid-week breath of life on their way to the weekend.

Christina Huygh seemed even more rattled than Haley.

"So I still don't get it," Haley said. "Some woman in New York goes into a suicide-by-bus routine. Derek Bennett calls her a dumb bitch and agrees with whoever it was on the other end of the phone that things are reaching critical mass—his words, *critical mass*."

Christina took a sip of wine.

No, not a sip, a drink.

"Bennett's turning out to be one strange dude," she said. "And that gun. Why does a lawyer need a gun in his office? It gives me the creeps just knowing it's in the building, much less that he's the one who has it."

She shuttered.

"That was a stroke of genius, by the way. That whole battery thing."

Christina frowned.

"Sorry I didn't think of it sooner," she said. "I was a heartbeat away from pulling the fire alarm when I thought of it."

"That would have been subtle."

Two men came over, wearing suits, very polite, and wanted to buy them drinks.

They let them.

Then headed back to Christina's.

WHILE CHRISTINA WENT TO SHOWER THE DAY OFF, Haley fired up her laptop and plugged into the Internet to do a little research. The suicide-by-bus woman, Rebecca Yates, turned out to be a still-gorgeous ex-model who landed a full time job as a trophy wife ten years ago. Other than giving her husband's money away to charities, and parading her face in every high-society function this side of the moon, she really didn't have many other dimensions.

Her husband—Robert Yates—on the other hand, turned out to be quite the story. A self-made man who worked his way up to Harvard and later said it was the most boring four years of his life. It did, however, springboard him onto a path that eventually landed him as the President, CEO and majority shareholder of Tomorrow, Inc., a satellite communications company.

He and eight-year-old daughter Amanda Yates were playing Frisbee in Central Park on a nice July afternoon earlier this summer, a common ritual. Except this time they died.

Both had been ripped open with a jagged knife.

The prevailing theory being that a robbery had gone bad.

The father resisted and ended up on the wrong side of the blade.

That left the girl.

A witness.

So she had to go too.

There were no solid leads or suspects.

Even to this day.

Ordinarily it wouldn't have been much of a story, except the guy was richer than God and everyone wondered what the wife would do afterwards. Most expected her to live it up. Who wouldn't? She was young, beautiful, filthy rich and single.

But, strangely, she actually grew despondent instead.

And then threw herself in front of a bus.

WHEN CHRISTINA CAME OUT OF THE SHOWER, Haley told her the story.

"He was President of Tomorrow, Inc.?"

"Right."

She scrunched her face.

"We had major litigation against that company," she said. "We represented Omega in a federal case in D.C. against Tomorrow. An antitrust case based on predatory pricing. Our client got a judgment against Tomorrow for over a hundred million dollars."

"Wow."

"They appealed and managed to dodge having to post a supersedeas bond," she added. "But the case comes up for oral argument next month."

"Do they have any basis for reversal?"

"According to the powers that be, no. So Tomorrow's on

the verge of writing a very big check to our client."

Haley spun around in her chair.

"This is getting too complicated," she said.

"Forget about it," Christina said. "Obviously it has nothing to do with Renee Rand. We need to stay focused on Derek Bennett the weirdo sadist and not Derek Bennett the antitrust lawyer."

"You're right."

She looked at her watch.

10:42.

"I'm ready to hit the sack."

"Let's do it."

CHRISTINA HAD ONLY ONE BED, but it was big enough that neither of them felt uncomfortable sharing it. They said goodnight and snuggled in. Five minutes later Haley said, in a very low voice, "Are you sleeping yet?"

"Yes."

"Robert Yates got killed on July 22nd. We need to find out if anyone from the law firm was in New York at that time."

Christina moaned.

"Go to sleep."

Chapter Fifty-Seven

Day Nine – September 13
Tuesday Morning

WITH A GUT FULL OF PANCAKES, Jack Degan kissed Gretchen goodbye under a cloudless Colorado sky, pulled her T-shirt up and licked her left nipple, and then pointed the front end of the Granada towards the cabin, intent on getting everything done today that he needed to get done. In a perfect world he would have just waited at the farmhouse until Swofford called and said the coast was clear. But he figured it would be smarter to head out now and get Mia Avila the hell out of there before Gretchen started to freak out again, or came up with some wild idea to bring the woman inside and feed her.

His story was already thin.

He didn't know how long she'd actually believe it.

Better to not press his luck.

So he headed down the road.

It was times like this that he wished he had Swofford's number, or—better yet—actually knew who Swofford was. But the rules had been set up long ago, and the communications only went one direction, and always came to him from a mystery voice calling from a public phone.

"It's safer for everyone that way," Swofford said.

So far the arrangement had been good.

Swofford always came through with the money.

How the hell did Swofford get the clients?

That was the question.

Degan could cut Swofford out of the deal altogether if he could just solve that little puzzle. And why shouldn't he? After all, he was the one doing all the heavy work and taking all the risk.

Well, most of the risk, anyway.

HE SKIRTED AROUND DOWNTOWN GOLDEN and headed west, winding into Clear Creek Canyon, one of the most beautiful places on the face of the earth, with its steep rock walls and frothing mountain river. The radio reception immediately went to hell.

Then, shit!

He noticed that the gas gauge read full. There was no way that could be right, not with all the miles he'd driven. The goddamn thing must be broken.

So how much gas did he have left?

Probably not much.

He could be riding on fumes for all he knew.

So, what to do?

Suddenly the bitch Mia Avila moaned and started to move.

He was just about to tell her to shut up when the engine sputtered and died.

Goddamn it!

He managed to get onto the shoulder, barely clear of the road. When the woman moaned again something exploded in

Degan's brain and he punched her in the head so hard that his hand felt like it broke.

The moaning immediately stopped.

He wasn't sure if he'd killed her or not.

Ten seconds later a cop car pulled behind him and turned on the light bar.

DEGAN WAVED AT THEM, as friendly as he could, and walked over. "No problems," he said. "I just ran out of gas. Someone's bringing some up and should be here pretty quick."

The driver got out.

"You're awful close to the road," he said.

"I'm over as far as I can get," Degan said, which was true. "Like I said, they should be here pretty soon."

The cop scratched his nose and surveyed the area.

"I'm just worried that someone's going to come around the corner a little too tight and clip you."

Degan shook his head and said, "I think I'm okay."

The cop studied the other side of the road, which had twice the shoulder, maybe even three times. "I'd feel better if you were over there," he said. Then to his partner: "Jake, watch the traffic for a moment, will you? I'm going to push this guy across the street." Back to Degan: "What I need you to do is put the car in neutral and steer it into that spot over there. Can you do that?"

Degan nodded.

"Sure, no problem."

The cop walked to the front end of the car. "Did you just buy this?" he asked.

"Yesterday," Degan said.

"Next time talk to me first," the cop said. "My neighbor had one of these. Bought it new and it fell apart in about three months."

Degan swallowed and tried to look amused.

"Now you tell me," he said.

Then the cop started pushing.

At that exact second Mia Avila groaned.

DEGAN COUGHED TO MASK THE SOUND, then punched the radio button and worked the dial until he found a station, filled with static but good enough for what he needed.

He knew the song.

"Johnny B. Goode," by Chuck Berry.

Must be an oldies station.

"Take your foot off the brake," the cop shouted.

Degan did.

Pay attention you dumb shit.

The cop couldn't move the vehicle by himself so his partner came over to assist. Two minutes later the rust-bucket of a car sat on the other side of the road, far enough from the pavement to where it wouldn't be clipped.

Degan thanked them and said goodbye.

The woman was making noises again.

As the cops started across the road a Hummer sped around the bend, going too fast and hugging the inside track. It clipped the rear end of the police car, only catching it by a foot or so, but crushing the metal and spinning the vehicle into the middle of the road. The cops dived for cover. The taillight shattered and the rear tire exploded.

"Goddamn it!" one of the cops shouted.

THE HUMMER HARDLY GOT SCRATCHED but the cop car ended up in the middle of the twisty canyon road, blocking traffic in both directions. The rear quarter-panel had bent into the tire, not only flattening it but also locking it in place so that the vehicle couldn't be pushed.

Cars were already backing up.

Degan's first instinct was to just calmly walk down the road until he was out of sight and then run. But he was at least five miles into the canyon. If anyone found the woman, there would be no way he could make it back to town before they caught him.

Unless he confiscated a car.

Say the last one in line.

He walked back to the Granada, slipped behind the wheel and closed the door. The woman made no sounds but he had no idea if it was because she was unconscious or she was just being careful.

"You're not going to die," he said. "I'm going to let you go, just like always. Unless you screw up and do something stupid. If you do that I'll take you out. You'll give me no choice. Do you understand?"

Silence.

Not a word.

He poked her.

She didn't respond.

He twisted the knife in his hands. Maybe he should just stick it in her head, right here right now, and get it over with. True he'd have a body in the car with him, but at least it would be a guaranteed quiet one.

But then again, if he did get caught, a charge of kidnapping would be a whole lot better than murder.

Shit.

What to do?

Just then one of the cops walked over.

"We're going to push you a little farther onto the shoulder," he said. "See if we can open up a lane and get this traffic moving."

Degan nodded.

"Good idea."

They pushed him farther onto the shoulder while he steered and did his best to not take his knife and just start slashing everyone in sight.

Then he called a tow truck.

Chapter Fifty-Eight

Day Nine – September 13
Tuesday Morning

DEGAN'S TOW TRUCK SHOWED UP forty minutes later, not long after the cop car got pulled onto a flatbed and disappeared down the canyon. A big-boned woman climbed out. The sleeves of her shirt had been ripped off, displaying thick, muscular arms.

Tattooed arms.

Biker-Mama arms.

"You the call I'm looking for?" she asked.

"That's me."

She studied him up and down, and then said, "You got quite the body going there. I might have to give you a discount."

She wasn't his type, but he smiled, not wanting to piss her off.

"Thanks for coming so fast."

She focused on his scar but didn't say anything about it. Instead she motioned to her body. "It's all muscle under these clothes," she said.

"You look good," Degan said.

She chuckled.

"Of course it doesn't just fall out of the sky and land on me," she said. "I work my ass off in the gym. Monday I squatted four ninety-five. A personal best."

Degan nodded, actually impressed.

"Five plates on each side," he said.

"Very good."

It took her only a few minutes to hook up the Granada, and then they headed down the canyon.

THE RADIO PLAYED A COUNTRY-WESTERN SONG that Degan had never heard before. He tapped his hand to it, feeling good and watching the scenery roll by.

"We used to tube here quite a bit," he said, referring to Clear Creek. "A good ten of the times I've come the closest to death were right there in that water."

She shook her head with disapproval.

"You got to be nuts to mess with that river," she said. "You'd never catch me on it in a million years. I'd rather be on a Harley any day of the week."

Degan chuckled.

"Statistically the river's safer. Every other driver's an asshole."

"That's true," she said. "But I don't know too many people who have drowned on a Harley. I don't know how I'm going, but it isn't going to be by drowning. That's one thing for sure."

At the bottom of the canyon they took Highway 93 north towards Boulder, running through the rolling plains at 50 mph, parallel to the foothills. Clouds were building over the mountains.

In another ten minutes they'd be at the farmhouse.

He'd be home free.

Then the woman repeatedly looked in the rearview mirror, so many times that Degan turned around to see what had her attention all of a sudden. He saw normal traffic, nothing unusual, and most importantly no cops.

"What?" he asked.

"I thought I saw something move inside your car."

HIS MIND SCRAMBLED, NEEDING A STORY, FAST. But nothing good came to the surface.

"Yes!" she said. "I just saw movement. I'm sure of it. There's someone in your car."

She looked at him for an explanation.

He stared back and then put on a face as if he just realized what the situation was all about. "Oh, that," he said. "Nothing to worry about. That's just my girlfriend. She's major drunk, sleeping it off." He chuckled. "She probably got a little freaked out with the car tilted up and me not in it. She'll be fine."

The woman didn't seem satisfied.

"I can't have a passenger in a car under tow," she said. "It's against the law."

Degan pulled a hundred dollar bill out of his pocket and held it out towards her.

"For your inconvenience," he said. "We're almost there anyway."

She looked at the bill.

But didn't take it.

"You don't understand," she said. "If I get busted I lose my license."

"We won't get busted. We'll be at my place in five minutes.

If we get stopped I'll just say you knew nothing about it."

She looked in the rearview mirror again.

Then started to slow down.

"We need to move her up here in the cab," she said.

Degan shook his head with disapproval.

"She's been throwing up for two hours. You sure you want that in here?"

She grimaced.

"Unfortunately we got no choice. I'm down to the last few points on my license."

They continued to decelerate.

Then pulled onto the shoulder and stopped.

DEGAN SURVEYED THE TRAFFIC and found it moderate, flying by at sixty or more. Even if someone did think they needed assistance, no one would want to slow down from that speed and stop.

He knew what he had to do.

But tried to think of another way out.

Nothing good came to mind though.

He opened the door and stepped out. "She's pretty heavy," he said. "I'm going to need your help."

She hopped out and met him at the passenger door of the Granada, on the side of the vehicle facing away from the traffic. He opened the door and said, "Can you pull her out? I strained my back a couple of days ago."

The woman bent inside and said, "It looks like her hands are tied."

That's when Degan drove the knife into her spine.

Chapter Fifty-Nine

Day Ten – September 14
Wednesday Morning

WEDNESDAY MORNING, INSTEAD OF HEADING to the office, Bryson Coventry drove straight to the railroad spur where the four bodies had been dumped. By the time he got there the first thermos of coffee started to run through him and he made a quick detour behind the 55-gallon drum.

This time, though, he didn't uncover a body.

Under a warm cerulean sky he pulled down the tailgate of the truck and set a map of Denver on it, looking for an industrial area that had passed its prime.

Shalifa Netherwood called and asked where he was.

He told her and she said to wait there.

Ten minutes later she showed up.

"Here's my theory," he said. "No one drives too far with four bodies in the car, meaning the building's around here somewhere. So I'm going to drive around until I find it."

She shook her head in disbelief.

"You're just going to drive around aimlessly and try to bump into it?"

He nodded.

"That's my plan."

"I'm glad I didn't come up with it," she said. "You'd fire me."

He agreed, but added, "Sometimes you just have to turn yourself into a monkey and peck at the keypad. Then hope you get lucky enough to spell a word."

"I better come with you," she said. "Otherwise you're going to get yourself into trouble today. I can already tell."

AS THEY POKED AND PRODDED the never-ending industrial areas north of the railroad spur, occasionally stopping to piss behind a dumpster—Coventry, not Shalifa—he got a call from Kate Katona.

"I have a list of all the BMW owners," she said. "By the end of the day I should have background checks on all of them. But get this. Eight of them are registered to Hart, Sanders & Day, where Renee Rand worked."

"Interesting."

"I thought you'd say that."

He hung up and told Shalifa.

"That law firm's involved in all this up to its ass," Coventry said. "I just don't know how." He studied the buildings as he drove and tried to pay enough attention to the road to keep from running into anyone. "Haley Wilde's been snooping around," he said. "She overhead two of the lawyers talking about a death."

"Which lawyers?"

Coventry tried to remember.

"I have it written down," he said. "Anyway, one of them, the guy lawyer, is turning out to be seriously strange. According to

Haley Wilde, he frequents an S&M place called Tops & Bottoms where he sticks pins into the girls."

"That's goddamn sick."

Coventry agreed.

"I mean, how does a guy get to be like that?"

"I don't know, but a mind that thinks that's okay probably wouldn't flinch at cutting someone's head off."

"So you think he killed Renee Rand?"

"He's got my attention," Coventry said. "Especially now that we know the firm has lots of BMWs. We need to find that building and confirm that's where the killings took place. Then squeeze it for evidence."

Three blocks later they came to an abandoned building enclosed in a chain-link fence.

Coventry held the picture up and compared it to the structure in front of them.

"Bingo," he said. "The monkey spells a word."

Chapter Sixty

Day Ten – September 14
Wednesday Morning

ALL MORNING LONG, HALEY WILDE expected someone to walk into her office and ask what she was doing in Derek Bennett's office last night. When no one came she started to feel better. That changed when Austin Gray called shortly after ten and asked if she was available for lunch today.

"Of course. What's the occasion?"

"Nothing special. Why don't you swing by my office at 11:30 and we'll try to beat the crowd."

As soon as she hung up she ducked into Christina Huygh's office, closed the door and told her.

"Somehow he knows," she said. "I can feel it."

Christina didn't seem concerned.

"How could he?"

"They could have this place bugged a million different ways and we'd never know it."

Christina rolled a pencil in her hand.

"Now you're getting paranoid," she said. "Just calm down, go to lunch and see what he has to say. It's probably nothing."

She looked amused.

"What?" Haley asked, curious.

"Here's a list of things to not bring up," she said. "Tops & Bottoms, Rebecca Yates, Robert Yates, flashlights, coat closets, and guns in drawers."

"And Derek Bennett," Haley added.

"Right. And me too, for that matter."

HALEY KEPT HER NOSE to the grindstone all morning and then inconspicuously went to the billing room and pulled the time sheets for Jacqueline Moore and Derek Bennett, to see if either of them were in New York on July 22nd when Robert Yates got murdered.

Both were right here in Denver.

Billing clients like there was no tomorrow.

For the week before and the week after as well.

Just for grins she checked on Austin Gray too.

Same thing.

IN A CORNER BOOTH AT THE PARAMOUNT CAFÉ, over the lunch special—salmon and salad—Austin Gray gave Haley the inside track on how to survive life in a big law firm. Then he got to the point of the meeting.

She shouldn't let her guard down.

He still firmly believed her life was in danger.

She should go to the firm's D.C. office until everything blew over.

She listened carefully, thanked him overwhelmingly for his concern, and then politely rejected the offer. Then she changed the subject.

"Christina was telling me about this huge antitrust case that the firm won, over a hundred million," she said. "I can't even imagine what that must feel like."

"Ask Derek Bennett," Austin said. "He spearheaded the whole thing."

She bit her lower lip.

Trying to not visibly react.

"Talk about your nasty kick-'em-in-the-balls fight, this was the granddaddy of them all. It was the legal equivalent of two packs of junkyard dogs ripping each other wide open. Lucky for us Derek Bennett was the biggest dog in the bunch."

"Wow."

"Bow wow. As usual though," Austin added, "the drama behind the scenes was a whole lot more interesting than the case itself."

"How's that?"

Austin finished chewing and then said, "The defendant, Tomorrow Inc., was owned and run by a guy named Robert Yates, an insanely rich guy, at least on paper. Have you ever heard of him?"

She shook her head.

"I don't remember him being at my last party."

"Mine either," he said. "Anyway, he makes a slick move and convinces the trial judge to stay execution of the judgment without posting a supersedeas bond. So he's temporarily off the hook. Then while the case is on appeal he starts to secretly buy the stock of our client, Omega, which is publicly traded. He's doing it in small chunks, through a lot of dummy corporations, friends and brokers, to keep everything under the radar so the price doesn't go up."

"A takeover," she said.

"Exactly," he said. "A takeover, but not by the company itself, since it wasn't Tomorrow buying the stock, but a takeover by a private party."

"Why?"

"My theory is that he wanted to get control of Omega and then have it drop the case against Tomorrow, or at least settle it for some ridiculously small amount. It's called, *If you can't beat your opponent, eat him.*"

"But how could he have Omega drop the case? There are other shareholders besides him. Whoever's on the board of Omega has a fiduciary duty to *all* the shareholders, to maximize the amount of the judgment."

Austin laughed.

"That's the difference between someone fresh out of law school like you and a crusty old guy like me," he said. "You're absolutely right, in theory. In reality though, it would have worked very differently." He nodded with respect. "You got to hand it to the guy, he was a genius. The interesting thing was, both companies would have come out stronger. But then, out of the blue, Yates gets robbed one day. It turns out he had about twenty dollars in his pocket. He decides to resist instead of handing it over and gets both himself and his daughter killed. Then, in an even stranger twist, his wife walks in front of a bus. That, by the way, just happened a day or two ago."

She sighed.

"How tragic."

He seemed to chew on the words.

Then looked at her.

"Yeah. It really was."

BACK AT HER OFFICE AFTER LUNCH, she found a sealed envelope sitting on her chair where she'd be sure to find it. Inside she found a sheet of paper. A LITTLE BIRDIE TOLD ME YOU COULD USE A FRIEND, SO HERE'S YOUR SHOT OF REALITY FOR THE DAY. DON'T TRUST CHRISTINA HUYGH. SHE'S A SPY. MY ADVICE IS TO GET OUT OF THE FIRM WHILE YOU STILL CAN. AND WHATEVER YOU DO, DON'T SHOW THIS NOTE TO ANYONE. I'M THE ONLY ONE YOU HAVE WATCHING YOUR BACK.

She read it six more times.

Then swallowed hard and shredded it.

As soon as she did she wished she hadn't.

Chapter Sixty-One

Day Ten – September 14
Wednesday Morning

SLIGHTLY HUNG OVER, JACK DEGAN crawled out of bed before dawn, being careful to not wake Gretchen. He carried his jeans and T-shirt outside and put them on, then walked over to the barn and took a heaven-sent piss in the dirt. Crickets chirped. Something small rustled in the brush, maybe a mouse or a snake. He zipped up, unlocked the barn and inched his way into the blackness.

He couldn't remember a darker dark.

Nothing was visible.

Not even the outline of the tow truck. He held his arm out until he felt steel, and then followed the cold body of the vehicle around until he reached the door. When he opened it the dome light came to life and shined on the driver's dead body.

He grimaced at the sight.

Shit.

The dumb bitch.

Why'd she have to go and screw everything up?

He moved her arm to see how much stiffness had settled into the body since yesterday afternoon—not enough to make a difference. He opened the door as far as it would go and then pulled on her arm until she dropped to the ground with a thud. Then he dragged her out of the barn over to the Nissan, where he muscled her into the trunk. The whole thing took less than three minutes but left him covered in sweat.

He locked the barn and double-checked the lock.

It was important that Gretchen didn't stumble across the tow truck today while he was gone. He'd come up with a plan to dispose of it later, but right now he had to concentrate on first things first.

He checked on the tattoo woman, chained to the seat frame in the back of the Granada. She was still wonderfully unconscious, thanks to the injection. He moved her into the back seat of the Nissan, re-chained her to the frame and covered her with a blanket. Then he left a note on the kitchen table for Gretchen, telling her he had business but would be back this afternoon.

Finally at ease, he pointed the Nissan towards the cabin.

He arrived at the structure just as dawn broke.

It looked deserted, as it should.

No lights were on.

No cars were parked in front.

Perfect.

Everything was back on track.

HE FOUND THE STRIPPER—CHASE—NAKED AND DEAD in the bedroom, brutally dead to be precise, the victim of multiple bloody wounds. In addition to all that, a nail had been pounded into her forehead.

The hammer sat on the dresser, next to a box of 3" galvanized nails.

"Goddamn sicko," he muttered.

For a split second, he had half a mind to hunt the guy down and do the same thing to him, to see how he liked it. But the feeling passed after he wrapped the woman in a bed sheet and made a pot of coffee. Out in the garage, he confirmed that the satellite DVD recorder—the one that the clients never knew about—had done its job. He watched for a few seconds, just long enough to tell that it had worked properly, and then popped the DVD out. He put it in a plastic case, carried it into the cabin and set it on the kitchen counter where he wouldn't forget it.

Okay.

Good.

He filled the cup back up with piping hot coffee and then sipped it on the front steps. The sun was already taking the chill out of the air and washing the mountains with a yellow hue.

It'd be a nice day.

Autumn in Colorado.

It doesn't get much better than that.

AS BAD AS YESTERDAY HAD BEEN, things still worked out pretty good in the end. After the stupid tow-truck driver forced him to kill her, Degan drove the rig straight to the farmhouse. Luckily, Gretchen wasn't home. He figured out how to unhook the Granada, and stashed the truck in the barn, long before Gretchen showed up.

Then she cooked hotdogs and chili for him, and jumped up and down on the couch until he promised he'd take her to a bar.

Which he did.

A dive with cheap beer and a crappy jukebox.

Then they drove back home with guts full of alcohol and managed to screw like crazy before passing out.

BUT THAT WAS LAST NIGHT. Now, today, he had work to do. He put the tow-truck driver in a wheelbarrow and muscled her into the mountains as far as he could, ending up a good five or six hundred yards from the cabin. Then he buried her a foot down, fighting rocks the whole way.

In a perfect world she'd be deeper.

But the effort was too much.

The ground was almost all stone with hardly any dirt.

In any event, a foot ought to be good enough to keep the stench in and the animals out, especially after he piled a ton of rocks on top.

Then he went back to the cabin and ate a sandwich and a half box of cookies, thinking about how he should kill the tattoo woman.

Then he heard her moan out in the Nissan.

Perfect.

She was waking up.

Just in time to die.

He unchained her and carried her into the bedroom, where he tied her on her back with her arms over her head. Then he gagged her, straddled her chest and slapped her face until she was fully awake.

The hammer kept drawing his attention.

He pulled up a vision of driving a nail into her forehead.

On the one hand, death would be quicker than she deserved for all the pain she'd put him through. On the other hand, he wouldn't have to fuss around with her all day.

She must have read something in his eyes, judging by the way she pulled so frantically at the ropes.

"Yeah, it's that time," he said.

She tried to plead with him, through the gag, but everything came out scrambled.

He leaned over far enough to get the hammer and a couple of nails.

Then dangled them in front of her face.

"I can't lie to you," he said. "This is going to hurt."

Chapter Sixty-Two

Day Ten – September 14
Wednesday Morning

AFTER WORKING UP A SEARCH WARRANT and taking it down to the D.A.'s office for review and processing, Bryson Coventry drove back to the wooden building and paced back and forth outside the chain-link fence.

The four women had been killed inside that structure.

He was sure of it.

The question is whether it would give up its secrets.

Mid-afternoon Shalifa Netherwood pulled up, dangling a thermos of coffee out the window. Coventry immediately ran to his truck and searched around in the back seat until he found a used Styrofoam cup.

"You got the warrant?" he asked, relieving her of the thermos and pouring much needed caffeine into the cup.

"Nope."

He shook his head in wonder.

"I'm going to enter Clay in a snail race," he said. "See if he can at least move that fast."

She grinned and then paced with him, for some time, for so long in fact that he brought up a subject that he didn't think he would.

"Tianca Holland blindsided me this morning," he said.

"How so?"

"Well, you know she's bi, right?"

"So you say."

"This morning she said she misses women," he said. "I know I shouldn't have said anything, but of course I did, and we ended up in a little discussion. The bottom line is this. If I give her my approval to sleep with other women, she's going to look around. If I don't, she won't." He picked up a stick and snapped it. "This has nothing to do with men. She's crystal clear that she isn't interested in other men."

He studied Shalifa to get her reaction.

"Does this mean you're sleeping with her?"

"No."

"Are you sure?"

"Trust me, that's the kind of thing I'd remember."

She laughed.

"Well, this is quite the dilemma," she said.

"I want her to be happy. On the other hand, if I give her the go-ahead to get intimate with a woman, I'm afraid she'll end up falling in love."

"Think of the bright side," Shalifa said. "Unlimited three-somes."

He chuckled.

"Been there," he said. "They were fine in their day, but now I think they'd be more work than they're worth." He kicked a stone.

Shalifa cocked her head.

"What if she did get feelings for another woman?" she asked. "Do you think that would mean she would feel differently about you?"

"I'm don't know. And I don't want to find out."

He stopped, laced his fingers through the chain-link fence and stared at the building. "I'm jealous of someone who doesn't even exist yet," he said. "A woman no less. How pathetic is that?"

She looked amused.

"It'll either work out or it won't," she said. "There are no guarantees. Personally, I think you have a better chance with a woman if you give her what she wants instead of trying to herd her in."

He kicked the fence.

"I know that," he said. "It's just going to be hard."

"Maybe there's a compromise," Shalifa said. "She can do other women but only if you're there."

He thought about it.

"Maybe," he said. "In the meantime, this is our secret."

"I'll tell the chief. No one else."

"Not funny."

Just then Paul Kubiak pulled up in a Crime Unit van, waving the search warrant out the window.

"Is anyone ready to have some fun?" he asked.

THEY FINGERPRINTED THE PADLOCK on the fence, got nothing useable, then cut if off and bagged it. Coventry's heart pounded as they walked over the dirty, weed-infested asphalt towards the building. "I know none of us would ever make a mistake," he said, "but especially don't make it today."

All the doors had padlocks so they cut one off and entered.

The lights didn't work.

They wandered around the outside perimeter until they found the main electrical box. The breaker was closed, meaning there was no electricity coming to it. Paul Kubiak scratched his gut and frowned.

"Looks like we're going to have to fire up the generators and set up some halogen stands," he said.

Coventry nodded.

"Go ahead and start on that," he said. "Do you have any flashlights in your van?"

"A couple."

Coventry and Shalifa entered using flashlights. The building was broken down into a large room and several smaller ones. Most of them were cluttered with old rusty parts, no doubt left-over remnants of machines that no longer existed.

"I want the eyes," Coventry said. "I'll be a happy man if I can find the eyes."

"Don't get your hopes up," Shalifa said. "I always pictured them floating in a formaldehyde pickle jar on someone's mantle."

Coventry grunted.

They searched the place thoroughly but didn't find the room that had been in Brad Ripley's snuff video.

"Damn it," Coventry said. "I can't believe this isn't the place."

One of the metal racks seemed odd and Coventry studied it as they walked past. It didn't seem as dirty as the others. On closer inspection it seemed as though the boxes and parts on the shelves had been taken off and then put back on. There were scratches and smudges in the dirt. Then he spotted a door hidden behind it and started pulling things off the shelves and setting them over to the side.

"Help me with this stuff," he said.

When they finally got everything moved and opened the door, they found a room unlike the others, empty except for a bed. "Bingo," Coventry said, shining the light around. He paused the beam on a black smudge on the back wall. "I remember that mark from Ripley's snuff film."

On closer examination they saw blood splatters.

On the floor.

And the walls.

Not as many as Coventry anticipated, but enough to give them all the DNA they wanted.

"So this is where it all happened," Shalifa said.

"Yeah. Nice, huh?"

They didn't enter, but instead went back outside to talk to Paul Kubiak. "I got some good news and some bad news," Coventry said. "The good news is, we have a whole room that we're going to take apart inch by inch."

Kubiak's face brightened.

"You found it?"

"*We* found it," Coventry said.

"Well I'll be damned."

"That's true but not relevant right now."

Coventry walked towards his truck.

"Hey," Kubiak shouted, "What's the bad news?"

"The bad news is I have to piss like you can't believe, so turn your back."

"Just don't turn up any more bodies."

Chapter Sixty-Three

Day Ten – September 14
Wednesday Afternoon

HALEY WILDE ALMOST WALKED into Christina Huygh's office fifteen different times to tell her someone was running around accusing her of being a spy. But she didn't.

Instead she continued to think it through.

If she was a spy, who for? Clearly not Derek Bennett. Christina's disgust at what they found at Tops & Bottoms was genuine. No one can fake those kinds of facial expressions.

As for Jacqueline Moore, Christina's personality conflict with the woman was on record. Plus Cruella wouldn't ever help anyone other than herself. She particularly wouldn't go out of her way to help Haley after the blow-up last Wednesday, even though things had supposedly smoothed over.

So rule her out too.

What about Austin Gray?

He had, after all, saved Christina's ass after she botched a case by failing to timely disclose an expert. So, technically, she owed him big time. Plus Austin is the kind of guy who wants to know what's going on in his little kingdom. Still, even though the pieces could technically fit, it didn't feel right. And, now that she thought about it more, Haley was with Austin at lunch when the envelope got put on her chair.

So rule him out.

Who, then?

Either someone else altogether or—more likely—Christina wasn't a spy at all. Maybe someone was just trying to drive a wedge between Haley and her.

But who would want to keep them apart?

The person who had the most to lose by them being together. Meaning the person who they had their sights on, namely Derek Bennett.

Did that mean he knew what they'd been doing?

Did he see them at Tops & Bottoms?

Or in his office?

Interesting questions.

He was just the kind of guy who would be clever enough to sneak through the back door and try to drive them apart instead of confronting them head on.

If he knew what they were up to, and his wedge plan didn't work, maybe he had something more sinister up his sleeve. Maybe both she and Christina were in his crosshairs. If that was the case, then Christina deserved to know.

So confusing.

For now, she decided to not tell Christina about the note, but to watch her back for her, especially as to Derek Bennett.

THAT EVENING, SHORTLY AFTER DARK, it rained—starting as a light drizzle but quickly taking on a harder edge, pounding against the windows. Christina got a weird look on her face, grabbed an umbrella from the closet, pointed it at Haley and opened and closed it as if flapping a wing.

"I'm taking a walk. You want to come?"

Haley studied her, decided she was actually serious, and listened to the storm.

"We'll get drenched," she said.

"That's the point."

They headed outside, jammed under the one umbrella, keeping their heads dry but not much else. After five blocks, when they were near Colfax, Christina said, "I have an idea."

They walked to Colfax and then south for a couple of hundred yards, ending up at the Old Town Tavern. Although the place didn't seem that big from the outside, cars filled the parking lot and the surrounding streets. A sign announced "Live Music Every Wednesday." As they walked toward the entrance Haley said, "I didn't bring a wallet."

That didn't slow Christina who said, "Me either."

At the door the bouncer hugged Christina, lifting her off the ground and spinning her around. Then he kissed her on the lips, cupped her ass with a strong hand and squeezed. Christina said, "Do you have enough beer here to get me drunk?" He laughed, waved them through the five-dollar cover charge and said, "Probably not. But go ahead and try."

"You're too sweet."

"You have no idea," he said. "Maybe some day you'll want to find out."

"You never know."

Inside, everyone seemed to be on the move, elbowing through the crowd, on the hunt for the night's catch. A stage band belted out a country-western song with a lets-get-drunk attitude. The singer—a blond cowgirl wearing Daisy Duke shorts—looked and sounded like she just got off the bus from

Texas. Countless half-empty bottles of beer sat on black Fender amps.

Christina grabbed Haley's hand and started to muscle her way to the bar.

"Are you going to get drunk with me, girlfriend, or what?"

"We don't have any money," Haley said.

"We don't need any. The owner's a client of mine."

An hour later, beers in hand—their third—and exhausted from dancing, they got lucky enough to be standing near a booth just as bodies were leaving. They jumped in and leaned back, stretching their legs.

"God that feels good."

They clanked glasses.

Then Haley's mind wandered to Robert Yates, knifed down in Central Park, in the middle of a private takeover of Omega. "Got a question for you," she said. "About Robert Yates. What would happen to Omega if he succeeded in buying enough stock to get control?"

Christina looked puzzled. "What do you mean?"

"I don't know," she said. "I'm just looking for a motive, in case he didn't get killed by a random robbery."

"A motive?"

"Right."

Christina laughed. "Is your grandmother Nancy Drew or something? Give it a rest, girlfriend."

"Seriously," Haley said. "Suppose Robert Yates goes on breathing, buys up a boatload of Omega stock and then gets control."

Christina leaned back and studied her.

"So you're asking who would suffer, if everything had gone according to plan."

"Right."

"Well, let's play it through." Christina said. "First, he'd fire everyone on the board of Omega and set up his own puppets. Then he'd have them elect new officers—President, VPs, etc. Most of those people would bring in their own upper-level support staff, meaning the old ones go bye-bye. Then, of course, the operations of the two companies would be consolidated to cut costs, not immediately but at some point down the road. Lots of upper management types at both companies would end up losing their jobs. So if you're looking for someone who wouldn't want the takeover to go though, you have a couple of hundred faces right there."

Haley frowned.

"That's a lot of people."

"Right."

"No wonder the police just went with a robbery theory."

"That's what I would have done."

Then thunder cracked as if it was right on them.

A bright flash exploded at the windows and disappeared just as fast.

The building rattled.

Then the lights went out.

Hundreds of drunken voices simultaneously howled and cheered. Haley couldn't see two feet in front of her nose.

She said, "Someone told me you're a spy."

But Christina didn't hear.

And Haley changed her mind about saying it again.

Chapter Sixty-Four

Day Ten – September 14
Wednesday

WITH THE 3" GALVANIZED NAIL IN HIS LEFT HAND and the hammer in his right, Jack Degan looked into his victim's face one last time. She struggled beneath him and pulled wildly at her bonds but it did no good.

She was stuck.

There was nothing she could do to avoid the ugliness that was upon her.

There were no magic words she could say.

There was no hero racing through the front door to save her.

Degan knew that he should feel remorse, or excitement, or something. But if he felt anything, it was curiosity—seeing what it looked like to be on the ragged edge of death with absolutely no way out.

Her life wasn't passing before her eyes. She wasn't remembering loved ones, or good times, or any shit like that. The horror on her face clearly said otherwise. No, she'd fallen into a first-rate adrenalin panic.

Degan recognized the look.

And knew the feeling.

He'd been there a few times himself, although not to this extreme of course, fighting for his life in the cold waters of Clear Creek after getting thrown out of a tube and being bashed in rocky rapids. At times like that you don't think about anything but survival, pure and simple.

He positioned the nail on her forehead, with the tip against her skin, as if he was about to drive it into a two-by-four. He raised the hammer, looked in her eyes, and said, "See you in hell."

At that moment his cell phone rang.

HE ALMOST DROVE THE NAIL INTO HER SKULL but instead got off and answered the phone. Swofford's voice came through.

"Is that tattooed woman still alive?"

"Yes. Why?"

"Good," Swofford said. "Keep her that way. The client's going to come back into town and finish the job."

"He is?"

"Yeah. He called me, just to be sure everything was being taken care of, and I told him what happened."

Degan paced.

"That's going to screw everything up," he said. "I already got plans to bury her and the stripper today."

"So the stripper's dead—"

"Right. No problems there."

"Okay, do this," Swofford said. "Bury the stripper somewhere today so we have her wrapped up. Leave the tattooed woman tied up in the cabin. The client should be there by nightfall. Just be absolutely sure she can't get away. I'll call you tomorrow when the coast is clear."

Degan felt his voice rising.

"Look," he said. "I need to get out of town, today. I'm too hot right now. Yesterday I had a complication."

"What kind of complication?"

"The car I was using broke down," he said. "I had to call a tow truck. The tattoo woman was in the back and apparently woke up during the tow. The driver—a female—saw her and stopped. She said she couldn't have a passenger in a car that was being towed. I had no choice but to kill her."

Swofford breathed into the phone, thinking.

"Is that the case all over the news?"

"I don't know," Degan said. "I haven't been watching the news. But here's the problem. When I was broken down, lots of people saw me, including a couple of cops. I'm going to get tied to the tow truck real quick. I wouldn't be surprised if they had a composite sketch of me on the news before the day's over."

Swofford said nothing.

Thinking it through.

"Where are you staying?"

Degan explained and then added, "Luckily, a woman I've been seeing is the one who rented the place. The owner never saw me."

"Good," Swofford said. "Just lie low there, it's as good a place as any for right now. We have to let the client finish up with the tattoo woman, so you need to stay in town at least that long. Just keep your eyes open."

Degan said, "Fine," hung up, and kicked a chair.

AN HOUR LATER SWOFFORD CALLED AGAIN. "We have another client. He wants a specific person. Have you still got enough balls to hang around and make some more money?"

Money.

Right.

There was nothing wrong with money.

"Who's the person?" he asked.

"Someone by the name of Tianca Holland, apparently some rich bitch. So are you up for it, or should I get someone else to do it?"

Someone else?

Screw that.

Someone else this time might turn into someone else every time.

"I'm always up for it," he said.

"Good. I'm going to do a little research on the woman this afternoon and will call you later with more details."

Chapter Sixty-Five

Day Ten – September 14
Wednesday Afternoon

A NEWLY-FOUND CRIME SCENE always comes with a sense of exuberance. If you don't contaminate it to death, it usually turns out to be the trailhead of the critical path to justice. The clues are always there. More importantly, the forensic ties are there—small, obscure and hidden at first; then the size of mountains by the time they get paraded before the jury.

Fingerprints.

Fibers.

DNA.

But today Bryson Coventry was looking for bigger things. "I'm not leaving this place until we find the eyes," he said.

Shalifa studied him, as if contemplating a question.

"What?" he asked.

She shrugged. "I just don't understand this obsession with the eyes. That's all."

Coventry kicked a rock, sending it skipping thirty feet down the asphalt driveway.

"I keep getting an image of the guy eating them," he said. "I need to know that didn't happen."

She laughed.

"Coventry, no more pizza before bed for you."

He grunted.

"I didn't say a dream, I said an image."

But he had to admit she was right.

The concept was stupid.

"The guy probably didn't like the way she was looking at him, after she was dead," Shalifa said. "So he took them out. I doubt there's anything more to it than that."

He knew she was probably right but still couldn't get the image out of his brain. "I'll make you a bet," he said. "If you're right I'll take you out to lunch or dinner at the restaurant of your choice."

"Cool."

"If I'm right, you have to keep my coffee cup filled up for a week."

She shook her head.

"No way," she said. "That's twenty hours of work."

He grinned.

"Okay, one day then."

"A morning," she said.

"Okay. But you have to get to work when I do."

"No way. I'll start at eight—eight till noon. That's the deal."

AFTER PAUL KUBIAK GOT THE LIGHT STANDS IN PLACE, they processed the murder room, slowly and methodically. But it was the things that weren't there that tugged harder and harder at Coventry. For example, Brad Ripley's snuff film showed a sheet on the mattress.

Where was that?

And the pillow?

And the rope?

He wandered outside and found a rusty dumpster in the back of the building, the old dangerous kind with the steel lid that'll slam down and take your finger off if you give it half a chance. He muscled it up and propped it in place with a piece of wood. Inside he found several black plastic bags.

He put his gloves back on and pulled one out. Then ripped the side open.

Bloody sheets.

Bingo.

Then his cell phone rang and Tianca Holland's voice came through. She called for no reason other than to say hi. "I've been thinking about our conversation this morning," he said. "If being with a woman is important to you then go for it."

"You sure?"

"Pretty sure."

"You don't sound sure."

"To be honest, it'll be a little hard. But I can handle it."

"Do you want to be there?" she asked.

"Not really."

A pause.

"I'm not so sure I want to anymore. But I do know one thing. I'm not going to let you fight me off much longer."

Coventry chuckled.

"I'll warn the little guy."

"You do that."

THREE MINUTES LATER Shalifa Netherwood appeared.

"There you are," she said.

He nodded at the black plastic bag.

"The mother lode," he said. "There are more in the dumpster." Then he told her about the conversation with Tianca.

She listened patiently and then said, "Congratulations."

"On what?"

"You just passed your first major test."

"What does that mean?"

"It means she was trying to find out if you'd put her happiness above your own," she said. "And you did. I'm impressed."

"So this was just a big test?"

"I thought it might have been all along."

"Then why didn't you say something?"

"Because that would have been cheating."

"I thought you were on my side," he said.

"Not when it comes to another woman. Besides, aren't you glad you passed fair and square?"

He thought about it.

Yeah.

He was.

"Don't go breaking her heart, Coventry," she added. "If she's testing you that means there's a whole lot more going on than she's letting on."

"That's fine with me," he said. Which was true.

Then he looked at the dumpster. "If the eyes are anywhere, they're in one of these plastic bags. If they're not there, he ate them."

She cocked her head.

"Okay, I'll buy that, at least for the purpose of settling our bet."

Chapter Sixty-Six

Day Ten – September 14
Wednesday

BRYSON COVENTRY ORDERED SIX LARGE PIZZAS, enough to feed everyone working at the crime scene, and even paid out of his own pocket, causing Kubiak to note that somewhere down below hell just froze over. They sat on the driveway and ate, in good moods, having already processed a ton of forensic evidence with a lot more to go.

Clouds filled the sky.

Warning of rain later this evening.

They found four black trash bags in the dumpster, which appeared to represent separate throwaways for each of the four murders. Three of them contained blood-soaked bed sheets. Later, they'd run DNA tests to confirm that the blood belonged to Angela Pfeifer, Renee Rand and Catherine Carmichael, but no one had a doubt at this point.

The bed sheet in the fourth trash bag didn't have blood and no doubt correlated to Tonya Obenchain, who was suffocated. With any luck they'd find Brad Ripley's DNA on it and confirm beyond any reasonable doubt that he was the masked person in the snuff film.

From what Coventry could tell, each woman was brought into the murder room separately. After each killing the sheets were changed and the space was cleaned up, at least cosmetically, in preparation of the next session.

Very well organized.

By who?

WITH TOO MUCH PIZZA IN THE GUT, Coventry walked over to the Tundra and brushed his teeth. Shalifa Netherwood joined him just as he spit toothpaste onto the ground.

"Lovely," she said.

"Hey, I've been meaning to ask you, what's going on with that Pueblo woman? Has she shown up yet or anything?"

She shrugged.

"I don't know. I haven't touched base down there for a couple of days." He must have had an unhappy look on his face, because she added, "I'll put it on my to-do list. Which reminds me, by the way, we might have someone else missing too."

Coventry didn't like the sound of that.

"Who?"

"Emphasis on the *might*. A woman by the name of Samantha Stamp," she said. "She's a stripper at some place out north on Federal called Cheeks. One of the other dancers reported her missing this afternoon. Supposedly she hasn't shown up for work for the last couple of evenings and isn't answering her cell phone."

"Probably strung out somewhere," Coventry said. "But keep it on your radar screen, just in case."

THEY WORKED THE SCENE until the streetlights came on and the rain plummeted down, and then called it a night. Coventry drove straight to Tianca's. She was waiting for him with dimmed lights, cold white wine, a stomach-to-stomach body hug and a long, deep kiss.

"I'm your slave," she said. "Command me."

She wore a long-sleeve white shirt. She must have sensed his question—whether she wore anything underneath—and pulled the ends up and tied them together, just under her breasts.

Question answered.

In the affirmative.

A white thong.

He raised an eyebrow and sipped the wine.

"My slave, huh."

"Utterly and completely."

"What are the boundaries?"

"Only your imagination."

He cocked his head.

"Okay," he said. "But no turning back."

"Yes, master."

Lightning crackled. He grabbed the bottle of wine and two glasses, and then led her out the front door, into the back seat of the Tundra. The rain pelted the roof and, in the dark, seemed louder than it probably was. He filled their glasses, put his arm around her shoulders and leaned back.

"Now this is perfect."

She stayed quiet and snuggled in.

"You're always full of surprises."

They talked about whatever came to mind, with no subject too big or too small. The rain didn't let up. Not a bit. In fact, if anything, it got stronger.

"Tell me about Shalifa Netherwood," Tianca said.

"What do you want to know?"

"I don't know. Just something."

"Something, huh?"

"Yeah, whatever."

"She said you were testing me this morning, to see if I'd put you above me," he said. "By the way, was she right?"

"Maybe a little."

"But she wouldn't help me figure out the answer," he said. "She said that would be cheating."

Tianca chuckled.

"I'm starting to like this woman," she said.

"There's a lot to like."

"But you never screwed her?"

He shook his head. "I bounced a quarter off her ass a couple of times at a bar once when we were all drunk," he said. "But that's about it."

"How high did it go?"

"What?"

"The quarter."

He laughed. "I don't know. I think it knocked down a chandelier or something. All I remember is, there was a lot of damage."

She punched him in the arm.

"Actually, I handpicked her out of vice last year and brought her over to homicide. There are still a few people over in vice who won't talk to me because of that. Anyway, it started out that I was going to take her under my wing and show her the ropes. Now she's showing them to me."

"She seems competent."

"Take a good look," he said. "She's the first female chief."

THEN HIS CELL PHONE RANG. He reached for it but she grabbed his hand. He pulled it out anyway and looked at the incoming number. It was Haley Wilde. "This is the attorney whose face I put on the news and turned into a target," he said. "The one whose apartment got ransacked. I better see what she wants."

Chapter Sixty-Seven

Day Ten – September 14
Wednesday Night

THE LIGHTS AT THE OLD TOWN TAVERN never did come back on, not after a minute, or ten or even fifteen. Incredibly, almost no one left, apparently determined to drink the beer they paid for. Lighters ignited everywhere, reminding Haley of the final scene in Frankenstein. The band pulled out acoustical guitars and sang without mics. Haley and Christina stayed in the booth until their beer was gone and then muscled through the crowd to the front door, alive and without incident, except for a few invisible hands that managed to grope them pretty good. The umbrella, of course, was long gone, and the storm outside now plummeted down even more intensely than before.

They ran through the weather.

Cold, tipsy and incredibly alive.

Feeling like wild animals.

Thirty minutes later, in dry clothes and sipping hot chocolate, they settled in on the couch to watch TV for a half hour before heading to bed, flicking the channels until they eventually landed on *A Perfect Murder.* Michael Douglas was in the process of pressuring his wife's boyfriend to kill her.

"See, never get married," Christina said.

"Gee, I better remember that," Haley said. "I get asked so often."

A HALF HOUR LATER, while Christina was in the bathroom getting ready for bed, a mental picture of Derek Bennett sticking pins into women jumped into Haley's brain. It was so vivid and unsettling that she called Bryson Coventry, who had earlier said he'd do a background check on Bennett. When he answered he didn't seem eager to talk, almost as if she was interrupting him. She heard rain in the background, as if he was in a car.

"It's me, Haley Wilde," she said. "Is this a bad time?"

No.

No problem.

She thought she heard a woman's voice in the background but couldn't be sure.

"I just wondered if you found out anything on Derek Bennett yet."

A pause, then, "We haven't had a chance yet. Why?"

"Nothing, really. I was just curious, that's all."

"He's on the to-do list," Coventry said.

"Okay. Thanks."

They said goodbye, and she almost hung up, when his voice came back again. "Are you still there?" She was. "Let me ask you something. Apparently your law firm owns several BMWs. Do you know who in the firm uses them? Who they're assigned to?"

She didn't.

"Can you do me a favor and find out?"

"Sure."

"Do it quietly, though. Don't let anyone know," he added.

He sounded serious.

"Are they connected to the four murders?"

"We'll see."

"Wait a minute. I just remembered. I'm pretty sure Derek Bennett drives a BMW. Silver, I think."

Chapter Sixty-Eight

Day Ten – September 14
Wednesday Night

TIANCA HOLLAND, IT TURNED OUT, LIVED in a filthy-rich house on a filthy-rich street in a filthy-rich neighborhood southwest of Denver. Jack Degan drove past her place after dark and studied it through windshield wipers that were doing their best to beat back an incredibly heavy rain. A white Toyota Tundra pickup sat in the bend of a long, circular cobblestone driveway in front of the house, half hidden behind a water feature. It almost appeared as if two people sat inside it, although he couldn't be sure.

Then the shadows moved.

So, someone was definitely inside.

He made only one pass and then got the hell out of there.

He knew the type of place.

Security cameras galore.

And not just on this house, but all of 'em.

One thing for sure—he'd have to snatch the woman from some place other than her house, unless there was a way to get in from the back, through a field or something. That was a question he could better answer tomorrow by the light of day. Either way, she'd be tricky to get.

Maybe he should hit Swofford up for an additional twenty-five, on account of the complications.

Yeah.

That'd be worth a try.

He unscrewed the flask, took a hit of Jack, and then headed back home to Gretchen.

SHE WAS ASLEEP ON THE COUCH when he got there and the sight made him warm inside. He sat down gently, without waking her, and ran his fingers through her hair. After a while, he moved her up until she was nestled under his arm, and then sat there in the dark and listened to the rain pound on the house.

If everything was going according to plan, the tattoo woman—Mia Avila—was in the process of dying right about now. Tomorrow Degan would do the cleanup and bring that phase of events to an end.

Then he'd be able to concentrate all of his attention on the new victim.

Tianca Holland.

After that he'd take Gretchen to Malibu.

Chapter Sixty-Nine

Day Eleven – September 15
Thursday Morning

NOT SCREWING TIANCA HOLLAND LAST NIGHT, after they sat in the Tundra in the rain drinking wine for more than two hours, was definitely, without a doubt, the hardest thing Coventry had ever done in his entire male adult life.

The morning didn't turn out to be any easier.

There in the dark, before the dawn broke, Tianca rolled him onto his back, straddled him and pined his arms above his head before he even knew he was awake.

Then she ground on him.

He let her.

He wouldn't let her put it in, but let her grind.

Until she screamed and came in a long, rolling orgasm.

Then she fell off and collapsed on her back. "Damn I needed that," she said.

"You're bad," he said.

She propped her head up with one hand and looked at him. "So when do I get the whole deal?"

"When the case is over."

"Which is when? Never?"

"As soon as I can get it that way, believe me."

She ran her fingers through his hair.

"You're so old-fashioned sometimes," she said.

"Not old-fashioned," he said, "just experienced in how the courts work. I can't end up catching this guy and then having some sleazy defense attorney muck everything up and get him off by being able to tell the jury that the detective—me—and a person of interest—you—were banging each other's socks off."

"Simple solution," she said, "we just don't tell anyone. It's called a First Amendment right to privacy."

Coventry shook his head, got out of bed and headed for the shower. "It's not that simple," he said over his shoulder.

"Why? Don't you know how to lie?"

He stopped and turned.

"Oh, I can lie all right, but that's not the question," he said. "The question is, do you feel like going for a jog?"

She laughed.

"You just gave me a workout, in case you didn't notice."

"Come on," he said. "Two miles."

She got out of bed.

"I guess I owe you that."

"I'll go slow," he added.

She laughed.

"As if you have any other speed."

They actually ended up doing three miles, and showered together afterwards. Then Coventry ate a bowl of cereal in the Tundra as he drove to headquarters.

MID-MORNING HE GOT A VERY UNEXPECTED and strange phone call. When he hung up, he swung by Shalifa Netherwood's desk and said, "You got time to take a ride?"

"No, not really."

"Good, come on."

"Why, what's going on?"

"Fresh blood."

They took the 6th Avenue freeway west into Golden, then headed north on Highway 93, riding parallel to the Rocky Mountain foothills under a cloudless Colorado sky. Five miles later, in unincorporated Jefferson County, they turned west on a gravel road that rolled towards the mountains through a treeless terrain.

A mile or so later they came to where they were headed.

Six or seven police cars punctuated the spot.

Coventry pulled in at the end of the line and killed the engine.

They checked in with a scribe and then got escorted by a small but serious looking sheriff by the name of Ben Baxter out to the gravesite, which was about fifty yards off the road.

"The dumb shit buried her in an arroyo," Baxter said. "The rain last night uncovered her."

Coventry nodded.

The gravesite, so far, hadn't been disturbed.

The woman still laid in the ravine, her face sticking out, plus one hand and part of an arm. The rest of her still laid under the dirt, which would have been mud last night, but had mostly dried at this point.

A nail had been pounded into her forehead.

"Looks like he buried her about eight or twelve inches down, is all," Coventry said.

"Right. Not too deep," Baxter said, "which is one of the reasons we called you."

"This is our guy," Coventry said. "No question in my mind."

Baxter nodded.

"It's your case if you want to take the lead," Baxter said. "You guys are better equipped for this stuff anyway. We don't get much of this out here."

"Lucky you," Coventry said. "Sure, we'll take it. You want us to process the scene?"

Baxter shrugged.

"You may as well. We'll support you, of course—whatever you want, just holler."

"Fine," Coventry said. "The first thing I want is everyone back on the road and then move a half mile down, people and vehicles. We'll need casts of everyone's boots, so don't let anyone go anywhere." He looked at a hawk, circling high, riding a wind current. "The interesting thing will be whether there's another body stacked underneath."

"Or nearby," Shalifa added.

Paul Kubiak came out with a Crime Unit and processed the scene in that slow, methodical way of his. As near as they could tell, the body had been buried last night before the rain started, meaning that none of the countless boot marks now in the area were likely to be relevant.

No stacked body was found underneath.

No other gravesites were found nearby.

No pop cans, cigarettes or other such items were discovered in the vicinity.

The grave had been dug with a shovel.

The shovel was no longer there.

With any luck, it got put into the trunk of a car or the back of an SUV after the event, dropping residue. Kubiak took several soil samples to use for comparison later if the opportunity ever arose.

Watching, off to the side, Coventry told Shalifa, "The victim's got a good body. I wouldn't doubt it a bit if she's that stripper you were telling me about."

"Agreed."

"What was her name?"

"I don't remember it off the top of my head, but I have it written down."

"Where?"

She tilted her head, thinking. "In a notepad, on my desk."

"Call headquarters and see if someone can find it," Coventry said. "Then have them run a background check on her."

She wandered off and talked into a cell phone.

Five minutes later she came back. "The stripper's name is Samantha Stamp—stage name Chase," she said. "I called the club to see if she'd shown up for work yet. When I told the guy I was a detective he muttered *bitch* under his breath and hung up."

Coventry frowned.

"That wasn't very nice."

Chapter Seventy

Day Eleven – September 15
Thursday Morning

WHEN HALEY WILDE GOT TO WORK AT 7:15 Thursday morning, she found an envelope on her chair. Inside was an unsigned piece of paper that said: *Go to the Starbucks on the 16th Street Mall at 9:00 a.m. Come alone and don't tell anyone.*

She suspected the note came from the same person who accused Christina Huygh of being a spy.

Fine.

Let's find out who it was.

She showed up five minutes early, didn't see anyone she knew, ordered a latte and took a table by the wall. A Billie Holiday song dripped down from ceiling speakers, painful and lamenting. A few minutes later a man walked over and sat down. He looked vaguely familiar and wore an expensive gray pinstriped suit over a red silk power-tie. He looked to be in his early thirties, thin set, and balder than he should be.

"I'm Conrad Conrad," he said.

She recognized the name.

He was an attorney in the firm.

In the environmental section.

"Sorry to be so mysterious," he said, "but I felt it best that we met somewhere away from the firm. I hope you don't mind."

She shook her head.

"No, this is fine. So what's going on?"

The man looked around, apparently saw no one of interest, and refocused on her. "The word's going around that you're asking questions about Renee Rand," he said. "Maybe even doing an ad hoc investigation of some sort."

She didn't know whether to admit it or not.

But did.

"Of some sort," she said. "Maybe."

"I have some information for you," he said. "But first you have to promise that you won't tell anyone that I told you."

She considered it.

"I don't know what you're going to tell me. So I'm not sure I can promise that."

He frowned.

"It's for your own good," he said.

"Why don't you just tell me what's on your mind?"

He slurped the coffee.

And paused, deciding whether to talk or not.

Then he looked her in the eyes.

"This happened back in March of this year," he said. "I was working late one night, after nine o'clock, and one of the cleaning ladies—an older Hispanic woman—stepped into my office to empty my trash can. I could tell she was upset about something and asked her what was wrong. She said she was in the hallway passing by one of the offices upstairs. The door was closed. She heard a commotion inside and stopped to listen. To her, it sounded like a man was forcing himself on a woman. The woman was telling him to stop. He didn't and she got louder, yelling for him to stop. Then the cleaning lady heard stuff breaking."

"What are you saying? That someone in the firm was raped?"

The man shifted in his seat.

"Let me finish," he said. "I had the cleaning lady take me up and show me the office she was talking about. It turned out to be the office of Renee Rand. When we got there, though, the door was open and no one was inside. There didn't appear to be anything broken."

"Renee Rand?"

"Right."

"Are you saying she was raped?"

The man held up his hands in surrender. "I asked her about it the next day. She said the cleaning lady must have been hallucinating because no such thing happened. She said she wasn't even in the office last night."

"So someone else got raped, then, in Renee's office?"

"Maybe," the man said, "maybe not. I had the feeling that Renee wasn't telling me the truth. So I snooped around a little and found out that her keycard had in fact been used for an exit that evening, meaning she had been there. I never told her that I found out about that, though."

"So she lied to you."

He nodded. "That's my feeling. I don't know if she was actually raped, however, or whether someone just came on to her extra strong. In any event, whatever happened, it was clear that she didn't want to talk about it or do anything about it. Since she didn't press it, I didn't either. You're the only person I've ever told."

"What about the police? After she disappeared? You didn't tell them any of this?"

He shook his head.

"No. And I'm not real proud of that, for the record. I guess I was more concerned about not making a tidal wave inside the firm that would come back to drown me."

She shifted in her seat.

"I have kids in private schools," he added.

"I have to take this to the police," she said. "I'll leave your name out of it. Do you have a problem with that?"

"No. I should have done it myself."

"Okay. By the way, are you the one who left me a note saying that Christina Huygh is a spy?"

No.

He wasn't.

In fact, he hardly even knew Christina Huygh.

CONRAD CONRAD LEFT AND WAS ALMOST OUT THE DOOR when Haley caught up to him. "Who was the man in Renee's office that night?" she asked.

"I don't have a clue."

"Do you remember the date when it happened?"

"Not really."

"You said you were staying late," she said. "Would you be able to look on your calendar and figure out what day it was?"

He cocked his head.

"Probably."

"Good. Let me know."

Chapter Seventy-One

Day Eleven – September 15
Thursday Morning

JACK DEGAN WOKE AROUND 9:00 A.M., feeling like a dried leather shoe. His muscles screamed from burying the tow-truck woman out in the goddamned rock-infested mountains yesterday. Burying the stripper later in the day had been a lot easier, but had still taken its toll.

He looked at Gretchen, still sleeping.

Nice.

He stretched and hit the shower, getting the water as hot as he could stand it. Unfortunately, today he'd need those same muscles again, to bury the tattoo woman.

He didn't care.

Putting an end to that phase of his life would be worth it, whatever the cost.

When he got out of the shower Gretchen was up and dressed in jeans and a T-shirt, with hot coffee made.

"So what's the plan today?" she asked.

"I have some surveillance work I need to do," he said.

"Can I come?"

He laughed.

"No," he said. "It's all confidential stuff."

"Can you drop me off downtown first, then?"

"Why?"

"The Granada won't start," she said. "And I don't feel like sitting around here by myself all day."

He nodded.

Then pulled out his wallet and gave her a thousand dollars.

"In case you see something you need to have," he said.

They ate breakfast.

Then she gave him a long slow blowjob, until he came in her mouth.

He dropped her off downtown, gave her a long sloppy kiss, turned the radio to an oldies station, and then wove his way into the mountains towards the cabin.

ON THE WAY SWOFFORD CALLED WITH BAD NEWS.

"The client's schedule got all jacked up yesterday and he didn't make it into town," Swofford said. "So we're going to Plan B, which is, you go up to the cabin and feed the woman, let her go to the bathroom, walk her around a little, etcetera. Basically, just keep her alive and in relatively good shape."

Degan slammed his hand on the dashboard.

"This is nuts," he said.

Swofford couldn't agree more but said, "We have no choice."

"Yeah?" Degan said. "Well you know what I think? I think that when I get up there this morning I'm going to find that the poor woman choked on her own tongue last night."

Swofford laughed.

"I hear you, but this guy's paid a lot of money. We owe him

some indulgence."

"This is more trouble than it's worth," Degan said.

"Sometimes that's the way it works," Swofford said.

Degan shifted thoughts.

"I scooped out this new one—Tianca Holland—last night," he said. "She's a rich bitch, meaning she's going to be a lot trickier than the average snatch."

"I know that."

"A *lot* trickier," Degan emphasized. "I'm thinking twenty-five grand trickier."

Swofford laughed.

"Nice try, but I've already given the client a fixed price. Here's the good news, though. No rush with her. Take your time, do it right, and then let me know when you have her. The client's totally flexible on the timing. Don't hurt her, though. She can't be marked up."

"Has he paid yet?"

"Yep, cold hard cash."

"Good."

"As soon as you have her, let me know and I'll get your cut to you."

Suddenly a deer appeared on the road.

From out of nowhere.

Just standing there, staring at the vehicle.

Degan hit the brakes as hard as he could.

Chapter Seventy-Two

Day Eleven – September 15
Thursday Evening

THE CLUB, CHEEKS, WAS PACKED when Bryson Coventry showed up shortly after six o'clock. Strippers were on all five stages and lots more were grinding out in the crowd, giving table dances. He ordered a Bud Light, leaned against the bar and then called Shalifa Netherwood at home.

"Do me a favor," he said. "Call Cheeks again and see if the same guy answers who called you a bitch before. Then call me back and let me know."

"Why? What's going on?"

"Just a little something."

A minute later the phone behind the bar rang. A large man with a shaved head and a muscle shirt answered, muttered a few words, and then hung up. Ten seconds later Coventry's phone rang.

"The same guy answered," she said.

"Okay. Thanks."

He watched the dancers, particularly the ones giving the table dances. They were friendly, very friendly in fact, rubbing their crotches in the guys' faces and occasionally sticking a hand down someone's pants.

Suddenly a woman appeared in front of him. By the time he registered her as there, she had already put her arms around his neck and brought her lips to within inches of his.

"I've got a special table dance that I've been saving just for you," she said.

"Oh yeah?"

She rubbed her stomach against his.

"We can go over there, in the corner," she said, pointing. "You can feel my pussy if you want."

"How much?"

"Only ten dollars."

Coventry pulled out his wallet and handed her a ten-dollar bill, but remained leaning against the bar. "There's a dancer who works here called Chase," he said. "Do you know her?"

"No."

"Her real name's Samantha Stamp."

"Don't know her."

Coventry pulled a photograph out of his shirt pocket. "This is her," he said.

She looked at it, then at him. "She works nights," she said. "I work days."

Coventry nodded.

"Who's in charge around here?"

COVENTRY ENDED UP IN A BACK ROOM three times smaller than it should have been. The walls closed in as soon as the manager, a man named John Stevens, shut the door. Coventry explained that the body of a woman had been found today, a woman who they subsequently identified as Samantha Stamp—

Chase. He explained that he'd be in the club tonight talking to the dancers to see if anyone had any information.

The manager himself had none.

But had no problem with Coventry talking to the women.

"You can use my office if you want," he added.

Coventry chuckled and stood up. "One more thing," he said. "One of my associates called here today. The man who answered hung up on her when she identified herself as a detective. He called her a bitch."

The manager stared at Coventry and said nothing.

"It turns out that it's the guy behind the bar, the one with the shaved head," Coventry said. "I'm sure that's not the way you do business around here."

The manager agreed.

"Absolutely not," he said.

"So my suspicion is that you're going to walk out there right now and fire his ass," Coventry said. "The rest of my suspicion is that I won't call vice and have them live down here for the next month."

The man considered it.

"Both your suspicions are right," he said.

Coventry shook his hand. "Good. Be sure he knows why you're letting him go. And be sure to point me out to him. If he has a problem with anything, he can come over and talk to me about it face-to-face."

The manager frowned.

"The guy's dangerous," he said.

Coventry headed out of the room and said over his shoulder, "Be sure you point me out."

The day dancers knew nothing. The night shift started wandering into the club shortly before seven and disappeared into a back room. They showed up in the crowd a half hour later, looking drunk and stoned and loose. Coventry talked to six of them before he finally found someone with something to say, a petite black-haired beauty who went by the name of Mercedes.

She had actually talked to Chase on Monday, the day she disappeared, because they were supposed to go to the gym together. Chase told her that she had to cancel to do a trick that afternoon, someone from the club who was paying her big bucks.

"That's all I know," she added. "I never heard from her again."

"What'd she say about the guy she was going to meet?"

Mercedes shrugged.

"Nothing. Just that she was going to meet him."

"She didn't mention a name?"

"No."

"Or describe him?"

"No."

"Where were they going to meet?"

She held her hands up in surrender.

"I don't know."

The shaved-head man wasn't behind the bar any more—now he sat on the other side of it, getting drunk and staring Coventry down. Coventry looked him dead in the eyes and then headed for the men's room.

Come on, asshole. Bring it on.

Chapter Seventy-Three

Day Eleven – September 15
Thursday Noon

OVER THE LUNCH HOUR HALEY WILDE left the office early, ran the six blocks to her car, took I-25 northbound to the Boulder Turnpike and then headed west. She tried to call Bryson Coventry several times on the way but he never answered. Directly ahead through the windshield loomed the Rocky Mountains, getting bigger with each passing mile. Boulder sat at the foot of the mountains, with good views of the Flatirons from almost everywhere.

She drove around until she found a free two-hour parking spot, several blocks beyond The Hill, across Broadway. Then she hoofed it down to the University of Colorado campus.

The day was gorgeous.

Students were everywhere.

Every single one of them was dressed for comfort.

Sarah Rand was waiting for her on the front steps of the library. While she wasn't the splitting image of her sister, Renee Rand, there was enough of a resemblance that Haley recognized her. She looked to be about twenty-three, tanned and fit. After greetings and chitchat they walked through campus, surrounded by the timelessly beautiful rock buildings.

"Like I indicated on the phone," Haley said, "I'm trying to figure out what happened to Renee. This morning I got a disturbing report that Renee might have been raped one night at the law firm, on March 14th to be precise."

Then she told Conrad Conrad's story, without disclosing his name.

"If that's true," Haley said, "I have to think that it's somehow involved in why she disappeared, which was only two weeks later. My gut tells me that if she confided in anyone about what happened that night, it was you."

Over in a grass field, four guys played Frisbee.

Carefree.

"If she did tell me something," Sarah said, "why would I tell you?"

Haley shrugged.

"Because I'm trying to find out what happened. She was my friend."

Sarah shifted a worn backpack to her other shoulder.

"Let me think about it for a minute," Sarah said. "I need to figure out if Renee would want me to talk to you or not."

They walked in silence.

Then Sarah said, "She was sexually assaulted, but not raped, at least technically, since there was no penetration."

"By who?"

"She wouldn't say but I always had the impression it was someone she knew. My guess is either another attorney in the firm or a client. Anyway, the whole thing really had an impact on her, but at the same time she almost seemed to defend the guy, saying he was drunk, lonely, stuff like that. She couldn't stay at the firm though, she knew that much. She was already floating her resume when she disappeared."

"Did she report it?"

"You mean to the police? No."

"How about to the law firm?"

Sarah exhaled.

"I told her to," Sarah said, "but I don't know if she ever did or not. She was ashamed by the whole thing. She said that if word ever got out then her career as a lawyer would be over, especially if someone put a spin on it and put the blame on her. I told her she was nuts but couldn't get her to see things the way she should." Sarah looked into Haley's eyes. "I'm only telling you this now because if it does have something to do with her death, then it's time to get it out in the open. You seem like a genuinely good person."

"I don't know if I'd say *genuinely*."

Sarah laughed.

"I'm not even sure I'd say *good*."

"But *person*," Sarah said. "You'd at least say that."

Haley nodded.

"That much I can admit to."

Haley had a ton of work on her desk and would already be cutting the day short, even if she headed back to the office right now. But it looked like Sarah needed to talk.

"You want to get some coffee?" Haley asked.

Chapter Seventy-Four

Day Eleven – September 15
Thursday Afternoon

Jack Degan's vechicle almost stopped in time but didn't, hitting the deer directly in the chest. The animal shot backwards, landed on its side, muscled itself up in a panic and then limped into the mountainside.

"Shit!"

Degan got out and found the front end nearly destroyed. The hood had buckled and couldn't be opened. Antifreeze dripped onto the ground, not a lot, but enough to indicate a puncture in the radiator or a hose.

"Dumb-ass animal!"

He picked up a rock and threw it at the deer. Astonishingly, he actually hit it, and not just anywhere, but right in the back of the head. The animal immediately fell to the ground and didn't get up.

"Serves you right."

He got back in the car and squealed off. He already had enough goddamn stuff on his plate without this. When he arrived at the cabin twenty minutes later he left the engine running and looked under the front end, trying to determine how fast the radiator was draining. The leak, while still present, was barely perceptible. The gauges reported a normal engine temperature.

Okay.

Good.

Maybe things weren't as bad as he thought.

He turned off the engine and stepped to the front door of the cabin. It was locked, as it should be. Everything appeared to be exactly as he'd left it. He used his key to enter and walked straight into the bedroom.

The tattoo woman—Mia Avila—was still tied to the bed, exactly as she should be. Except unlike the last time he'd seen her, she was awake now.

The drugs would have worn off long ago.

"Visitor," he said.

Her face twisted into a panic.

But he focused more on the urine smell coming from the sheets. He almost slapped her but reminded himself that it wasn't her fault. No one could have held it that long.

He untied her and let her shower while he watched. Then he put her in a fresh T-shirt and let her eat until she'd had her fill—cereal, fruit, a sandwich, yogurt and lots of coffee. He made her remove all the old bedding. Then he flipped the mattress over and let her put fresh sheets on.

She must have sensed that he wasn't there to kill her because the stress fell off her face.

She looked pretty, actually.

Especially considering what she'd been through.

"Can we go outside?" she asked.

Degan didn't like the idea.

"Just for a few minutes?" she added. "I won't try anything, I promise. There's no air in here. I can hardly breathe."

She was right, actually.

It was stuffy as hell.

"Fine," he said. "But first I'm going to tie your hands behind your back."

She nodded.

"No problem."

"And if you try anything . . ."

"I won't, you have my word."

As he tied her hands he wondered if he should tie her feet too. No, that wasn't necessary. She couldn't go anywhere barefoot. The mountains would eat her feet alive within ten steps. They ended up sitting on the steps of the back porch, with the sun on their faces. Degan took his knife out and tossed it from one hand to the other. Then he spotted a fairly straight stick and whittled it into a spear.

"Thanks," the woman said. "I really appreciate this."

"No problem."

His thoughts drifted to the things he needed to do—keep Mia secured until the client killed her, and then dispose of her body; snatch the rich-bitch Tianca Holland; dispose of the tow truck; deal with the damage to the car; get Gretchen out to California where they could finally kick back and relax.

Suddenly he heard a vehicle.

It pulled to the front of the cabin and stopped.

Degan immediately put the knife to Mia's throat.

"Don't make a goddamn sound!"

She nodded.

DEGAN JERKED HER UP BY THE ARM to get her back into the cabin. Then something bad happened. The doorknob wouldn't turn. The little shit was locked! He'd left the keys on the kitchen counter.

He pulled off his T-shirt, ripped off a section and gagged the woman.

She didn't resist.

In fact she held perfectly still.

Someone knocked on the front door. "Anyone home?"

Degan poked the knife into Mia's throat. "Lay down on your stomach and don't move!"

She obeyed.

Degan walked around the side of the house, gave her one last threatening look before he disappeared around the corner, and found the owner's son standing at the front door—the same kid who met Degan at the cabin initially, to show him around and get his money.

Degan stuffed the knife behind his back and smiled as nonchalantly as he could.

"Hey, what's up?"

"There you are," the kid said.

"Right. What's going on?"

"My dad wanted me to swing by and give you a heads up that someone from the state's going to be coming by to take a sample from the well," the kid said.

"Why?"

"I don't know."

"My dad just wanted to be sure you knew it was coming, in case you came back and found a car here or something like that."

Degan nodded.

"Tell your dad thanks, I really appreciate it."

The kid headed towards his car.

"When are they coming?" Degan asked.

The kid stopped walking and tried to think. Finally he gave up. "I can't remember. Sometime within the next week, I think."

"Okay. Thanks again."

As soon as the kid pulled away, Degan ran around the side of the cabin.

The woman was gone.

He looked at the mountains.

In every direction.

And saw her nowhere.

"Bitch!" he shouted as loud as he could. "Get your ass back here right now!"

Chapter Seventy-Five

Day Eleven – September 15
Thursday Evening

IT WAS DARK OUTSIDE AND BRYSON COVENTRY was alone in homicide, feeling the weight of the day, when the phone company finally faxed over Chase's cell phone records. On Monday she'd received about fifteen calls.

Monday was the day she disappeared.

Coventry dialed the people who had called the woman and got their stories as to why they called, what they talked about and whether Chase mentioned anything about meeting a man for sex.

He took notes, but none of substance.

One of the calls came from a payphone north of Pueblo.

Coventry dialed the number.

No one answered.

The oversized industrial clock on the wall, the one with the twitchy second hand, said 9:10 p.m. Overhead, a florescent bulb hummed. He stood up, dumped a cup of cold coffee into the snake plant, and turned the lights out as he left.

Then he headed south on I-25.

HE WAS PASSING THROUGH THE TECH CENTER, trying to stay out of the way of maniac drivers, when Shalifa Netherwood called for an update. He filled her in and was almost about to hang up when a stray thought entered his head.

"Hey," he said, "before you go, help me out on something. One of the calls to Chase on Monday came from a public phone north of Pueblo. For some reason, that's been nagging me. It means something but I don't know what."

"Pueblo?"

"Right."

"We have a missing person down there," she said.

Coventry knew he should have remembered that as soon as she said it. Early in the case he'd asked Shalifa to keep track of anyone who turned up missing in Colorado. She subsequently told him about a Pueblo woman. He'd dismissed it as not much more than a curiosity at the time because the location was too far away and all of the bodies found at the railroad spur had been white.

"I remember," he said. "What's her status? Did she ever show back up?"

"I don't know."

"It'd be interesting, if she hasn't."

FIFTEEN MINUTES LATER, when he arrived at Tianca's, a strange car sat in the driveway—a white Jaguar. When he knocked on the door no one answered. He tried the doorknob, found it unlocked and stepped inside.

He called for her.

No answer.

He grabbed a Bud Light out of the fridge, took off his weapon and put it on the kitchen counter, and finally found Tianca out back in the hot tub, naked, in the company of another equally naked and well-endowed young woman with long, wet, jet-black hair.

"Hey, stranger," Tianca said. "We've been waiting for you. This is Monica."

The woman stood up, displaying a totally shaved body, and leaned over to shake his hand. When she did, she suddenly grabbed his arm with both hands and yanked him into the water.

When his head came to the surface both of the women were laughing.

"Be careful of her," Tianca warned. "She has a bit of a wild side."

Coventry shook water out of his ear.

"So I see."

"Now get out of those clothes," she said.

He hesitated.

"You said I could have another woman," Tianca said. "This is her. But we haven't done anything yet, because I'm not going to do anything unless you're with me." She squeezed Monica's breast and then looked back at Coventry. "And now you are."

The two women kissed.

Long and deep and passionately.

Then Tianca looked back at Coventry.

"You can join in or you can watch. Your choice."

Chapter Seventy-Six

Day Eleven – September 15
Thursday Evening

WHEN HALEY WILDE ARRIVED back at the law firm after meeting with Sarah Rand at CU, she called Austin Gray and asked if his office door was still open.

He laughed.

"Yeah, but not until tonight," he said. "I'm totally slammed all day."

"Tonight's fine. That way if you fire me, at least I can sleep in."

"Let me tell you where I'll be."

That evening, after supper, she headed to Chatfield State Park, paid an expensive entry fee, and then drove all the way around the lake to the marina. The Accord ran sluggish, as if twenty horses had been pulled from under the hood and were now being dragged behind instead.

"If you break, I'm leaving your ass here," she said.

The car sputtered.

"I'm serious," she added.

The marina turned out to be a lot bigger than she expected. There must have been three or four hundred slips. Tons of geese walked around, not showing a bit of fear. A gentle but steady wind blew out of the northwest, surprisingly warm. Austin Gray met her at the gate, escorted her to a thirty-foot sailboat moored at the end of D-Dock, and helped her aboard.

"When I want to forget everything, this is where I come," he said. "This isn't mine, by the way. It belongs to Nick Willoughby, the CEO of Omega."

Haley recognized the name—Omega.

That was the client that had the big antitrust judgment against Tomorrow, Inc. The one Derek Bennett represented. The one that Robert Yates was going to take over, before he and his daughter got killed while playing Frisbee in Central Park.

Haley couldn't believe the vessel and headed for the cabin.

"Can I go inside?" she asked.

"Absolutely."

FIFTEEN MINUTES LATER THEY HAD THE BOAT on the lake, tilted fifteen degrees to starboard, with the mainsail and jib taut with wind.

He let her take the wheel, disappeared below, and then returned with two glasses of white wine.

They passed a small fishing boat.

"See that guy over there, baiting that hook?" Austin asked. "I've know him for years. At one time he was just an amateur baiter. Now he's a master baiter."

She laughed.

They sailed for over an hour, long enough for her to learn how to work the lines. Then they dropped the sails and bobbed. A flock of eight or ten geese floated over looking for a handout. Austin went below and returned with a loaf of bread. Haley threw pieces into the water and decided that this was as good a time as any to get to the point of the meeting.

"I had some information fall into my lap today," she said. "The long and short of it is, Renee Rand was sexually assaulted in her office on March 14th. It happened late, after nine o'clock or thereabouts. It wasn't rape but it was definitely an assault."

Austin frowned.

"What makes you think so?"

"Renee's sister told me."

"Sarah?"

"Right."

He took a long swallow of wine. "I already know about it," he said. "She reported it to me back when it happened."

"She did?"

"Yes," he said.

"Who did it to her?"

He looked blank. "She wouldn't say. I told her to take it to the police but she didn't want to. She was embarrassed and felt it would hurt her career if the word got out. She didn't want me to press it so, out of respect for her and against my better judgment, I didn't."

"She disappeared just two weeks after that," Haley said.

"I know."

"There's got to be a connection."

He didn't seem convinced.

"Maybe, in theory. But keep in mind that she got killed by some psycho maniac who cut her head off," he said. "That's a guy in a totally different league."

She stopped throwing bread.

Every goose on the water watched her, waiting.

SHE WASN'T SURE WHETHER SHE SHOULD BRING UP what she was about to, but couldn't hold back any longer.

"I followed Derek Bennett the other night," she said. "He goes to a place called Tops & Bottoms, which is an S&M place, and sticks pins into women."

Austin looked shocked and studied her face, as if trying to decide if she was messing with him.

She wasn't.

"That's the kind of guy who could saw someone's head off," she said.

Austin didn't disagree.

"Assume he's the one who sexually assaulted Renee," she said. "Two weeks pass and she hasn't reported it to the police yet, but then he finds out that she's in the process of leaving the firm. He starts to get nervous about whether she'll change her mind after he doesn't have so much of a grip on her any more."

"So he takes her out," Austin said, finishing the concept.

"Exactly. And has fun doing it."

Chapter Seventy-Seven

Day Eleven – September 15
Thursday Afternoon

JACK DEGAN FRANTICALLY SEARCHED the mountainside for Mia Avila, gripping the knife so tight that his fingers hurt, already planning what he'd do to her for putting him through this.

"Get back here you bitch!"

No response.

"All you're doing is making me mad!"

Silence.

There were too many trees, too many boulders, too many goddamn places to hide. He ran from one to the next, hoping beyond hope to find her cowering on the ground and scared out of her mind.

His lungs burned from the mad dashing but he didn't care.

She couldn't have gone far, not in those shoeless little feet of hers. The whole mountain was covered in rocks and twigs and pine needles and other pointy things. She might start out with enough feet to go for a ways, but before long they'd be raw and bloody and stuck full of needles. She'd have to stop no matter how desperate she might be.

She was here somewhere.

Where?

He covered ground as quickly as he could, no longer shouting now that he realized he was only giving his position away.

He hunted quietly, quickly, trying to remain confident that sooner or later he'd spring around the corner and grab her by the hair.

His legs grew increasingly heavy.

His lungs no longer got enough oxygen.

He was no longer just tired.

He was slipping into a deeper and deeper state of exhaustion.

He stopped and sat on a boulder, just to catch his breath for a second. Bad thoughts pounded his brain. *He might not catch her. She might actually escape.*

He knew he should stand up and continue the search.

He was too tired to move.

But muscled himself up anyway.

HE SEARCHED EVERY NOOK AND CRANNY that she could have possibly made it to without being seen, found her nowhere, and then finally gave up and went back to the cabin.

Time to get the hell out of there.

Then, shit!

A large puddle of green antifreeze sat under the car. He kicked the side of the door, giving it a huge dent while sending a bone-compressing shockwave up his leg, all the way up to his hip.

"Goddamn it!"

He'd have to get the hood up to fill the radiator with water.

He opened the driver's door, reached under the dash and

activated the hood release, and then tried to muscle the hood up. It didn't budge.

"Son of a bitch!"

He picked up a rock and threw it at the vehicle, shattering the windshield.

Then he stormed into the cabin and punched a hole in the wall. He was shaking the pain out of his knuckles when he noticed that the woman's shoes were missing.

They should be on the floor.

Right there next to the couch.

He'd put them there himself.

And then almost tripped over 'em ten times.

Clever girl.

But not clever enough.

He immediately bolted out the front door and ran down the gravel driveway towards the road.

Chapter Seventy-Eight

Day Twelve – September 16
Friday Morning

BRYSON COVENTRY WAS ALREADY UP AND DRIVING south on I-25, heading towards Pueblo, when the sun broke over the eastern plains and washed the Front Range with a soft golden hue. He saw about fifteen different places where he would like nothing more than to pull over and set up an easel. There was something about the light in the fall, particularly the early morning light, that brought out the color of things.

Shalifa Netherwood slept in the passenger seat.

His thoughts turned to the hot tub incident last night, the one he didn't participate in but did watch. The sex show with Tianca and the black-haired beauty had been erotic and intense, and should have aroused him, but didn't. All he could think of the entire time was that he wished she didn't need things like that in her life.

Maybe she was too wild for him.

Maybe no one person could satisfy her.

He raked his hair back with his fingers and decided to just take things one day at a time.

When he passed the Air Force Academy lots of small single-engine planes buzzed the sky. Shortly thereafter he got bogged down in the Colorado Springs rush hour, but finally broke out the other side and entered that arid stretch of undeveloped land that escorted weary travelers into Pueblo.

He didn't know much yet about the missing Pueblo woman, Mia Avila, other than she was fairly young, ran a tattoo shop, and vanished without a trace eight days ago—Thursday of last week, to be precise.

The stripper—Chase—disappeared four days later.

On Monday.

The same day she received a telephone call from payphone just north of Pueblo.

Then showed up later with a nail in her forehead.

The big question is whether Mia Avila got one of the other nails in the box.

SHALIFA NETHERWOOD WOKE UP just as they passed Eagleridge Drive on the northern edge of the city.

She yawned, stretched, and said, "I'm starved."

Twenty minutes later they were in a booth at the Grand Prix Restaurant, with smothered burritos and piping hot coffee, meeting with a young Hispanic woman by the name of Detective Julia Torres.

She had a good dose of hunt in her blood.

Whereas most relatively fresh detectives might get overly excited at the possibility of being connected to a case as big as the one in Denver, she stayed focused on the facts.

The way a seasoned hunter would.

"Everything in the tattoo shop was pretty much normal," Torres said. "There was no indication of a struggle or abduction.

Nothing was broken. There was no blood on the floor. Nothing was taken, even though there was lots of stuff that would have been, if it had been a burglary. The sign in the window was flipped to Closed and the front door was locked. Her car was still parked out front."

"So she left with someone," Shalifa offered.

The woman sipped coffee and nodded.

"It appears that way, which of course suggests that she knew the person," Torres said. "Maybe she shut down for lunch but never made it back for some reason. We just don't know."

Coventry frowned.

"Did she keep an appointment book?" he asked.

"We didn't find one."

He raised an eyebrow.

"You think she'd have one to schedule tattoos," he said.

Torres agreed and said, "That's one of the things so far that doesn't fit."

"Maybe someone knew he wasn't going to bring her back, and also knew he was in her appointment book, so he took that too," Coventry suggested.

"Possibly and maybe even likely," Torres said. "But we haven't been able to come up with a brilliant plan to recreate it."

Coventry nodded.

And couldn't shine any bright ideas on the subject either.

"Can we have a look at the place, after breakfast?"

"Absolutely. I brought the key with me."

Coventry took a swallow of coffee.

"Good stuff."

Shalifa chuckled. "As if you've *ever* seen a cup of coffee you didn't like."

INSIDE THE MISSING WOMAN'S TATTOO SHOP, following a thorough walk around, Coventry agreed that there was no indication of foul play.

In the back room he spotted a safe.

"Have you opened that yet?" he asked.

Torres shook her head. "Not yet."

Coventry cocked his head, wondered if there was any reason why the shop's appointment book would be inside, and decided that there wasn't.

"We lifted some prints off the front door and matched a few of them to names," Torres added. "We interviewed those people but didn't find anything that got us excited. It's all in the file."

Coventry nodded.

He'd read every word of it later.

Okay.

Now what?

The scene at the railroad spur jumped into his thoughts—four women in two graves. Assuming that Chase and Mia Avila were somehow connected, that still only made two women.

"Have any other women in Pueblo shown up missing?" he asked.

The young detective retreated in thought.

"Not that I'm aware of," she said.

They stepped outside and locked the door behind them. Three Harleys rumbled up the street and then disappeared in the other direction.

"Oh, that reminds me," Torres said, "there is one other woman who has technically dropped off the radar screen, but we're pretty sure why."

Coventry spotted a twig on the ground, picked it up and snapped it.

"Who's that?"

"A local prostitute named Gretchen Smith."

Coventry looked her straight in the eyes, because Chase had been a prostitute in a way, and in fact disappeared the day she went to meet a client.

"Tell me about Gretchen Smith."

"WE'RE WORKING ANOTHER CASE INVOLVING A BIKER who got beat to death on his driveway," Torres said. "First he got his face punched in, almost beyond recognition, and then got his head smashed in—we think with a rock, although we never found it. Anyway, it turns out that he had a fairly serious altercation with an Indian in a bar a couple of nights before that."

"An Indian?"

"Well," she said, "maybe I spoke too fast because we don't know that for sure. What we do know is dark skin and a long black ponytail, and half the people we talked to thought he was an Indian. Anyway, he's a person of interest."

"Okay."

"He's apparently big enough and strong enough to do what got done," she added.

"Got it."

"But there's a side issue," she said. "The victim and a couple of his friends reportedly raped Gretchen Smith at some point in the past, although nothing ever came of it legally. It was pretty common knowledge that she'd take her revenge if she ever got a chance. So, some of the victim's biker friends were looking to 'interview' her to find out if she was behind it somehow. When we found that out, we contacted her and told her she'd probably be safer if she got out of town until the whole thing blew over. As far as we can tell, she took our advice, because she checked out of the hotel she was staying at and no one's seen her since."

"Maybe the bikers found her," Coventry suggested.

Torres shrugged.

"I doubt it," she said. "There's no buzz around town to that effect."

Chapter Seventy-Nine

Day Twelve – September 16
Friday Morning

ON THE WAY TO WORK FRIDAY MORNING, Haley Wilde noticed that the Accord's gas gauge was on empty, below empty in fact. Luckily she had enough fumes left to get her to a station where she prepaid $20 cash and filled up while "Sweet Child of Mine" played on the radio. She wore dark green Dockers and a white cotton blouse, after learning last week that Fridays were casual dress at the firm. When she got to the parking lot twenty minutes later she discovered she was a dollar short. So she drove over to the side streets on the far side of Broadway until she found a 2-hour parking spot and then hoofed it double-time to the firm.

When she got there she didn't go up to the office.

Instead, she went to Parking Level 3, where the firm had several reserved spots, and hid behind a van in the corner. She stayed there for over an hour.

Feeling a lot more like a thief than a lawyer.

But she eventually got what she wanted.

Namely, a look at the faces of the people who drove the law firm's silver BMWs.

When she finally arrived at her office an envelope sat on her chair. Inside, as before, she found a computer-printed piece of paper warning her that Christina Huygh was a spy. This time, however, instead of shredding it she marched into Christina's office, shut the door, and handed it to her.

"This is the second one of these that someone left on my chair," she said.

CHRISTINA HUYGH HAD NO IDEA what the letter meant. She did know, however, that she wasn't a spy and that the whole thing was a lie.

A vicious lie.

Totally preposterous.

Obviously spread by someone with an agenda—Derek Bennett, no doubt, since he was the one with something to gain by driving a wedge between Haley and Christina.

"That means he knows what we're up to," Haley said.

"Agreed. But how much? And how does he know?"

Haley had no idea.

Unless he had a camera in his office, or something like that.

Then she changed subjects.

SHE TOLD CHRISTINA about her meeting yesterday with Sarah Rand at CU, who reported that her sister Renee had been sexually attacked in her office.

"I know in my heart that Derek Bennett was the one who did it," Haley said. "My guess is that he threatened her life to keep her quiet."

Christina frowned.

"Agreed," she said. "But it will be impossible to prove it, now that Renee's dead and we no longer have her testimony."

"Fine. We get him for her murder, then."

LATER THAT MORNING, Haley shut her office door, dialed Bryson Coventry and told him everything she knew, including her theory that Derek Bennett sexually assaulted Renee Rand one night in her office. And then later cut her head off when she started to leave the firm, just to be absolutely sure that she didn't change her mind about going to the police.

Coventry asked her a lot of questions.

But he was all over the board.

As if struggling with a way to fit it into a bigger picture.

He was almost about to hang up when he said, "What about the BMWs?"

"Oh, right, I almost forgot. Derek Bennett definitely has one of them, the one with Colorado plate number BMW 4."

"Hold on, I'm writing it down . . ."

"By the way," she added. "You can't tell anybody about any of this."

Chapter Eighty

Day Twelve – September 16
Friday Morning

JACK DEGAN SLOWLY MUSCLED HIS WAY OUT OF BED, the victim of too much alcohol last night. At first he couldn't get his bearings, then recognized the farmhouse. Gretchen was already awake and making noise in the kitchen.

He couldn't remember his mouth ever being this dry. He drank a full glass of water, then another.

It tasted like crap.

But already his mouth didn't feel quite so much like sandpaper.

He took a hot shower and then Gretchen filled his stomach with pancakes and coffee, after which he started to feel like a human being again.

To top it off, she led him into the bedroom and gave him a really good blowjob.

YESTERDAY HAD BEEN A BITCH, but someone must like him because everything turned out okay in the end. He managed to catch the woman, Mia Avila, before she made it down to Highway 119. Then he dragged her ass back to the cabin, beat the shit out of her and tied her to the bed.

With some effort, he finally managed to pry the hood of the car up and got the radiator filled with water. Then he put the bitch in the trunk, drove her to the farmhouse, pumped her full of drugs and chained her securely in the cab of the tow truck in the barn.

He limped the Nissan back to Avis, explained what had happened, and learned that the damage was covered under rental insurance that they'd tacked on without him knowing it. He rented another car, this time a green VW Jetta, and picked Gretchen up downtown as if nothing had happened.

He celebrated by getting drunk with Gretchen last night.

Although she didn't know they were celebrating.

She thought they were just having a good time.

THAT WAS YESTERDAY. Now, today, he had all that behind him and was the owner of a happy gut and an even happier dick.

"So what's the plan?" Gretchen asked.

He smiled and slapped her ass.

"Get in the car and you'll find out."

She wrestled him to the floor and pinned his arms above his head. "Why? Where we going?"

"Nowhere, if you don't get off."

"Not 'till you tell me."

"Someplace you're going to like."

She rubbed her crotch on his chin.

"I'm already someplace I like."

They took Highway 93 south into downtown Golden, where the air smelled like hops and barley. Degan found a liquor store—one with a sign in the window that said No Fresher Coors Sold Anywhere—and bought enough Jack to get them through the next few days. Then they took Old Golden Road east and ended up a Lexus dealership across the street from the Colorado Mills Mall.

"What's going on?" Gretchen asked as they pulled in.

Degan put a confused look on his face.

"I don't know, but as long as we're here why don't we have a look around?"

He wore tattered jeans and a black muscle shirt that showed off his tattoo. Throw in the ponytail and the scar and he looked like the last person on the face of the earth who would want, or could afford, a Lexus. He chatted it up with the salesman and the manager, took a long test drive, and waited for a derogatory insinuation that he couldn't afford it.

When he didn't get it he closed the deal, titled the car in Gretchen's name, had funds wired in from one of his California bank accounts, and then strolled outside with his woman to drink coffee and wait while the dealership detailed the vehicle and gave it a final prep.

Gretchen's face made it all worthwhile.

No one had ever done anything like this for her before.

Not once in her whole life.

Not even close.

"God are you going to get some sex tonight," she said. "Be warned." Then she hugged him tight and cried. He ran his fingers through her hair.

"I love you," she said. "And not just because of the car."

She kept her eyes down.

As if she was afraid she might see a reaction on his face that she didn't want to see.

He looked into her eyes.

"Me too," he said.

"Really?"

He nodded. "I think I have from the start, to tell you the truth."

She buried her head in his chest.

"Of course, I did have a second thought when you bashed that guy's head in with a rock. But that was only for a moment."

She punched him on the arm and said, "Not funny." Then she looked into his eyes and said, "Till death do us part?"

He squeezed her.

"Sounds good to me."

Chapter Eighty-One

Day Twelve – September 16
Friday Morning

WHILE HEADING BACK TO DENVER FROM PUEBLO, Bryson Coventry couldn't get away from maniac drivers to save his life. No matter what lane he was in, or how fast or slow he was going, the rearview mirror always showed some idiot riding his ass. An 18-wheeler looked like it was actually trying to get into the bed of Coventry's truck just as Kate Katona called to report on her investigation of Chase's apartment.

"We found an appointment book," she said. "Unfortunately, nothing was written in it for the day she disappeared."

"Figures."

Coventry swung into the high-speed lane.

The trucker followed.

Goddamn it.

"If I'm reading it right," Katona said, "she did some freelance hooking on the side, but I wouldn't say a lot. When she wrote those appointments down she only used first names. Some had phone numbers and we're checking them out. There are also some appointments for something called T&B, where time is blocked out, anywhere from four to eight hours."

"T&B?" he asked.

"Right."

For some reason that resonated in his brain.

"What's that mean?"

"I don't know. Tim and Bob?"

He chuckled. "That's not giving me a good visual," he said. "Let's make it Tina and Brenda."

They hung up.

Katona called again thirty minutes later, just as Coventry passed Castle Rock.

"Hey," she said. "We found a scrap piece of paper that had a phone number for T&B. It turns out to be a place called Tops & Bottoms."

"Thanks," he said. "You just gave us another tie to our lawyer friend, Derek Bennett."

INSTEAD OF GOING TO THE OFFICE, Coventry and Shalifa went straight to Tops & Bottoms and ended up meeting with a curvy, feminine woman with a soft voice and liquid blue eyes named Rose Abbott. They left an hour later with more than they hoped for. Coventry also had a standing invitation for a free session with the lovely Ms. Abbott any time he wanted.

"We all have fantasies," she said. "Even you."

"Me?"

"Right."

"What are my fantasies?"

She ran her fingers through his hair.

"You call me when you're ready."

HALF AN HOUR LATER they sat in the reception area of Hart, Sanders & Day, LLC, sipping coffee and waiting.

Coventry wasn't sure that this was the smartest thing to do.

His gut told him to slow down, stay hidden, get more evidence, maybe even enough to bring charges. His other gut told him to ignore his first gut, and to stomp on the guy now with hope that he'd crawl under a rock and at least not hurt anyone else for the immediate future.

A contemporary abstract oil painting on the opposite side of the room kept drawing his eye, so he wandered over past the leather chairs, the coffee tables and the fresh flower arrangements to take a look at it. The signature said RABBY. The paint was scooped on with a pallet knife, a half-inch thick in some places. Most of the canvas was fairly smooth and earth toned, a backdrop for the strategically placed pops and rivers of thick bright colors.

A lot of thought had gone into it.

And passion.

It was the kind of piece where the average Joe Blow on the street would look at it and say, *I could do that.*

It was that good.

That deceptively good.

Shalifa walked over and checked out the signature.

"Rabby," she said. "I've heard of that guy. I think his first name's Jim."

"I couldn't paint like that," Coventry said. "Not because it's abstract but because you can tell that he had to set it down and let some parts of it dry before going on. I need to get it done in one sitting and see I have a dud or a keeper."

"Men," she said. "Instant gratification."

He sipped coffee and said, "You make that sound like a bad

thing."

"No, it's okay, except when you're with a woman in the bedroom."

He chuckled, picturing it. "You don't want it there."

"No. Not even close."

THEY FINALLY ENDED UP in Derek Bennett's office with the door closed, sitting in expensive leather chairs. The man was Coventry's size, six-two, maybe even bigger. His suit was loose, but not so loose as to totally hide the troll-like muscles underneath. His shirt was white and stiff. His eyes protruded too far, as if someone tried to suck them out with a vacuum tube.

Paint his head green and he'd be a frog.

"Thanks for seeing us without an appointment," Coventry said. "I'm going to get right to the point. We're investigating two homicides and we noticed that you have connections to both of the victims."

Bennett looked insulted. "Are you saying I'm a suspect?"

"No, nothing like that," Coventry said. "We just have a few questions."

The stress lines on Bennett's face didn't lighten.

"What kind of questions?"

"Well, one of the victims is Renee Rand, and you know her of course," Coventry said.

"*Everyone* who works here knows her," Bennett said.

"I appreciate that."

"Meaning I'm one person of about two hundred and fifty."

Coventry nodded and fought the urge to bring up the other connectors—someone, probably Bennett, half raped Renee one night; Bennett drove a silver BMW, the same kind of car in the photograph from Brad Ripley's safe, the photograph of the building where the four women were killed; and the conversation between Bennett and Jacqueline Moore about a killing, overheard by Haley Wilde. As fun as it would be to whip those little facts out and slap the smugness off Bennett's face, Coventry couldn't do it without fear of implicating the help he'd received from Haley Wilde. So he smiled instead and changed subjects.

"Right," he said. "Lots of people knew Renee. The more curious question I have involves a dead woman by the name of Samantha Stamp, also known as Chase. She was a dancer at a strip club called Cheeks. But that's not what interests me. What interests me is that she also worked part time at a place called Tops & Bottoms. Have you ever heard of that place? Tops & Bottoms?"

The smug expression was gone now.

Totally gone.

Coventry could tell that the man was trying to decide if he should lie or not.

"Why do you ask?"

"Because we talked to the proprietor of that establishment. Certain names came up during that conversation. Yours was one of them." He sipped coffee, letting the implications hang. "The rumor is that you like to stick pins in the girls."

Bennett shot out of his chair, his hands balled in fists, and violently pushed a pile of papers off the desk.

They landed halfway across the room.

Coventry didn't move.

Instead he took another sip of coffee.

"Get your ass out of my office!" Bennett said. Then he looked directly at Shalifa. "That means your ass too."

Coventry stood up, drank the last of the coffee and set the cup gently on the desk. Then he looked Bennett directly in the eyes. "You really shouldn't talk to ladies like that. It could come back to haunt you."

SHALIFA NETHERWOOD DIDN'T SPEAK MUCH on the walk back to the car. Then, right after they almost got run over at Welton by a car bursting through the wrong end of a yellow light, she said, "I think it worked."

Coventry agreed.

"He's running scared. Hopefully scared enough that he'll think twice about doing anything else stupid. I almost decked him, when he talked to you that way," Coventry added.

"I want to be there when we catch his ass," she said. "I want to look him right in the eyes."

ON THE DRIVE BACK TO THE OFFICE Coventry flicked the radio stations as he pulled his phone out to call Haley Wilde. He paused at a song he'd never heard before. The singer had a nasally voice that sounded like Bob Dylan. The lyrics were something about a pump that didn't work because the handles got taken by the vandals. He waited until it finished then dialed Haley.

"I don't know if you heard," he said, "but me and Shalifa were at the firm just a little bit ago, meeting with Derek Bennett. We put some heat on him." He filled her in on the details, including the fact that he'd been careful to keep her out of it. "Here's the reason I'm calling. The guy's a powder keg and he's going to start exploding. If you hear of him doing anything out of the ordinary, and want to tell us about it, that would be fine with us."

"Done deal," she said. "Count on it."

"Thanks." Coventry almost hung up, but said, "Are you still there?"

"Yes."

"Don't do anything stupid," he added. "Just keep your ear to the ground. And don't let anyone know you're doing it. Things are going to start getting really dicey from this point on."

Chapter Eighty-Two

Day Twelve – September 16
Friday Afternoon

HALEY WILDE BROUGHT CHRISTINA HUYGH up to speed on the noose that Coventry was dangling around Bennett's neck. Then they took turns going up to the 45th Floor, ostensibly to visit the dead files room but actually to see if anything weird was happening in Derek Bennett's neck of the woods.

Nothing was.

Nothing obvious, at least.

Bennett was in his office with the door closed.

Mid-afternoon, Haley took a stroll down the 16th Street Mall to clear her head, hugging the sunny side of the street. The city vibrated, with lots more people around than usual, poised on the edge of the weekend.

A deep blue, totally cloudless sky floated overhead.

She ended up sitting on a bench by California Street.

Someone sat down next to her.

When she looked over she couldn't believe who it was.

Jacqueline Moore.

Cruella.

Clearly this wasn't a chance encounter. The power lawyer

must have discovered that Haley was feeding information to Coventry. She was here to fire her.

"We need to talk," Moore said. The tone of her voice was serious. Haley bit her lower lip and tried to appear as if she wasn't afraid.

"Sure," she said. "What's up?"

Moore didn't answer.

Instead she looked around. Her hair appeared to be slightly disheveled and her makeup wasn't as crisp and sharp as normal. Her blouse sagged out of her skirt and could have been tucked in better. The normal confident look in her eyes wasn't there.

"I'm leaving the firm," she said.

Haley studied her, to see if this was some kind of a joke, but found no lies.

"You are?"

Moore nodded. "As soon as I leave here I'm heading back to the office to type up a resignation. With the grapevine the way it is, I have no doubt that everyone will be celebrating by the end of the day."

"Why are you leaving?"

The woman let out a nervous chuckle, as if there was so much to the answer that she didn't even know where to begin. "That's not the question," she said. "The question is, why am I telling you before anyone else?"

Haley cocked her head.

Good point.

"Okay, why?"

"Because I want to be sure I get a chance to warn you before all hell breaks loose. You need to get out of the firm. My advice to you is to go and go quickly, while you still can."

The words shocked Haley.

"Why? What's going on?"

Moore shook her head. "I can't get into it. Just trust me. Your life is in danger." Then she stood up and looked at Haley one last time. "I've done what I could to warn you. If something happens after this, it's not on my shoulders."

Then she walked away.

HALEY SAT THERE FOR A FEW MOMENTS and then stood up and walked in the direction away from the firm. She called Coventry from Civic Center Park and told him what just happened.

"My suspicion is that this is some kind of fallout from the heat we put on Bennett," he said. "Something's going on and I have no idea what it is. But I do know that things are in motion and that I can't have you in harm's way. I don't want you snooping around anymore."

"But . . ."

"No buts," he said. "At this point you're officially out of it."

"But I'm your only inside source."

"Forget it," he said. "It's not going to happen. If I were you I'd think very seriously about getting out of the firm. Right now. Today. In fact if you don't, you're crazy."

SHE HEADED BACK TO THE FIRM, walked into Christina Huygh's office, closed the door and filled her in on everything. Then added, "I had a stray thought, walking back here."

"Oh? What kind of stray thought?"

"It relates to the dead guy in New York—Robert Yates," she said. "Do you remember when we were talking about who might have a motive to kill him, if he was successful in taking over Omega and then merging it with Tomorrow?"

"Yes."

"Well I thought of someone else who has a motive."

"Who?"

"Derek Bennett."

Christina tried to find the connection but couldn't. "I don't follow," she said.

Haley stood up. "I got to make a run to the restroom. You'll figure it out by the time I get back."

BUT CHRISTINA DIDN'T FIGURE IT OUT, so Haley told her. Bennett spent almost all of his time working on Omega cases, his bread-and-butter client. In the antitrust suit brought by Omega against Tomorrow, Bennett had been Omega's pit bull, the dirty dog who didn't play fair, the driving force behind the mega-judgment in favor of Omega and against Tomorrow. If Robert Yates succeeded in his goal of gaining control of Omega and bringing it under the umbrella of Tomorrow, then he'd control Omega's legal work.

Robert Yates, of course, hating Bennett the way he no doubt did, wouldn't give Bennett an ounce of work to save his life.

Bennett would be washed up.

Even Austin Gray wouldn't be able to protect him.

Robert Yates, no doubt, would demand that Bennett be completely removed from the firm as a condition of giving the firm any further work.

"So Bennett killed him. He was smart enough to look into the future and figure out that he was boxed in. So he took Yates out as early as he could, before anyone could figure out that he had a motive."

Christina worked out the details, looking for an inconsistency or a flaw in the theory. "How the hell do you think this stuff up?"

Haley laughed.

"I don't know. It just comes to me."

"You're in the wrong business, lady. There's only one thing that doesn't make sense. Bennett was in Denver when Robert Yates got killed, so he couldn't have done it." She smiled. "Other than that little fact, very good theory."

Haley stood up, put her hands on the desk and leaned across. "Let me rephrase it," she said. "Bennett killed Yates. *By hiring someone to do it.*"

Chapter Eighty-Three

Day Twelve – September 16
Friday Afternoon

JACK DEGAN FOUND A PERFECT GROVE OF TREES in the open space about a half mile behind Tianca Holland's house. He looked around one last time, still saw no one even remotely close, and then laid down flat next to a log. A stick pushed against his stomach. He pulled it out and threw it to the side.

There.

Perfect.

This would work.

He got up long enough to pull a pair of Bushnell binoculars out of the backpack, then flopped back on his belly and pulled in the view.

Damn!

Tianca Holland was in the backyard by the pool, reclined in a lounger, facing his direction, pointing her chin at the sun.

Totally naked.

Nicely tanned.

Her feet were comfortably apart. He studied the area between her legs and decided that he was actually seeing her pussy.

The corner of his mouth turned up.

"Sweet."

The woman was hot. And not just mildly hot, sizzling hot. He already knew that after he snatched her, before he turned her over to the client, he'd spend more than a little quality time with her.

Maybe even a full day.

In fact, definitely a full day.

Maybe two.

He could already feel his cock between her legs.

And sandwiched between her tits.

"Oh, man."

She shifted in the lounger, pulling her arms over her head to tan her armpits.

So nice.

So incredibly sexy.

He pulled the lens away from her long enough to train on the house, looking for a way in. From what he could tell, there were at least three doors on this side of the house. Also, there was a window well on the south edge of the structure, near the back. He could hop down into it and be out of sight, then pry open the window with a crowbar.

Lots of options.

The big issue is whether she had an alarm system. He hadn't seen any signs in her front yard warning of one. Even if she had one, he'd probably be able to get to her pretty fast if he came for her while she was sleeping. Then he could get her out the back, through the open space to his car, and be gone by the time anyone pulled up to the front of the house.

He trained the binoculars back on her.

She was masturbating now.

Keeping the binoculars in his right hand, he shoved his left hand down his pants and rubbed his cock, picturing his cum on her face.

In one minute he was rock hard.

He maintained control, timing it so that he came exactly when she did.

LATER THAT AFTERNOON, Degan was back at the farmhouse, throwing rocks at squirrels and anything else that moved, when Swofford called. "The client's supposed to be getting into Denver soon to finish off the tattoo woman."

"He better be," Degan said. "I'm sick of having her around. She's a serous liability at this point."

"Agreed. I told him twenty-four hours, max. We can't wait any longer than that."

"Good," Degan said. A robin perched on a limb, about fifty feet away, chirping. Degan threw a rock at it, missing by more than five feet but scaring it enough to send it scrambling into the sky. "Also, we got a slight complication at the cabin. Apparently some water guys are going to be coming around to check out the well for some stupid reason. They're only going to be there a couple of minutes and won't need to go into the house or anything, but I'm not sure when they're coming so I moved the woman over to the place I'm staying at in the meantime."

"Smart move. God, nothing's easy."

"You got that right," Degan said. "Anyway, I positioned some wood by the well which they'll have to move, so I'll know when they've been there."

"Well, tomorrow's Saturday," Swofford said. "We won't have to worry about them over the weekend."

Degan agreed.

"Changing subjects, how are you coming along with Tianca Holland?"

"Circling and closing," Degan said.

"Good."

"She's a looker," he added.

"So I hear. Just remember to not mark her up. That's for the client to do. He's very insistent on that."

Chapter Eighty-Four

Day Twelve – September 16
Friday Evening

Jacqueline Moore lived in an expensive penthouse loft on Larimer Street, not far from Coors Field in the heart of LoDo—a place befitting the stature of a senior partner in one of Denver's most established law firms. After work, about six o'clock, Coventry pointed the Tundra towards that loft to have a chat with her.

Mean charcoal clouds blew in and filled the sky.

And dropped rain on the city.

He set the windshield wipers to intermittent, but they made a god-awful noise every time they raked back, so he turned them off and made a mental note to replace the blades.

He wanted to know exactly why Moore had quit the firm. And why she'd warned Haley Wilde that her life was in danger. More importantly, he wanted to confirm that the source of that danger was Derek Bennett. And find out if she had any information as to how or when he might strike.

Jacqueline Moore was definitely in the mix of things.

Dirty.

That was obvious from the conversation in the hallway that

she had with Derek Bennett, referencing a murder, overheard by Haley Wilde and Christina Huygh—that and her strange behavior today. If it turned out that she was only nominally involved, however, maybe he could scare her into turning state's evidence.

Either way he needed to squeeze her.

He circled around the area, caught up in a claustrophobic press of traffic, finally finding an empty spot on Walnut. He used to carry an umbrella in the Tundra but it mysteriously disappeared more than a year ago.

He stepped into the rain, making a mental note for the fifth or sixth time to get another umbrella, and then hoofed it over to the building.

By the time he got there he was soaked.

A security guard sat behind a desk in the lobby, strategically positioned to protect the elevators. She was a woman in her mid-twenties, dressed in a dark blue uniform with her hair pulled into a no-nonsense ponytail.

Put her in makeup and nice clothes and she'd be a looker, though.

Coventry flashed his badge. "I need to see Jacqueline Moore," he said.

She studied his eyes and then said, "She's not in."

"You sure?"

She was.

She would have seen her. Also, there was no elevator activity going to the penthouse since early this morning.

"How late are you on duty today?" he asked.

"Two."

"In the morning?"

"Right."

He handed her his card. "Do me a favor," he said. "As soon

as she shows up, call me on my cell phone, no matter what time it is. Also, I'd appreciate it if she didn't know I'm looking for her. Do you think you could help me out with that?"

She could

And would.

And stuffed the card in her pocket.

"I like your eyes," she said. "Especially the green one."

FROM THERE HE WENT STRAIGHT TO Tianca Holland's place. They took a long run in the rain and then showered together. She kept trying to message his cock and he let her, but only a little.

"As soon as I have this case buttoned up," he said, "you're going to get more of the little fellow than you ever wanted."

She frowned and rubbed soap on his chest.

"You're driving me nuts. I can't wait that long."

"Me either," he said. "But it may be any day now. Let's just give it a little more time."

She rubbed her stomach on his.

"You're the biggest tease I've ever met in my life."

"Trust me, I'm not trying to be."

WHILE TIANCA WENT INTO THE KITCHEN to see if she could find anything edible in the freezer to microwave, Coventry went into the garage and sat behind the wheel of the Corvette.

A plan came to him.

A plan precipitated by the fear that Derek Bennett might actually strike Haley Wilde tonight.

Or if not tonight, then this weekend.

He pulled out his cell phone and made a number of calls to set it in motion. Everyone cooperated and sprang into action, even though it was Friday night.

Then Tianca opened the passenger door and stuck her head in. “There you are,” she said. “I found food.”

“Excellent.”

He was starved and would need the energy for tonight.

“You look weird,” she added.

“I’m just thinking.”

“About what?”

“Whether I should bring you with me tonight or not.”

“You better,” she said. “You owe me something after the way you keep teasing me. So where are we going, exactly?”

He stepped out of the mid-year beauty and carefully closed the door.

“You’ll see.”

Chapter Eighty-Five

Day Twelve – September 16
Friday Evening

WHEN HALEY WILDE GOT A CALL from Coventry early Friday evening, she was shocked to find that he was taking Jacqueline Moore's warning so seriously.

She was even more shocked at what he proposed.

But she agreed to go along with it.

And so did Christina Huygh.

They packed, threw two suitcases in the trunk of Christina's car, and met Coventry at the Table Mountain Inn in downtown Golden. He checked them in under an alias, paid cash, and helped carry their stuff up to the room.

It was a nice two-bed suite with a New Mexico décor.

"You guys don't have to stay holed up here," he said. "I can't see how anyone would trace you here. But if you feel the need to go out, stay within walking distance."

"I need to get drunk," Haley said. "I'm getting totally stressed out."

"Go for it if you want," Coventry said. "Just be sure you keep your cell phone with you." He cocked his head. "So you're pretty sure that Bennett knows you're staying with Christina?"

Haley nodded.

"It's common knowledge in the firm, after my apartment got busted into," she said. "I can't image Bennett not knowing."

Coventry looked at Christina.

"He'd know where you live, right?"

"Right. There's a firm directory. Plus I'm in the phone book."

"Okay. Looks like we're set then."

He started for the door but Haley grabbed his arm. "Who are you using for the decoy?"

"I don't know, vice is going to get someone for us about your age and size," he said. "I told them to be sure she's pretty so we keep it as real as possible."

She smiled.

"You are such a flirt."

He shrugged. "Actually, I really did say that."

"See what I mean?"

AFTER COVENTRY LEFT, Haley and Christina walked down Washington Street until they found a dark place with upbeat music and ordered Margaritas at the bar.

"I just hope that the people inside the house don't go snooping around to kill time," Christina said.

"Why?"

"You know."

"No, what?"

"My dresser drawer," Christina said.

"Why, what's in there?"

"You know, my vibrator." Christina punched Haley on the arm. "Don't pretend like you don't know."

Haley laughed.

"Okay, busted. I think that I might have taken one short peek in there once."

"As long as you didn't use it," Christina said.

"No need. I have my own."

They clinked glasses.

Chapter Eighty-Six

Day Twelve – September 16
Friday Night

ON FRIDAY NIGHT GRETCHEN wanted to go out and get drunk, so Degan decided to take her to an old biker bar that he used to frequent in downtown Golden, up the street a block from Foss Drug. It turned out to still be a bar, but the ragged edge was gone.

Someone had civilized the place.

Shit.

Nothing ever stayed the same anymore.

Still, it wasn't bad, so they grabbed a booth, sat on the same side next to each other, and drank Jack while they talked about what life would be like in California.

A couple of women sat at the bar drinking Margaritas.

One of them looked familiar.

The Asian one.

The one with the designer glasses.

Outside lightning cracked and the sky dropped rain with a vengeance.

Gretchen reached under the table and rubbed Degan's dick.

"I love the rain," she said.

Chapter Eighty-Seven

Day Twelve – September 16
Friday Night

BRYSON COVENTRY HADN'T BEEN on more than two or three stakeouts in his entire career, largely because they almost always represented too much of an investment of time for the potential return. So it was weird, sitting out here in the dark a half block down from Derek Bennett's house, waiting for something to happen.

Having Tianca with him made all the difference.

Without her, he wouldn't have had the patience.

The rain beat down and sounded incredibly nice.

Better than any song ever made.

Except maybe "Brown Eyed Girl."

They sipped coffee. The first thermos was only half gone and they still had a second full one in the back.

"I need to tell you something weird," Tianca said.

He raised an eyebrow.

"You're not going to say you used to be a guy, are you?"

She laughed. "I don't think so."

"Okay. Good."

"It has to do with last night in the hot tub with Monica," she said. "Before it all started I was really excited about it."

Coventry chuckled.

"You looked pretty excited during it, too," he noted.

"Right," she said. "I was. But not as much as I thought I would be. I kept thinking that she shouldn't be there, that she was invading our space. I felt guilty, being the one who brought her in."

"*Our* space, huh?"

She nodded. "The space of you and me; our private space. The bottom line is that I don't think there are going to be any more Monicas."

"Your choice," he said. "Either way, I'm going to support you."

HE CALLED SHALIFA and when she answered he said, "Talk to me."

"We got Haley's car in the driveway to make it look like she's home," she said. "We have most of the curtains partially open and the decoy's walking around, turning lights on and off, stuff like that, to make it obvious someone's there. I'm sitting a half block down the street. It's raining like hell."

"Here too," Coventry said.

"So far, no activity."

"Same here."

"How will Bennett know the car in the driveway is Haley's?"

"The information is in her H.R. file. Plus I'm sure he's already been stalking her."

FORTY-FIVE MINUTES LATER A SILVER BMW pulled out of

Derek Bennett's driveway and started to wind its way out of the neighborhood.

Coventry followed.

And called Shalifa to tell her he was in motion.

Being this far off the main roads, the traffic was sparse. So Coventry had to hang back. Unfortunately he had to hang back so far that Bennett slipped away.

He called Shalifa.

"I lost him," he said. "Watch for him at your end. I'm headed that way."

"What do you mean you lost him?"

"I had to hang back."

"Well don't hang back *that far*," she said.

"Now you tell me."

TWENTY MINUTES LATER, when Coventry was only a few minutes away from Christina's house, he got a call from Shalifa Netherwood.

"We just had a drive by," she said. "A light colored BMW. It could have been silver."

"That little shit," Coventry said.

"The driver might have looked my way when he passed," Shalifa added.

"Then go ahead and get out of there," he said. "I'll take the watch."

"Done."

He heard an engine start before the phone went dead.

He drove by the house and saw no suspicious cars and definitely no BMWs. He circled the block twice, took a spot all the way at the end of the street under a burned out streetlight, and killed the engine.

The sound of the storm immediately intensified.

The coffee was suddenly going right through him so he stepped outside and pissed by the side of the truck. By the time he got back inside he was soaked.

"Goddamn hurricane out there," he told Tianca.

"So I see."

He stared down the street.

"Come on asshole. Take the bait."

Nothing happened for the next hour.

Except that Coventry had to step back out into the storm two more times. Tianca did too, but only once.

Then a second hour went by.

Still nothing.

"Do you ever get the feeling like you're being watched or followed?" Tianca asked at one point.

"No, not really."

"I've had that feeling for the last couple of days," she said.

"That happens sometimes when you're around all this cloak and dagger stuff. It plays with your mind."

They were half asleep, listening to a country-western station, when Barb Winters called from dispatch. Coventry pulled up an image of her new implants, double Ds. "We got a dead body," she said.

Right now he could care less.

"Call Richardson," he said. "He's got duty tonight."

"Yeah, I already did," she said. "He wanted me to let you know that they have a preliminary identification. It's someone called Jacqueline Moore. He said she's a lawyer."

Coventry slammed his hand on the dashboard.

So hard that Tianca jumped.

Chapter Eighty-Eight

Day Twelve – September 16
Friday Night

Bryson Coventry cornered a cab downtown, stuck Tianca in it, and then headed straight to the Jacqueline Moore crime scene. The woman's body was still lying undisturbed in a dark Wynkoop alley not far from Union Station, about four blocks away from her LoDo loft.

The sky continued to spit rain.

Coventry was drenched, again.

And shivering.

The woman's neck had a deep knife wound.

Her purse was on the ground, looking as if someone had ransacked it before throwing it down.

"Looks like a robbery," Detective Richardson said as Coventry ducked under his umbrella. "All the money's gone from her purse and she doesn't have a shred of jewelry left."

"Actually it's a murder made to look like a robbery," Coventry said. "Get the tapes of every surveillance camera up and down this street and for the surrounding two blocks. I know who did it and I want to tie him to the location."

"You know who did it?"

"Yeah. A guy named Derek Bennett."

"How do you know that?"

Coventry was already walking away, but said over his shoulder, "It's a long story. I'll brief you tomorrow."

Shalifa Netherwood showed up, under an umbrella, just before he got out of the alley.

"Where you going?"

He ducked under with her.

"Bennett's," he said.

"You want company?"

"Come on."

On the way to the truck he called Haley Wilde, just to be sure she was okay.

She was.

He warned her to be careful because Jacqueline Moore had just been murdered.

THEY DETERMINED THAT BENNETT WASN'T HOME and then parked down the street from his house to wait. The plan was to cut him off before he could get in his driveway and then scare him into committing a traffic violation.

Then they'd pull him over and search his car.

And hope he still had some of the things he took from Jacqueline Moore.

WHEN BENNETT SHOWED UP an hour later, Coventry immediately fired up the Tundra and got on Bennett's ass, tailgating not more than ten feet away, blowing the horn and flashing the lights.

Bennett sped up.

Panicked.

Coventry hung with him, staying as close as he could without actually making contact.

Then Bennett did a beautiful thing.

He ran through the stop sign at the end of the street.

"Got you, asshole!" Coventry said.

He swung into the oncoming lane and pulled alongside. Shalifa powered down her window, flashed her badge and motioned for Bennett to pull over.

Instead of doing it, though, he slammed on the brakes, did a one-eighty and raced back the other way.

Coventry put all the muscles in his leg down on the brake pedal. The truck's ABS grinded and brought the vehicle to a straight-line stop.

He swung around as fast as he could.

But Bennett was way ahead.

"He's going to lose us," Shalifa said.

Coventry put the gas pedal to the floor.

"We'll see about that."

WHEN BENNETT GOT CAUGHT IN TRAFFIC up ahead, Coventry rammed him from behind. The Tundra's hood crinkled up and shot towards the windshield. Then the airbags went off.

A pain exploded in the middle of his face.

Coming from his nose.

Probably broken.

He had no time for it and charged out the door.

Bennett was out of his car now.

Running.

But not fast enough.

And when Coventry caught him, the little asshole made the mistake of throwing a punch that landed on Coventry's nose.

Chapter Eighty-Nine

Day Twelve – September 16
Friday Night

When Haley Wilde told Christina the news about Jacqueline Moore getting murdered, Christina hardly said anything and ordered another Margarita.

"I'm never going back that that firm," Haley said.

Christina studied her and said, "Me either."

"It isn't worth it," Haley added. "I'll work at McDonald's first."

Christina drank half the glass in one long swallow.

Then looked directly at Haley.

"I got a few things I should tell you," she said. "You asked me before if I was a spy. I said no. That was a lie."

A knot twisted in Haley's stomach.

"What?"

"I've been feeding information to Austin Gray the whole time," she said. "He wanted me to buddy-up to you, after you wouldn't drop your investigation, so he'd know what you were up to."

"Why?"

She shrugged.

"I'm not exactly sure," she said. "At first I thought it was just because he likes to know what's going on in the firm. But now, with Jacqueline Moore dead, maybe there's more to it."

"What do you mean?"

"I don't know what I mean, other than Renee Rand's dead and now so is Jacqueline Moore. What I can tell you, though, is that everything you and I did and everything we learned, I told him about it."

"That's disturbing. I thought we were friends."

"We are, but I owed him," she added. "He kept me in the firm after I screwed up that case I told you about. Plus, he was pretty clear that he'd grease the skids to be sure I made partner when the time came."

Haley pondered it.

And sipped the drink.

Then she asked, "Do you think Austin fed all that information to Derek Bennett?"

Christina shrugged.

"I'd have to believe so. They're pretty close."

Haley twisted the glass in her hand.

"So who put the note on my chair warning me that you were a spy?"

Christina didn't know but said, "It wasn't Austin, that's for sure. The more I think about it, it might have been Jacqueline Moore. She was close to both Austin and Bennett and would have known that I was working as a spy. If Bennett was getting the information from Austin, he might have been thinking that you were getting too close for comfort and needed to be taken out. So maybe Jacqueline warned you that I was a spy so you won't give me any more information. That way I couldn't feed it to Austin, who in turn couldn't feed it to Bennett. That way it would be less likely that Bennett would perceive you as a threat and would be less inclined to do something drastic." She frowned. "That's just a wild theory, though. I don't have any proof one way or the other."

A MAN AND A WOMAN climbed out of a booth and headed for the door. The man—who looked like an Indian—grabbed Christina's arm as he passed and asked, "Where do I know you from?"

She looked at him.

A scar ran down the side of his face.

His hair was long and thick and black, pulled into a ponytail.

She'd never seen him before.

She would have remembered.

"I don't know."

"You look familiar," he insisted.

"Sorry. I really don't think I know you."

He studied her, as if deciding whether she was lying, and then he looked at Haley.

Longer than he should have.

And then walked away.

Chapter Ninety

Day Twelve – September 16
Friday Night

WHEN GRETCHEN PASSED OUT back at the farmhouse, too drunk to even have sex, Jack Degan's thoughts turned to Tianca Holland. He got dressed in all things black, parked on the other side of the open space, and then crept towards her house through a pitch-black night.

Before he knew it he was in her backyard.

Then in the window well.

Prying open the window.

Listening for an alarm.

Hearing none.

Waiting there, nevertheless, for more than five minutes, just in case she had a silent alarm directly piped to a security company. When no cops came, he crept into the house.

He found her upstairs in the master bedroom.

Lying naked on top of the sheets.

Sound asleep.

He injected drugs into her ass and then held his hand over her mouth until she lost consciousness. Then he carried her naked body through the open space to the car, put her in the trunk and headed for the cabin.

WHEN THEY ARRIVED she was still unconscious. He tied her hands to the headboard and put a breathable gag in her mouth.

Then he pulled her legs up and stuck his dick in.

And pounded her as hard as he could.

Like the stud that he was.

Until he came like a madman.

He then tied her feet to the bed and wandered into the great room where he fell asleep on the couch.

An hour later he woke up and did it again.

Exactly the same, except this time she was awake which made it a lot more fun.

Chapter Ninety-One

Day Thirteen – September 17
Saturday—2:00 a.m.

BRYSON COVENTRY DIDN'T FIND a single thing belonging to Jacqueline Moore in Derek Bennett's BMW, even though he searched it meticulously three times.

No bloody knife.

No jewelry.

No nothing.

Maybe some of the bills in Bennett's wallet had come from Moore, and had her fingerprints on them, but at this point it seemed like a long shot.

"Looks like he was smart enough to dump everything," he told Shalifa.

"He's a slippery little bastard all right."

"Which means we got nothing," he added. "Except maybe a lawsuit for smashing his car. We're going to have to cut him loose."

"What about assaulting a police officer?"

Coventry frowned. "Hell, I'm the one who rammed him and chased him down. I'd have hit me too in his shoes."

So they cut him loose.

But then something weird happened.

Instead of leaving, Bennett wanted to talk and suggested that the three of them go to Denny's for a bite.

Coventry hated the thought of actually breaking bread with the guy. But hated the thought of not getting valuable information even more. So the three of them ended up in a red vinyl booth eating a 2:00 a.m. breakfast and drinking hot decaf coffee while it rained outside.

"SLOOP JOHN B" DROPPED FROM CEILING SPEAKERS. "We're not here because I'm trying to save my own ass," Bennett said. "We're here because Austin Gray is out of control. He's been my law partner for more than twenty years. So trust me, this hurts. But it has to be done."

Coventry shoved a forkful of pancakes in his mouth.

"Go on," he said.

"It all started when we got a big judgment for one of our clients called Omega," he said. "It was against a competitor of Omega's called Tomorrow, Inc. After we got that judgment the CEO of Tomorrow, a guy by the name of Robert Yates, started buying up Omega's stock. His plan was to get control of Omega and then bring it under the umbrella of Tomorrow. He'd be able to make the judgment go away, in effect, plus the two companies would be stronger together than either one was on its own."

Coventry nodded.

"All right."

"This was big trouble for the law firm," Bennett said. "If Yates succeeded we'd lose Omega as a client. Omega would be a part of Tomorrow and all of Tomorrow's legal work is done by a big Wall Street firm. So me and Austin Gray and Jacqueline Moore got together to see if we could figure out a way to prevent the takeover from happening."

"Makes sense," Coventry said.

"We had the name of a guy who might be able to help," Bennett said. "A psychologist by the name of Beverly Twenhofel, who also teaches at the University of Denver, was speaking to a group of students at an off-campus session at an Einstein Bros. They were talking about serial killers. After that meeting, a man who had been sitting at a nearby table approached her in the parking lot and asked her all kinds of weird questions. She got the distinct impression that he had killed and would kill again. She followed him and wrote down his license plate number. Then she came to our law firm and met with Jacqueline Moore to get a legal opinion as to whether the discussion with this man was within the physician-patient privilege. Jacqueline gave the case to Renee Rand, who handed the legal research down to Haley Wilde, a summer law clerk at the time. The firm ended up providing a legal opinion that the communication was indeed privileged, which is the correct answer by the way. However, we also had the license plate number of someone who might be a killer."

"Sloop John B" faded off and "Love Me Do" took its place.

"Austin Gray ran the plates, got the guy's name—Jack Degan—and actually met with him," Bennett said. "Then we hired him to go to New York and scare Robert Yates into abandoning the Omega takeover, under a threat that otherwise his daughter and wife would be killed."

Bennett looked at his food, lost in thought.

Then looked back at Coventry.

"I'm not proud of that," he said. "Nothing was supposed to

happen other than a threat. But things went wrong and Yates and his daughter, a little girl named Amanda, ended up stabbed to death in Central Park. We all felt like shit, especially Jacqueline Moore, who was having a hard time coping with the guilt."

He took a sip of coffee.

Interesting.

"Another series of events happened too," Bennett said. "Austin Gray got the hots for Renee Rand. He came on strong one night and almost raped her in her office. She came and told me about it and was going to go to the police. I actually encouraged her to, but somehow Austin talked her out of it and she didn't. But she was too uncomfortable to stay in the firm any more and started floating her resume around town. Then she turned up dead. Austin Gray never confessed to me that he did it, but the conclusion is inescapable. He was worried about loosing his power over her after she got away from the firm. He was scared she'd change her mind and go to the police."

"So you're saying Austin Gray killed Renee Rand?"

"Like I said, I don't have the proof, but I'm a hundred percent sure in my mind," Bennett said. "Either he killed her himself or he set someone else up to do it. Either way, she was a problem for him, and then the problem went away."

"I follow you."

"Then the firm hires Haley Wilde," he said. "She starts this stupid ad hoc Nancy Drew investigation into Renee Rand's death. The problem is that she's actually finding stuff out. We were worried that if she kept digging that she'd end up getting into the Robert Yates deal. So we tried to scare her off. Austin Gray hired someone to break into her apartment to make it look like she was in danger."

"So that was Gray's deal?"

"Right."

"I'll be damned."

"There's more," Bennett said. "He tried to get her to take a job in the D.C. office to get her nose out of our business. But she wouldn't go. So then Austin set up an associate attorney by the name of Christina Huygh to be his spy and to keep an eye on her. Haley Wilde kept digging and Christina Huygh keep giving us the updates. We kept getting more and more worried."

"Haley's a digger," Coventry said.

"Then something happens out in New York," Bennett said. "Robert Yates' widow—a society icon by the name of Rebecca Yates—threw herself in front of a bus. The rumor was that she was despondent over the death of her husband and daughter, and committed suicide-by-bus. Well, this hit Jacqueline Moore right in the gut. She was already feeling guilty and this put her over the edge. Austin and me were getting more and more worried that she'd crack any day."

"So you killed her?"

"Hold on," Bennett said. "I'm getting there. Anyway, then you walk into my office this afternoon and put the heat on me in connection with the deaths of both Renee Rand and that stripper, Chase. After you left, I met with Jacqueline Moore and Austin Gray because they had a right to know. I had to disclose to them that I've been frequenting Tops & Bottoms, including what I've been doing there. I also told them that I had a session with Chase about a year ago, which the cops would find out about sooner or later."

"You had a session with Chase?"

"Yeah, but I had nothing to do with her death," Bennett said. "Anyway, when Jacqueline Moore found out what I'd been doing down at Tops & Bottoms, that was the last straw. She turned in her resignation a couple of hours later. When Austin Gray found out about it he busted into my office, frantic that she was about to spill everything to the police. Then, tonight, she turns up murdered."

"So you're saying Austin Gray did it."

Bennett nodded.

"It was either him or me and I know it wasn't me," he said. "I'm not a perfect man, but that was even more than I can tolerate. That's why we're talking right now. The bottom line is that you got the wrong person. You want Austin Gray, not me."

Shalifa leaned on the table and looked at Bennett.

"Did you drive by Christina Huygh's house earlier this evening?"

Bennett looked at her as if she was nuts.

"No. Why would I do something like that?"

Coventry chewed a mouthful of pancakes.

Then cocked his head and said, "How do we know you're not making all this up? To try to put the blame on Austin Gray, now that we're closing in on you?"

Bennett chuckled.

"Well, for one thing, I was giving a speech in Colorado Springs this evening and have about two hundred people who will back me up. So if I didn't kill Jacqueline Moore, who do you think did?"

BACK IN THE TUNDRA, after the meeting, Shalifa asked, "So what do you think?"

Coventry wasn't sure.

"He might be telling the truth. On the other hand, he has all the same motivators that Austin Gray does. As far as his alibi for this evening goes, assuming it checks out, he could have hired someone to take Christina Moore out."

Chapter Ninety-Two

Day Thirteen – September 17
Saturday—2:00 a.m.

After Jack Degan screwed Tianca Holland the second time, he rolled onto his back and stared at the wood beams on the ceiling, amazed at how much her struggle had intensified the feeling.

He patted her stomach.

"You did good."

Then he pulled off the rubber and dropped it on the floor.

She tried to say something but the gag kept the words mumbled. No doubt she was telling him to let her go; and what an asshole he was.

Well, guess what?

He didn't give a shit.

He tweaked her left nipple. "What are you trying to say? How pretty I am?" He laughed. "Yeah, that's it. Save your breath, I already know."

Then he got curious.

And removed the gag.

She gasped for breath and then said, "You asshole!"

The words startled him. Not the words themselves but the

sound of her voice. He recognized that voice from somewhere. In fact, it was so familiar that he sat up, straddled her and brought his face in close. "Do I know you?"

"Jesus, asshole, it's me—Swofford."

The minute she said the word he knew she was right.

She was Swofford.

The boss-lady herself.

In the flesh.

"What the hell's going on?"

"I'm here to save your ass," she said. "Get me out of these goddamn ropes."

He stayed where he was.

"What do you mean, save my ass? How?"

"Let me loose."

"Sure. Just tell me first."

She pulled at the ropes and screamed. He let her struggle until she calmed down.

"Feel better now?"

She turned her head and said nothing.

"Tell me how you're saving my ass and what the hell you're doing here," he said. "Then I'll let you go."

SHE GRUNTED IN FRUSTRATION. "Things were getting too hot," she said. "The cops have been investigating the shit out of the four women at the railroad spur. They already figured out that Brad Ripley killed one of them. They even got their hands on his snuff film. And now they're on the edge of figuring out who killed Renee Rand."

"So what? Who gives a shit?"

"We do. The more they figure out, the closer they are to us," she said. "Then you went and killed that tow-truck woman. I'm not blaming you. You had to. But that's bringing even more heat."

"I don't get it," he said. "Even if you're right, I don't get why you're here."

"To give you an alibi," she said. "It goes like this. I called you and set myself up as a new victim. I did that so that when you took me it would be real. The detective in charge is too smart to fall for a charade. I didn't want to be hurt, though, which is why I kept telling you not to mark the woman up. Once you took me, then I'd stay with you for a day or two while the cops figured out I was missing. Then I'd show back up and tell them that I was abducted by a man who admitted being involved in all these murders that they're looking into. I'd say I escaped. Now here's the important part. I'd describe the person who took me. It wouldn't be a description of you. Then the cops would be looking for the totally wrong person. In the meantime, you go back to California and then we cool it for a while, until things are safer."

Degan smiled.

"Brilliant," he said. "Gutsy, too."

She tugged at the ropes.

"So this whole thing was to give you an alibi," she said. "Now say *Thank you* and untie me."

He ran his index fingers in circles on her nipples.

"I never pictured you to be this beautiful."

"Well I'm glad you enjoyed yourself, because you weren't supposed to. Now untie me."

THEY ENDED UP IN THE KITCHEN drinking Jack and eating

Lays potato chips, reminiscing about all the snuffs they'd been through together. Degan was particularly interested in knowing more about the clients and how Tianca got them.

But she wouldn't tell.

Not even close.

"Here's something you'll find interesting," she said. "Do you remember Angela Pfeifer?"

He nodded.

"Yeah. She was a knockout."

"Me and her were lovers," Tianca said. "She pissed me off and I decided she needed to die. So I told you that the client wanted her in particular and had you take her. Actually, he didn't care who he had as long as she was beautiful. The day you took her I was sure I had an alibi. Same thing for the day the guy snuffed her." She chuckled. "The cops won't figure out my involvement in ten million years."

"Remind me not to get on your bad side," Degan said.

She laughed. "You? Never. That's why I wanted you to bury all four of those women near each other. If the cops ever did find her body, she'd look like part of a bigger plan and they'd forget about lowly old me even though I had a motive. By the way, did you like the show I put on for you yesterday afternoon?"

"You mean in the backyard?"

"Right."

"So you knew I was watching you?"

She nodded. "You should be more careful."

Chapter Ninety-Three

Day Thirteen – September 17
Saturday—3:45 a.m.

IN THE MIDDLE OF THE NIGHT Tianca Holland walked on silent tiptoes from her bedroom to the other one and studied Jack Degan from the doorway. His body made a big lump under the covers. His breathing came deep and heavy. His clothes made a dark pile on the floor. She held her breath and snuck in.

She found his knife in the sheath, on the floor near the clothes.

She slipped it out.

Then she walked back into her bedroom and hid it under the pillow. She laid on her back in the bed, naked, and moved her hand under the pillow and got the knife properly positioned.

Moonlight filtered into the room.

"Jack, are you awake?" she shouted.

Mumbled words came from the other bedroom.

"Wake up and come over here," she said. "I need you to screw me."

Degan walked in, groggy, not much more than a naked shape in the dark.

She spread her legs and then raised her arms above her head.

"Come here," she said. "Make me feel good."

He straddled her chest and then inched up until his cock was on her mouth. "Get me hard," he said.

She did.

Using her tongue.

Then he slid down, put his arms under her legs and opened them wide. She bit her lower lip while he inserted himself. Then he rocked inside her with a steady up and down motion.

It was too bad for Jack Degan that he had raped her—twice—and made her change her mind about him. It was too bad that she was no longer interested in giving him an alibi or having him as a business partner. It was too bad that she no longer felt comfortable that he knew what she looked like.

It was too bad that she'd be better off if he was dead.

SHE REACHED UNDER THE PILLOW and got the knife in her hand. He didn't notice as she slipped it out. Then she raised it in the dark and brought it down as hard as she could into his back.

He immediately twitched and made an awful sound.

She pulled it out and stabbed him again.

Then again.

And again.

And again.

Then stuck it in one final time and twisted.

He went limp, no longer fighting death. Warm blood ran down his sides and onto her breasts and stomach. She fought to get out from under him and then rolled him off the bed.

"Asshole."

She brought his pants in from the other room, pulled his cell phone out of his front pocket, and then threw them on the floor at the foot of the bed.

She chained one of her ankles to the bed frame.

She made herself as hysterical as she could and then called Bryson Coventry.

Chapter Ninety-Four

Day Thirteen – September 17
Saturday—4:00 a.m.

WHEN BRYSON COVENTRY GOT BACK to Tianca's house at four in the morning she wasn't home and hadn't left a note. He called her cell phone and got no answer.

Weird.

Maybe she went to a girlfriend's.

He brushed his teeth, took out his contacts, dropped onto the bed and immediately fell asleep.

Then his cell phone woke him up.

He didn't answer.

Then it rang again.

He almost turned the power off but answered instead. Tianca's voice came though.

Hysterical.

Crying.

Talking a mile a minute.

Something about she'd been abducted.

And killed a man with a knife.

He got her calmed down enough to make sense. She was chained to a bed in a cabin in the mountains, but had no idea where it was. He threw on clothes, put his contacts back in and pointed the Tundra west.

On the way he woke up Shalifa Netherwood and had her work with the cell phone company to pinpoint the location of the phone that Tianca was calling from. Almost an hour later he pulled off Highway 119 onto a gravel road and took it west. In a mile it dead-ended at a cabin.

No lights were on inside.

A green VW Jetta sat out front.

He drew his weapon and approached.

Carefully.

Inside, he found Tianca Holland in a bedroom with an ankle chained to the bed frame, screaming for him to get her out of there. She was covered in blood. On the floor, next to the bed, lay a naked man with a knife in his back.

He looked like an Indian.

Chapter Ninety-Five

One Month Later
Friday Afternoon

BRYSON COVENTRY WAS ON A COUNTRY ROAD north of Denver, halfway to Loveland, when he found a pastoral scene that moved him. He pulled onto the shoulder, killed the engine and stepped out. The temperature was only about sixty, but under a full Colorado sun and without a wisp of wind, it seemed like seventy-five.

He felt a little guilty about taking off work early.

But not guilty enough to go back.

He set up the easel and positioned an eight-by-ten canvas on it. Then he squeezed Windsor & Newton oils onto a worn wooden pallet, limiting his selection to Alizarin Crimson, Cadmium Yellow Pale, Cadmium Red, French Ultramarine, Burnt Sienna and Titanium White.

From those six tubes he could mix any color he wanted.

And a few he didn't.

He solidified the composition in his mind and then laid in the lights and darks with a Burnt Sienna wash, until the painting looked like an old one-tone photograph.

Then he started to lay in the color.

The place was deserted.

There was no vehicle traffic at all.

Not a sound came from anywhere.

Off in the distance a hawk floated on large quiet wings. A butterfly fluttered to Coventry's left, one of the last summer holdouts. As he painted, his thoughts turned to the events of the last month.

Lots had happened.

THE SECURITY SYSTEM in Tianca Holland's house had recorded Jack Degan abducting her on that fatal Saturday night. There was no question that she shoved the knife in the guy's back in self-defense, while he was raping her. He had gotten himself too distracted to remember to keep the knife in his hand. Luckily, the events hadn't seemed to traumatize Tianca.

Why Degan had chosen her was still a mystery.

Maybe he did it to screw with Coventry.

JACK DEGAN, IT TURNED OUT, had made a duplicate DVD of a lot of the snuffs, if not all of them. Why? Who knows? Maybe he was going to use them for blackmail some day. Maybe he just liked to watch them.

One of the DVDs showed the murder of 19-year-old Catherine Carmichael. The resulting investigation led to a Kansas man named Porter Adams. The victim's eyes were found in a formaldehyde jar in Adams' basement. Adams was in the process of being extradited to Colorado to face the death penalty.

Another one of the DVDs showed Austin Gray sawing off Renee Rand's head. Gray was sitting in prison right now, without bail, facing the death penalty.

"He'll get it, too," Coventry told everyone.

Another one of the DVDs showed a man snuffing Angela Pfeifer, stabbing her repeatedly. So Tianca Holland was officially off the hook for that.

Coventry and Tianca had consummated their relationship that night in celebration.

And hadn't stopped since.

MIA AVILA, THE MISSING PUEBLO WOMAN, was found alive, chained in the cab of a tow truck, which was locked in a structure at the remote location off Highway 93 where Jack Degan had been staying.

She had suffered serious malnutrition and dehydration but in the end managed to pull herself back to normal.

The body of the tow-truck driver still hadn't been found.

Degan had been staying at the place with a Pueblo hooker named Gretchen Smith. She disappeared the day after she learned that Degan was dead.

No one knows where she went.

She left behind a brand new Lexus that was titled in her name.

DEREK BENNETT'S STORY CHECKED OUT. He had nothing to do with the deaths of Renee Rand, Chase, or Jacqueline Moore. The only thing he had done of an illegal nature was to conspire with Austin Gray and Jacqueline Moore to hire Jack Degan to threaten Robert Yates.

Although that was a felony, Coventry talked a New York

prosecutor into giving Bennett a plea bargain in exchange for Bennett testifying against Austin Gray at trial.

THE LAW FIRM OF HART, SANDERS & DAY, LLC, disintegrated. Coventry got Haley Wilde and Christina Huygh jobs in the D.A.'s office where they were thriving.

AS NEAR AS COVENTRY COULD TELL, Austin Gray was the one who had killed Brad Ripley. Coventry's theory was that Ripley learned from Degan that there would be more events at that same location after Ripley's.

Ripley then kept an eye on the place.

When Austin Gray showed up, Ripley took the pictures that were found in his safe, and also wrote down the license plate number of Gray's BMW. From there he learned who Gray was. When he lost money in Las Vegas and needed more, he blackmailed Austin Gray. But Gray traced the phone calls, found out who was blackmailing him, and shot him in the face.

MARILYN BLACK, THE HOOKER, WAS LIVING drug-free with her mother in Idaho, working as a cashier in a hardware store. She emailed Coventry almost every day.

COVENTRY WORKED THE PAINTBRUSHES for almost two hours and then stopped.

He was finished.

Anything more would just mess it up.

He packed up the Tundra and headed to Tianca's.

If she liked the painting he'd get it framed and give it to her.

Otherwise he'd sell it at the gallery.

It was good enough for that.

Tianca called while he was driving over and said, "Lets get drunk tonight and then take a cab home."

"Where?"

"I don't care, downtown somewhere, maybe one of those places on Larimer Street, somewhere dark and cozy. I'm going to wear a short black skirt and a white thong."

He chuckled.

"You're too wild for me. You know that, I hope."

"You have no idea," she said.

About The Author

Jim Michael Hansen, Esq., is a Colorado attorney. With over twenty years of high quality experience, he represents a wide variety of corporate and individual clients in civil matters, with an emphasis on civil litigation, employment law and OSHA.

www.JimHansenLawFirm.com.

Author Photo by Yvonne Melissa Hansen

For complete information on the *Laws* thrillers including upcoming titles, please visit Jim's website.

www.JimHansenBooks.com
Jim@JimHansenBooks.com